THE TRUTH NEVER SPOKEN

BAKER OAKS
BOOK 1

AMBAR CORDOVA

First edition 2025 – Cordova Chronicles LLC - Updated

Book Cover by Aliyah with Ever After Cover Design (Discreet) and Kim with KBG Designs (Illustrated)

Formatting and Illustrations by Ambar Cordova

Copy, Line, and Developmental Edits by Wonder and Wander Publishing

Proofreading by The Author Experience

Proofreading by Jen Bernacki

Hi friend,

I am so excited you picked up my book today. I hope you love it as much as I do, and that Allie and Jake will stay close to your heart forever. There is so much I could say about this book, but I just hope you give it a chance. Also, I would love to hear from you. Feel free to message me on social media, or shoot me an email. I love to chat!

The Truth Never Spoken is a contemporary romance, with on-page topics that may cause some difficulties for the reader. I will list them at the bottom of this page as they may be spoilers, and I want to allow those of you who don't care about content warnings to skip them if you want to. If you want to know what they are, just keep reading.

This is a work of imagination and completely fictional. Some medical scenes may not showcase what would happen in real life. It is okay to not believe real doctors would do that. The characters in this book are not real and some scenarios may not happen in real life either. Same with some of the football scenes and logistics.

This book is a romance with on-page spice. However, there

is an option to skip the explicit scenes. Some chapters have open door spice, so when this symbol ⮕ (signaling an open door) shows up, feel free to skip until the next chapter. It won't affect the timeline if you skip it in case reading closed door is your jam..

Now for the content warnings. There will be profanity, on-page violence toward a seventeen-year-old, a toxic parent relationship, and an on-page car accident. Some scenes feature an ambulance ride and a Code Blue situation at a hospital, as well as a football injury. There is some emotional abuse (neglect) in a marriage. There are on-page descriptions of alcohol, drugs, and sex (one particular scene in which the female main character is seventeen and the male main character is eighteen—both are seniors in high school).

Thank you again for giving this book a chance.

143,
Ambar.

To all the girlies who love a dirty-talking cinnamon roll who falls in love with his girl even when she's imperfect. The kind who would move mountains to see her smile. The kind who puts her first, every time, no matter what.

.... and to Joey, because in you, I found exactly that and so much more.

PLAYLIST

I LOVE MUSIC! I have been working on this playlist longer than I worked on plotting this book. There are no rules on how to listen to this. The music enhances the experience; each chapter has a song title that matches the overall feel of that chapter. Feel free to listen to them after you read the chapter (or during if your brain will let you do that <3) Playlists are available on Spotify & Apple Music.

Chapters:

1.Running with the Devil - Alexz Johnson

2.Miss Americana and The Heartbreak Prince - Taylor Swift

3.I Miss You, I'm Sorry - Gracie Abrams

4.Tennessee Fan - Morgan Wallen

5.Rockin' & Rollin' - Nashville Cast

6.Bejeweled - Taylor Swift

7.Meanwhile Back At Mama's - Tim McGraw ft. Faith Hill

8.Bicicleta - Carlos Vives Ft. Shakira

9.Back To December (Taylor's Version) - Taylor Swift

10.Robarte Un Beso - Carlos Vives Ft. Sebastian Yatra

11.Coney Island - Taylor Swift Ft. The National

12.Kiss Me - Ed Sheeran

13.Cornelia Street (Live from Paris) - Taylor Swift

14.Stay - Zedd Ft. Alessia Cara

15.Steal The Show - Lauv

16.You Are the Reason (Duet Version) - Callum Scott Ft. Leona Lewis

17.Ho! Hey! - Nashville Cast

18.Am I Wrong? - Nico & Vinz

19.when the party's over - Billie Eilish

20.Gold Rush - Taylor Swift

21.If The World Was Ending - JP Saxe Ft. Eva Luna Montaner (Spanglish Version)

22.Hey There Delilah - Plain White T's

23.Without You - David Guetta Ft. Usher

24.Hold On - Chord Overstreet

25.Heal - Tom Odell

26.This Love (Taylor's Version) - Taylor Swift

27.Take Me - Alex & Sierra

28.Dress - Taylor Swift

29.Epiphany - Taylor Swift

30.Back to You - Selena Gomez

31.Chasing Cars - Snow Patrol

32.Shivers - Ed Sheeran

33.Fingers Crossed - Elijah Woods

34.Champagne Problems - Taylor Swift

35.Heart Like Yours - Willamette Stone

36.The Last Time (Taylor's Version) - Taylor Swift ft. Gary Lightbody

37.Afterglow - Taylor Swift

38.I Almost Do (Taylor's version) - Taylor Swift

39.The Alcott - The National Ft. Taylor Swift

40.Stick Season - Noah Kahan

41.Little Did You Know - Alex & Sierra

42.See You Later (in ten years) - Jenna Raine

43.Tee Shirt - Birdy

44.All I Want - Kodaline

45.Big Girls Don't Cry - Fergie

46.21 - Gracie Abrams

47.Forget Me - Celina Sharma

48.Time to be your 21 - Alexz Johnson

49.Anyone, Justin Bieber

50.Say Don't Go (Taylor's Version) [From the Vault] - Taylor Swift

51.Take Me Home - Us the Duo

Epilogue: Timeless (Taylor's Version) [From the Vault] - Taylor Swift

PART 1

BRUISES, LEWIS CAPALDI

Without her, my world stops spinning.
My heart slows its beating.
My control fumbles out of my hands.
I cease to live, and I just exist.

1

———

NOW

RUNNING WITH THE DEVIL, ALEXZ JOHNSON

Allie

AFTER YEARS of traveling for work, I keep hoping flying will eventually feel easier, but it never does. The moment I step into the airport, my mind spins into overdrive—flooded with all the things that could go wrong, and all the things that have gone wrong today.

I move through the terminal in a blur of hurried footsteps and the cold sting of anxiety. My phone vibrates in my back pocket. Cara. Again. I check my list for the hundredth time, trying to make sense of it all. But I can't focus. Not with TSA ahead, not with the thought of another flight looming.

I pull my phone out to read her message, but it barely registers. I don't have the energy for her right now. The lines are long, the security checks endless, and my stomach is in knots. I speed-walk, trying to ignore everything, trying to silence the rush of thoughts that just won't stop.

CARA:

Bro, I'm sure the whole plane will wait for you.
Stop stressing pls

She knows I'm mad because I said so many times last night that I didn't want to go out. She never listens to me, especially when I've said no and she doesn't agree with me. She's so small, you would think after a glass of wine she would be ready to go home.

CARA:

I called the airline and you are ON TIME.

But no, this girl can drink a bar dry and still wake up like nothing happened. But I guess every yin needs their yang because, after just two glasses of wine, I'm completely dead and can sleep through everything–including my alarm.

CARA:

You will not miss this flight.

CARA:

I can sense how angry she's getting that I'm not answering, but right now my focus is on getting through this TSA line and to Gate B to catch my plane to Florida.

CARA:

For the love of Christ, Allie, can you at least let
a girl know you made it through?

CARA:

Or is this you telling me you are actually not
going to Florida anymore?

CARA:

You will not see him, OK? For all that you
know, he doesn't even live there anymore. You
need to relax ….

CARA:

and let me know you are ok. Jesus, Allie.

CARA:

ME:

Would you please stop? I'm next in line. I'll text
you while I'm on the plane. Stop blowing up
my phone. Ok? Love you, but chill the fuck out.

CARA:

You know you love me. Xoxo, C

Ugh, I seriously can't with her. We've known each other since we were kids because our dads used to work together. We were destined to be friends since our moms were pregnant at the same time. Essentially we grew up together, since Cara and I lived in the same area until we were twelve. My dad's promotion required him to move often and everywhere, so I guess he had to drag the whole family with him. My brothers and I were all born in the Dominican Republic, but since I can remember, we have constantly been moving all over the world.

We act like sisters, even though we look nothing alike. While I'm short and curvy with hazel eyes, Cara is taller, with thick thighs and green eyes. My skin is tanner than hers, giving me a soft caramel color, while she is a little more rosy-cheeked and pale. We couldn't be less alike, yet our friendship is one of the most beautiful things I have, and I will cherish it forever.

Cara is the definition of a free soul and the most loyal person I've ever met. She would move heaven and earth for those she loves, including her worthless boyfriend—but we're not getting into that. My child-loving, animal rescuer, level-headed, blunt bestie is almost the complete opposite of me. We went to the School of Education together at Stanford University, but she will probably finish her life as a special education teacher, whereas I ran away from the classroom as soon as I could.

The TSA agent calls for the next person, and I realize it's almost my turn to go through the checkpoint. I pull out my ID from my black, crossbody purse that I took to the bar with me last night. I wouldn't be surprised if I were to find some crazy things in there, like the condom Cara slipped in 'just in case' I was 'feeling lucky' last night. She got a call from that asshole boyfriend of hers, which put her in the crappiest mood, and she swore she was in her prime years, and it was time to have fun.

CARA:

Remember even though you're going to work this week, your job ends at 5. Go out and have fun!

CARA:

And by fun, I mean, act your age. Meet a guy and hang out. There doesn't have to be any strings attached, but you need to get out there. We made a pact last night, we both have to carry it.

I give the agent my phone so he can scan my boarding pass when I hear the soft hum of my phone vibrating in his hand with a new text. His eyes grow wide, and he blushes instantly. As he hands me back my things, he quietly says, "I didn't need to see that. But be careful—that can get you into trouble." He winks at me and signals for me to keep going.

WHAT. JUST. HAPPENED?

I go through the checkpoint, remove my shoes, and place them in the bin as I push them through the machine. I'm sweating everywhere at this point, trying to figure out what he meant by that, but I'm already late, so it has to wait.

The security guard asks me to step through, and when everything looks good, I grab my carry-on and phone from the belt, slip my shoes back on, and start walking to the gate.

I quickly look down to figure out Cara's issue, but stop as I read the message the agent saw.

CARA:

> Or even better, maybe find a hot stranger at the airport who can fuck you senseless before you hop on the plane.

CARA:

> God knows your grouchy ass needs to get laid ASAP.

SHE. DID. NOT.

ME:

> I just want you to know that this text popped up while the TSA guy was checking my boarding pass ON MY PHONE. Thanks for that.

CARA:

> SHUT UP. It did not

ME:

> Fml

CARA:

> Maybe he would like to volunteer? Was he cute?

I'm hunched over my phone, trying to type a reply, when I slam straight into something hard. No, not something—someone. A wall of human muscle who also didn't see me considering his face is on his phone too.

"Oh my gosh, I'm so sorry," I stammer, my words tripping over each other. "I wasn't paying attention. I just—"

But then my brain shorts out. I look up. And the world shifts.

The towering wall of muscle standing in front of me, blocking out everything else is not a stranger to me. Dark chocolate-colored eyes lock onto mine, deep and intense. They pierce me, like they can see into every corner of my soul. The kind of eyes I could never forget. And the scent—woodsy, fresh, and familiar in a way that makes my stomach tighten. I'd know that smell anywhere. Even after ten years.

"Allie," he says. His voice is rough, like gravel. It cuts deep and leaves a trail in my chest. Not a question. Just my name, a simple fact. An accusation and a torment at once.

I'm frozen. My heart's slamming against my ribs, my head spinning. I want to speak, to say something—anything. But nothing comes out. I just stare, caught in his gaze. The air between us feels thick, too thick.

If this were a movie, the subtitles would read, *Insert awkward silence here*, but it's not.

The seconds stretch on and on, each one longer than the last. I'm torn between wanting to run and wanting to cry. I should scream, or maybe... hug him? No, not fucking hug him, but something. I should definitely do something, but I can't move.

Finally, my mouth works, though it barely feels like mine. "Jake?" The word feels strange, uncertain, like I'm testing it for the first time. Like this boy—no, not a boy but a man now; taller, stronger, different—hadn't meant the world to me a lifetime ago.

I clear my throat, trying to salvage this situation and trying again. "Hey, Jake. So nice to see you."

I keep talking, and I can't stop. It's as if the words tumble out of their own accord. "Long time no see. You look great."

God, I sound like an idiot. I glance at him again, really seeing him. He looks... perfect. Perfect in a way I can't describe. The same boy I loved all those years ago, but grown. Taller. Broader. With a thick beard and tattoos snaking up his arm, every inch of him says, 'Fuck me now, please,' in a way that shouldn't even be legal. "How've you been? It's been so long—is everyone okay back home?"

And I'm still talking. *Why am I still talking?*

I finally stop myself. I force a breath and try one more time. "What brings you here? To this airport? On this day?"

I wait for him to answer, but my mind is racing too fast to process anything at all.

2

———

THEN

MISS AMERICANA AND THE HEARTBREAK PRINCE, TAYLOR SWIFT

Allie

"WAIT FOR ME," I call, panting as I run off the field, dragging the bag of pom-poms. I catch up to Cara, who is almost at my car, holding water bottles and our bags with the most annoying expression I've seen on her in a while.

"You don't have to look like you're going to puke. They just won a huge game—cheer up!" she instructs me while doing a little victory dance.

Shaking my head and staring at her like she's the last person I want to let down right now, I say, "I know, I know. But now we have to go and get ready for this last-minute victory party you decided to throw—at my house!"

"Allie, you need to let loose. Nobody cares what your house looks like. They just care that there won't be any parents around, and that tomorrow you have someone to clean up the mess. It's not my fault your hot-ass daddy has you in the biggest house in Baker Oaks."

Cringing, I throw a water bottle at Cara and shout, "STOP.

CALLING. MY. DAD. HOT." This girl has an issue with older dudes, I swear. Even though she has been dating the same guy for years, it doesn't stop her eyes from wandering every time an older man walks by—except when she's acting like a complete goof around one of my twin brothers. I don't think she even realizes she does it, but it's like her soul is comfortable with him around.

She hasn't stopped raising her eyebrows at me as I sigh. "You know we went to sleep so late last night, reviewing the routine and then the game. It's just a lot. I just want to go to bed for the next ten years."

I've known Cara since we were babies, and she has always been the ray of sunshine on my dark days. After the team won today, her boyfriend, Cole, picked her up and started spinning while she shouted, "Party at Allie's!" for the whole field to hear. So, even if I wanted to cancel, it's too late now. The other girls are supposed to be at my house within the hour, but all I want to do is curl up and read. I don't want to be friendly and nice tonight, I just want to let my social battery run out and forget about others for a minute.

"Allie, it'll be fine. Your parents aren't even there, and I'll kick everyone out as soon as you tell me to. Pinky promise," Cara adds, showing me her pinky and making me shake it. When I do, she squeals loudly and throws herself at me.

"Fine, but you owe me," I tell her, getting in my car and blasting the AC on high. It is hotter than hell outside, which means there is not much I can do to my hair without it becoming a lion's mane. Yet another thing to deal with tonight.

After driving home and spending three hours getting dressed, tidying things up, making snacks, and answering a million texts, the house looks somewhat put together. The people who came over seem to be having a blast. Everyone is dressed like they're at an after-party at a club, even though none of us are old enough to drink. I'm wearing a black sequin miniskirt with a see-through white top that makes me look way older than I am. Cara looks straight out of a magazine with her long legs, mini dress, straight golden hair, and cherry lips. She is smiling so brightly, and I wish I was enjoying this as much as she is. But I really don't drink, and the rest of the girls are all over their boys, congratulating them for the win.

The Sharks won today against their biggest rival, so they are all buzzing with excitement. Some of the girls are doing handstands while drinking beer, while others are just talking and dancing. Cara is all over Cole, like they haven't seen each other in years. She is so happy when she is with him, even when he tells her to tone it down sometimes. *That* I don't love. But seeing her happy around him? That I adore.

"You know, it wouldn't hurt you to go mingle," someone murmurs very close to my ear in a deep silky voice that has my skin prickling immediately. I stiffen before turning quickly to see Jake Clarke standing next to me with two cups in his hands.

"Sorry, didn't mean to scare you," he says with a smirk, roaming his eyes all over me. I feel my cheeks warm under his gaze. I've never had someone look at me like that before, and I don't know what to do with it.

"Well, try again," I sass back. Jake is one of Cole's friends. He plays center on the offensive line, and he is Baker's 'golden boy.' He's friends with pretty much the entire school, including the underdogs. He is unbelievably handsome: tall, dark hair, light skin with olive undertones, and chocolate eyes that make him look mysterious as shit. But then he smiles, and he looks every little bit the boy next door. He's in the same circle of friends I hang out with, but other than pleasant hellos, we don't really talk. He sure as hell has never looked at me like this before.

"Here, this is for you," Jake says, handing me one of the cups.

I grab it, take a sip, and almost spit it out. This is the worst thing I've ever had. I wince and ask, "Do you always drink nail polish remover or is this just a special occasion?"

He chuckles, and I suddenly find myself wanting to hear that sound forever. Holy shit, how come I've never heard this boy chuckle before?

"It's just vodka and lime, Allison. You'll be fine."

"Only my parents call me Allison, *Jacob*. At least add some juice to it or something," I quip as I stare back at him.

He's leaning against the table with his legs crossed, a Sharks T-shirt hugging his arms in all the right places, and with a smirk on his mouth. His dark hazelnut eyes are gleaming at me as he sips on his drink.

"Why aren't you mingling? I thought you were the queen bee around here?" Jake asks nonchalantly, as if he isn't standing there looking like a damn edible treat. *Get it together, Allie.*

"I'm just tired, okay? I wasn't planning on you guys winning, and I had a date planned already, so this," I say while pointing at the chaos in my house, "messed up my plans a bit."

He touches his chest like I stabbed him in the heart and dramatically moans, "A date? Oh my, you have so much faith in us, huh? Just kill me, why don't you?"

I smile and look at him, but I don't say anything. It's almost too much; the way he stares at me, the smile and the flirting. Is he flirting? Is this flirting? He finally breaks the silence and says in a low whisper, "I didn't know you were seeing anyone." I don't even know what he's referring to, so I just keep looking at him. I smile and take another sip—without wincing this time—and continue staring silently.

We both look away from each other as a loud noise comes from across the room. We see two of the players throwing their fists in the air and shouting, "Chug, chug, chug," at Cara and Tasha, who are drinking tall glasses of beer. I chuckle while looking at them as Jake gets closer and says, "You didn't answer my question."

"What question?" I ask, not looking at him. My cup stills on my lips as his scent engulfs all of my senses.

"Whether or not you're seeing someone, Allison. You said you had a date."

I'm getting so flustered at his use of 'Allison' that I snap back and say, "First of all, it's Allie. Second, how is *that* any of your business? Third, not that you need an explanation, but I had a date with a book, okay?"

Why am I being such a bitch to Jake? He barely talks to me at school, or at all—which is weird since he is best friends with Cole, and he and Cara are basically attached at the hip. This guy can have any girl he wants; why is he wasting time talking to me? And why is my stomach fluttering at his question?

"So, you aren't seeing anyone? I thought so," he boasts confidently. Not a question, but a statement.

I keep looking at him, waiting for him to say more, but he doesn't. He just looks all the way down to my toes and back up, probably noticing the very small amount of fabric that's draping my body. Between my outfit and my curves, there is probably very little left to the imagination. What is happening here? Why do I feel the air leaving my lungs? Why won't he stop looking at me? And why do I like it?

"Why are you so interested in whether or not I'm seeing someone?" I snap back.

As Jake lowers his now-empty cup, he stands up straight, leaning close to my ear to whisper, "I'm just glad I still have a chance to marry you one day. I seem to have been an idiot and not said something before." He is so close that I can smell the woodsy yet beachy scent on him again. He smells like a surfer boy who went to chop trees in the woods, and that's sexy as fuck.

"So, I'm taking my chance now," he adds. The smirk on his face makes my knees weak, and I can't breathe. The room is closing in. I blink rapidly and chug my almost-lethal drink to avoid looking at him again.

Jake waits, his presence almost a silent weight beside me as I set my cup down. Even though we're already so close, he somehow draws even closer before his hand brushes the small of my back, sending a shiver through me. The room suddenly feels suffocatingly warm; like the air itself has thickened around us. His fingers are gentle, barely there as they graze the skin at my lower back before slipping into the back pocket of my skirt. He pulls out my phone with a quiet, practiced ease.

His cheek presses to mine, the heat of his skin searing me as he angles the phone between us. I feel his breath against my ear, the weight of his proximity making my heart race. We both stare at the camera, a shared moment suspended in time. He's so close, too close, and his gaze is steady—smug, confident, and undeniably captivating. I, on the other hand, am lost and flustered, my thoughts jumbled.

"Smile, Allison," Jake murmurs, his voice low and commanding. I can't seem to do anything but obey.

I force a smile as he pulls away just as effortlessly as he'd come, slipping the phone back into my pocket before turning on his heel and walking out of the house—leaving me breathless, with a lingering warmth that has nothing to do with the room.

3

___

NOW

Allie

"ALLIE, you really think *what brings you to this airport* is what should be coming out of your mouth right now?" Jake asks with a straight face, still holding my life in his hands like no time has passed. His words are harsh, harsher than I remember him ever talking to me—or anyone for that matter. But then again, I don't know Jake. Not anymore, at least.

Taking a deep breath, I finally say, "Let me start over. Hey, Jake, nice to see you again."

"Allie," he replies simply, like my name is all he needs to convey his feelings. He doesn't need to tell me what I already know: I fucked up, and he's annoyed to see me.

"Hi," I answer with a smile, trying to cover my nerves.

"You owe me more than that." His tone is heavier than before, if that's even possible. His dark eyes are glued on mine, not letting me off the hook easily.

"I know, I'm sorry."

As much as I want to continue these short exchanges, an announcement over the PA system interrupts my thoughts.

"Now boarding Flight 904 to Jacksonville, Florida, at Gate 34B."

We both look up, trying to find where the sound came from and hoping to grasp some sense of what's happening right now when I say, "I'm sorry, Jake, but I have to go."

I quickly turn around, grab my bag, and speed walk to the gate, trying to run away from him and everything he brings with him. The future I thought I would have someday. All my buried hopes and dreams. All the love I had to give. All the love I still keep for him.

Get it together Allie, you were seventeen, nobody finds the love of their life in high school.

By the time I reach the kiosk, the line is gone. The attendant scans my ID without looking up, and I follow her through the gate, feeling the weight of my nerves pressing heavier with each step. As soon as I set foot on the plane, heat floods my body. Sweat prickles along my spine, my palms clammy. My throat tightens, a stubborn lump I can't swallow down. It's bad enough I had to fly today, but him? Running into him? Of all the places, of all the times.

I find my seat and sink into it quickly, hoping to disappear into the fabric of the chair. There's no one beside me yet, and I cling to that small mercy. I don't need anyone to witness the mess I'm trying not to be—no more stammering, no more fumbling over words. And certainly not the panic building in my chest. You'd think after all the miles I've logged, all the flights we took as kids, I'd be used to it by now. But I'm not. The feeling of being so out of control, so small, surrounded by strangers in this giant metal box, thousands of feet above the ground—nothing about it is comforting. It's suffocating. And no amount of frequent flyer miles will ever change that.

I grab my phone to read a text from Cara while people finish shoving their bags away and sitting down.

ME:

Guess who I ran into at the airport?

CARA:

Ricky Martin

ME:

Jake

CARA:

Which Jake?

ME:

Your friend, Jake.

CARA:

Holy shit, Allie. Are you ok?

The routine sounds of the compartments being closed and the high heels of the flight attendants as they walk the aisle checking seat belts invade my senses. My palms are sweating, so I lower my phone onto my lap and shove a piece of peppermint gum in my mouth. I close my eyes and lean against the window, hoping this will pass quickly. Praying it will be a smooth flight. Breathing so I don't shake. Counting so I don't cry. And we start moving down the runway.

In, one, two, three, hold.
Out, one, two, three, hold.
In, one, two, three, hold.
Out, one, two, three, hold.
In, one, two, three, hold.

We must be in the air already because I feel a fast jerk that makes me open my eyes suddenly. The seat belt sign is still on, and the pilot, with a raspy voice, announces that we are experiencing some turbulence and to remain seated with our seat belts fastened until the sign is turned off.

In and out Allie. You'll be fine. You can do anything. In and out.

Another jolt. The plane shudders beneath me, and my hands fly to the armrest without thinking. My knuckles are white, my grip almost painful as the plane jerks up and down, sways side to side. I squeeze my eyes shut, trying to breathe, trying to steady myself. *In and out. In and out.*

Then, suddenly, I feel it—a strong hand, warm and steady, wrapping around mine. My heart stops for a second, and I open my eyes, blinking hard to make sure I'm not imagining it.

There's Jake, sitting next to me. He's lifting the armrest in one effortless move, his other hand already holding mine. His eyes meet mine, and they are calm, steady—the kind of focus that cuts through the noise and the chaos of the plane's movements.

I blink again, but no—he's still there. Real. Just looking at me, his grip tightening ever so slightly. The noise of the plane fades into the background, replaced by the quiet, grounding pressure of his hand in mine. Just like *before.*

"You're okay, Allie, just breathe with me. Breathe in, one, two, three, four," Jake says as he fans his hand, encouraging me to breathe in with him. "And out, one, two, three, four. Come on, Allie, breathe for me." I let out a deep breath and continue to follow his directions, slowly relaxing my whole body as I lean into him, like the last ten years were ephemeral.

When it finally seems as though we're just cruising, I get the courage to whisper, "What are you doing here?" I'm afraid of any possible answer he might give me, so I keep my eyes away from his and stare at the hand he is holding.

Rubbing the top of my hand with his thumb, Jake answers, "I'm flying home. I was in Chicago for a conference."

Home?

Wait, does he still live in Baker?

Why didn't I Google this before I decided to take my next assignment in Jacksonville? I could have even gone on a social media hunt, or let Cara do her thing and tell me any of the information she has tried to share with me over the past few years. I'm so naive; of course he still lives in Baker. That's why Cara hasn't talked to me at all about him—or Baker, for that matter. When I left Baker Oaks, I made Cara promise she wouldn't tell me anything about the town we both love. I only wanted updates on her and her family—nothing else. Being without Jake wrecked me, and I swore I needed to forget he even existed to move on. I asked her ten years ago to never share what I'm missing, and my very loyal friend never has. She asked me a few years ago if I wanted to know something, but when I threatened to stop talking to her, she didn't continue. Childish of me, sure; but protecting my peace has been my number one goal the past few years.

"I could be asking you the same question, Allie. Last time I saw you, I thought you'd never step foot in Florida again." Jake looks at me with eyes that reflect what I'm feeling. *Hurt*. I not only hurt him, but I hurt myself when I decided to leave and never look back.

Taking a deep breath, I finally reply, "I'm going to Jax for work. I have a six-month assignment in a few of the school districts in the surrounding areas."

"You became a teacher after all?" he asks with pride in his voice. "I always knew you'd be great with children."

I sigh. "Yes, but I'm not in the classroom anymore. I'm a professional development specialist for an educational company that services K-12 schools. I'm sent to schools to help coach and train teachers. Then I get assigned to another district that needs me. You know me: always moving, never settling."

That hits him like a stab right in the heart, and I can see it. "I didn't mean it that way, Jake," I quickly add. After a few seconds, I ask, "Where is home for you now?"

"I still live in Baker Oaks. I'm one of the team's coaches now."

"Like, the Sharks? Are you a teacher?" I sound so surprised because Jake Clarke never wanted to coach anything—not even his own teammates, let alone children.

As I'm unraveling my thoughts, I hear him say, "Yes, I teach social studies, and I'm the offensive line coach. Still living in my small town, and I never want to leave."

And with that, I remember the main reason I told him why I needed to leave: he wanted to stay, I wanted to fly.

I have so many questions—too many—but I can see him holding something back. His lips are tight, like he's fighting to maintain some kind of control. Yet, he doesn't let go of my hand, even though it's slick with sweat. The weight of the tension hangs between us, thick and electric.

I pull my hand away slowly, but not too far. It's like I can't completely let go. My fingers curl back around his, and the gravity of it settles in my chest. I take a deep breath and force the words out, my voice quiet but steady. "Why did you come and sit here? How did you know I was struggling?"

Jake's eyes flicker briefly, as if he's trying to choose his words carefully. And then, with a low, almost raw tone, he answers, "Because even though you left with my heart ten years ago, I know you, Allie. Probably better than you know yourself, and definitely better than anyone else."

His words linger heavily in the air. "At least I did."

Before I can process them, the pilot's voice crackles through the intercom, announcing we're preparing to land. Jake's hand tightens around mine again, a firm grip that somehow feels both grounding and possessive. He doesn't look at me. He just stares straight ahead, his jaw clenched, eyes shut as if bracing himself.

I follow his lead and close my eyes, letting the surge of thoughts flood me. *How the hell did I end up here again?*

4

THEN
TENNESSEE FAN, MORGAN WALLEN

Allie

FUTURE HUSBAND:

Hey!

ME:

Since when?

FUTURE HUSBAND:

Since when what?

ME:

Since when did you decide you'll be my future husband, Jake?

FUTURE HUSBAND:

How do you know this is Jake? I could be a secret admirer.

ME:

Because you used the picture you took tonight as your contact photo.

ME:

Btw, I look like shit so I'm deleting it.

FUTURE HUSBAND:

You could never look like shit, Allie. I forgot I took that though. To answer your question, let's have dinner, and I'll tell you.

ME:

Dinner? It's 2:00 am, Jake, and I just got to bed after a day of hell.

FUTURE HUSBAND:

So sassy. Not tonight but soon.

ME:

We have the football banquet soon. That's dinner.

FUTURE HUSBAND:

Are you always this literal? I'm trying to have dinner with you.

ME:

Why? You can just tell me who you're interested in, and I can tell you if they're single. I know Tasha was talking to you at the game, and she is always twirling her hair when you are near. She's single for sure.

FUTURE HUSBAND:

...

FUTURE HUSBAND:

I don't want to ask you questions about other girls.

ME:

Then what? I don't speak football, and I'm sure your buddies are more entertaining at dinner than me.

FUTURE HUSBAND:

Let's try this again. Allie, would you go out to dinner with me? Like on a date.

ME:

Like dinner dinner? On a date dinner?

FUTURE HUSBAND:

Yes.

FUTURE HUSBAND:

I can see you typing Allison.

ME:

Sure

FUTURE HUSBAND:

Can I pick you up tomorrow?

ME:

6:00 pm. Don't be late. See you tomorrow, Jake.

I LIE IN BED, hugging the phone to my chest on top of my fast-beating heart. "What just happened?" I whisper to no one

Did Jake Clarke just ask me out? Did he really save his name in my phone as *Future Husband?* Since when is he interested in *me?* He did say earlier that his chances of marrying me one day weren't blown, but I thought he was just fucking with me.

I've been in and out of Baker Oaks all my life, but this is the first year I've actually set foot into the school as a student. It's different now—there's a heaviness to it, a newness I can't quite shake. Most of the kids here have lived in this town their whole lives, their roots running so deep they'll never leave. Of course, there's Jake. He's practically Baker royalty. Everyone knows his name, his family, their legacy. It's like he's been carved into the town's very bones.

Me? I'm the outsider, even if it doesn't feel that way on the surface. It's easy enough to blend in when my parents are best friends with Cara's family, and when I've spent countless weekends here, tagging along to visits and family dinners. Especially once Cara's little sister, Nellie, was born, our parents began to spend more summers than I can count visiting each other. We all took turns holding and helping with little Nellie. We don't live in Baker, but it's always felt like a comforting place—even if I feel more like a guest than a local.

When my dad got the opportunity to work at the Embassy in Jacksonville, my mom didn't even think twice. The chance to live closer to Cara's mom and soak up days of endless spa treatments were too good to pass up. So, we left. Now, I'm back in the town that feels like a second home, but with the added weight of needing to figure out who I am in this space.

My parents told me we'd be moving here around April, so I flew out early to try out for the cheerleading squad. I was a gymnast until my sophomore year, when I hurt my knee and couldn't take the conditioning or the long hours of gymnastics anymore, so I switched to cheer. I've always loved to dance, and that—plus my tumbling background—gave me the skills I needed and helped me make the Baker Oaks cheer squad.

I've seen Jake around—how could I not? He's always part of Cara's circle, slipping in and out of conversations, ever-present at the heart of whatever's going on. And I know his mom works at the daycare where I volunteer, reading stories to the kids every Tuesday afternoon. We hang out with the same people and share the same spaces, but it's always from different corners. He's Jake—*that* Jake, the one everyone knows, and I'm just me. We orbit the same world, but are never really in the same space.

He's the king of the offensive line, and sure, he could be the arrogant jerk type—tall and broad, with the kind of confidence that could turn heads and shatter egos—but he's not. He's the exact opposite. He's like a golden retriever: friendly, goofy, loyal, the kind of guy who always has a smile on his face and a laugh to share. You can tell by the way he is with his friends; the way he lifts the freshmen who can't even talk around him because they're so nervous. Everyone knows they're never going to win Jake's heart, but he's always kind, always patient. And it's not just them. It's the cafeteria lady who he greets every morning like she's his favorite person in the world. It's the band kids he helps load equipment for. It's the exchange students who are still trying to find their footing—he's always right there, making them feel like they belong.

And now... he wants to take *me* out?

How have I never noticed this before? How did I miss all the signals, or has he been sending them at all? I try to think back—has he ever looked at me the way he looks at everyone else? Has he always been this kind, this open with me, too? Or was I just too blind to see it?

I keep looking back at every interaction we've had, and I can't gather anything. He has always been nice to me, but not in a way that is different from how he treats everyone else.

As I continue thinking about it, I slowly close my eyes, take deep breaths, and drift off to sleep.

5

———

NOW

ROCKIN' & ROLLIN', NASHVILLE CAST

Allie

WE WALK off the plane in silence and wait by baggage claim. All I can think about is how I found myself in the situation I was trying to avoid at all costs. What the hell does the universe have against me? Out of all the damn flights to Jacksonville, I had to be on the one Jake was taking.

My suitcase finally appears on the conveyor belt, and Jake helps me grab it before it disappears. It seems polite to wait with him until his suitcase arrives too, but it isn't any less awkward. Once we have our bags, we start walking out of the terminal, and Jake asks, "Do you need a ride? I'm parked here, and I can take you wherever it is you're staying. Maybe we could grab a coffee or a drink and just talk?"

"Jake," I sigh, not dropping my gaze from his. He still looks like himself, just older, except there's no light in his brown eyes. There are fine lines next to them but they don't look alive anymore; not like they used to.

"Allie," he replies.

"I don't know if that's a good idea," I deadpan.

"Why not? You've made it seem like we're just acquaintances, so why not have a drink with me?" he asks seriously, staring straight at me and meaning every single word.

I won't tear my eyes from him. I refuse to back down now, even if I'm dying inside. "You know why."

"I'm not eighteen anymore, Allison. I can handle a drink with you." Jake stares at me, and I swear he can see right into my soul. There's nowhere to hide when he looks at me like that. He still has those beautiful eyes, perfect lips, and thick dark eyebrows that mark his face. His expression may have weathered the years, but I can still see that beautiful boy—the one I loved so many years ago, somewhere right beneath the surface.

"One drink," I say.

"Yes, ma'am," he replies, grabbing my suitcase as we start walking toward the parking garage.

THE DRIVE to the bar is awfully quiet. What once would've been a comfortable silence is now thick and full of angst. I can feel all the things we haven't said floating around us, just like that day ten years ago. It feels as though a lifetime, yet no time, has passed. We get to R&P, a local restaurant and bar that has a rooftop overlooking the St. Johns river. Jake drives to the valet and pulls over, where I get out of the truck. He meets me on the other side and grumbles, "I guess old habits die hard, huh?" as he nods to the truck door.

"Sorry," I wince. "Still a habit." He absolutely hated when I opened my own door. It took me a long time to get used to him opening it for me, and then, when there was no him anymore, I had to get used to opening doors for myself again.

"Still not dating? Or are you just dating jerks who won't open the door for you?" he muses.

"Jake," I fret.

"Allison," he challenges, and it hits me like a punch to the gut. Nobody calls me that anymore—not since... Well, not in a long time. He says it so easily, like it's just a name; but to me, it feels like a piece of the past I can't outrun.

He stares at me for a beat, his eyes searching, like he's trying to figure out something I'm not ready to share. Then, without another word, he turns and leads me through the door.

We settle at the bar, the low hum of conversation and clinking glasses surrounding us. Jake orders a beer on draft. I order a Moscato and a shot of tequila, because why not? It's one of those nights. Jake raises an eyebrow at my choice, but doesn't say a word. He just leans back against the bar, waiting for our drinks.

The silence is comfortable for a second, but then he breaks it. "So, are you going to answer the question?"

This man and his damn questions. I try to keep my cool. "Still not dating, Jake. Happy?"

He laughs—*laughs*—like I've told the funniest joke in the world. "Good one, Allie," he scoffs, his voice light. But I feel the sting of his laughter, a mix of amusement and something else I can't quite place.

The embarrassment creeps up my neck, a hot flush I can't shake. I clear my throat and try to regain some control. "Can we change the topic?" I ask, more out of necessity than desire.

For a moment, the conversation shifts, moving into safer territory. Jake tells me about his life—how he never expected to love teaching, but he does. He's also got an auto shop with his dad, a little family business. They do rebuilds in the summer, and during the school year, his dad and some guy named Thiago take care of the work.

It's strange to hear him talk about his life like this, but it's real. It's not the easy, surface-level chatter I'm used to. He asks about my job, but the questions are casual, light—almost as if he's testing the waters, gauging how much I want to share.

"How's Cara?" Jake asks as if he doesn't know the answer. I know they talk. I would be stupid to assume Cara spends her summers here and doesn't talk to *her boys*.

"Like you don't know," I choose to reply.

"Oh, so you do know?"

"That she comes to Baker every summer? Yes, Jake, I do. She's still my best friend; I just choose to stay out of it." I made the choice to limit my reminders. At first, I wanted to forget—but that has proven to be impossible, so at least I can pretend. I can tell he's good at this, at making conversation flow. Even the awkward, uncomfortable kind. As he always was.

I let the words come and go, letting myself feel, for just a moment, like maybe this night isn't going to be so strange after all.

The tequila shot is gone, but it gave me the courage I needed to whisper, "I'm sorry," as he looks at me with those big, puppy eyes. *I. Fucking. Can't.*

Jake breathes deeply and rubs his face, saying, "It looks like your life turned out okay, though," as he gives me a sad smile.

I look into his coffee-colored eyes, and after trying to fight it, I yawn. He pays for our drinks, and we leave. We haven't talked about anything important, but maybe that's what these drinks were about. Two old friends reconnecting and nothing more. No rehashing the past. No complicating things. He has clearly moved on.

We step outside and wait for the car. My skin prickles, and I'm instantly aware of his hand on my lower back. His presence is intoxicating, just as it always has been. I don't want to make him uncomfortable, so I don't say anything, but he moves his hand away and softly says, "Sorry, habit." I suddenly hate that word.

He tries to open the door for me, and this time I let him. I step in, and he closes it behind me before walking around to the driver's side. I give him directions to the B&B for his GPS, and we start driving. We're in silence for a while. Not even music is playing. It's a heavy silence, too; the type that pressure on your chest. The type that carries unspoken words.

"Jake, I'm sorry. I really don't know how many ways to say it," I insist, and it comes out shaky and breathy.

"What is it you say all the time? Sorry don't fix it." He holds the steering wheel tighter, and not once does he look my way.

I stare at him, take a deep breath, and add, "I think you're being a little dramatic, keeping a grudge all these years." Shit, maybe that wasn't the right thing to say, but I'm tired, and it *has* been a decade.

"Dramatic? You said goodbye and never looked back. After everything we shared. Like I was disposable. Like we were replaceable," Jake snaps with a deeper voice.

"It was not like that, and you know it. I said sorry then, and I'm saying sorry now. I can't change the past, and I didn't think you would even remember me by now."

He slows down rapidly, pulling to the side of the road. He puts the truck in park and turns to glare at me. His eyes are almost black as his jaw clenches tight. "Are you fucking kidding me right now, Allie?" he barks with a stern voice, and I can hear the hurt. "I'm not saying you need to fix everything right now because it can't be done," he continues, "but God damn it, can you at least acknowledge that we still need to have a conversation? We might have been young, but you know age doesn't matter when it comes to what we had. And if you think it meant nothing, then maybe I was just delusional." Jake starts driving again and adds, "Maybe I have been delusional all along."

I don't even know what to say, so I don't say anything at all. But as I look at him, I notice his scowl. "Alright. Yes, we can talk," I concede.

Jake doesn't say anything else as we approach the house where I am staying. It's a dark street, and the houses are all small and squished right next to each other. Not one light is on in any of them. Some have graffiti and damage on the outside, and the house the GPS is taking us to has a homeless person lying on a sheet of cardboard right by the door.

He keeps driving right past the house, shaking his head like he's made up his mind.

"What are you doing? That was the house," I protest, twisting in my seat, trying to get a glimpse of the place disappearing in the rearview.

"You're not staying there, Allie," Jake replies, his voice tinged with frustration, like I should know better.

"Oh yes, I am," I snap back, my own irritation bubbling up. "I have to report to work on Monday, and I only have tomorrow to get groceries and prep for the week. Turn around, Jake."

He lets out a long, exasperated breath. For a second, I swear I see his jaw tighten. "You are not staying there. It's not safe."

I blink, caught off guard. "What? What do you mean, it's not safe? My company won't pay for a hotel for long-term assignments," I argue, my voice rising just a little. "I have to stay there. I'm sure it's just a misunderstanding. I'll call the head office tomorrow, or Monday when they open, but I need to be there. I can't deal with this right now."

Jake doesn't even glance at me. His hands grip the wheel, knuckles white. "I'm not dropping you off there," he says, his tone final, like there's no room for discussion.

"So, where are you planning on taking me, then?" My voice

is quieter now, confusion starting to outweigh my frustration. I'm exhausted, my mind spinning, my thoughts a tangled mess. The last thing I need right now is to figure out some random hotel when I just want to get settled.

"Home," he answers, like it's the simplest thing in the world.

Home? The word hits me like a punch. Whose home? I haven't had a place I could call home in... I don't even know how long. And *his* house? Like, *why?*

"I'm not staying at your house, Jake," I say, the words coming out sharper than I mean.

He glances at me for the first time, a flicker of something—concern, maybe, or just annoyance—crossing his face. "I'm not letting you stay in that place. You can call your company tomorrow and figure it out, but it's getting late, and you're tired. I have an extra room. So, I'm taking you to my house."

I open my mouth to argue, but the tiredness weighs on me, and I feel too heavy to fight anymore. I forgot how bossy Jake can be and how protective he is when others are at risk. So, I just nod and wait.

6

———

THEN

BEJEWELED, TAYLOR SWIFT

Allie

THE SUN SHINES through the window I forgot to pull the blinds over, warming my face and reminding me how much I drank last night. I reach for the water cup on my nightstand. I can't forget to fill it up every night due to the panic attacks that wake me every so often. I've had anxiety for a long time, but as I get older, and since my grandparents' accident last summer, it's been getting worse. Especially at night. I started having panic attacks and waking up in the middle of the night, gasping for air. Other than my CPAP, having water readily available is the only thing that helps. A CPAP at seventeen—so classy, so demure.

I take a sip and open my nightstand drawer to grab some Tylenol that will likely help nurse me back to life. Without getting up all the way, I grab my phone to check the time. _10:30 a.m._ Shit; I was supposed to be ready by 9:00 a.m. to go into Jax with my mom. I guess it's another 'ask for forgiveness' kind of morning. My mom is usually pretty chill, especially because my brothers and I give her very few headaches in comparison to other teens, so she counts her blessings when she can.

I have a few unread texts, but only one catches my attention.

> **FUTURE HUSBAND:**
>
> Good morning, sunshine.

For a brief second, I scroll through our messages and quickly remember our conversation from only a few hours ago. *I have a date with Jake Clarke tonight.* I don't want to reply to his text immediately, so I go back to scrolling through the other texts.

> **CARA:**
>
> Are you dead?
>
> **CARA:**
>
> Don't make me call your asshole brother to go check on you.
>
> **CARA:**
>
> I realize I'm overreacting, but can you just answer the damn phone?

I also have five missed calls from her. Does that girl ever sleep? I swear she is powered by a motor—but also, asshole brother? Who is she even kidding? Those two have the best relationship, even if she acts like she wants to murder him half the time. She gets along with both of my brothers, but she and Manny are actually friends.

> **ME:**
>
> Barely alive.

> **CARA:**
>
> Bitch, I was walking out the door ready to come and revive you.

I get up from bed and walk to the bathroom. I hop in the shower, letting the hot water wash away the smell of sweat and booze clinging to my hair. Saturdays are for washing my mane of messy curls. It takes forever, but I do it as quickly as I can since Cara will be here shortly.

I step out of the shower, throw on an oversized T-shirt and some shorts, and head to my bedroom. She's already lying on my bed, scrolling through her phone when I walk in.

"You didn't tell me you and Jake are talking," Cara announces as she turns her phone to show me a picture. It's of her and Tasha with their cheeks pressed so close together, they are practically kissing. But if you look closely, you can see us talking in the back. Us, as in me and Jake. Jake is towering over me, and I am smiling like I'm completely smitten with the boy. Considering the butterflies in my stomach just looking at the picture, apparently I am.

"We talked for three minutes tops. Plus, you were too busy smooching your man to talk to anyone," I brush her off.

"Jealous?" she asks as she pouts and blows a kiss at me.

A soft chuckle escapes my lips, and I sit on my bed, grabbing the coffee from my nightstand. I take a long sip, close my eyes, and taste the salty caramel deliciousness in the cup. I slowly open my eyes, blow out a breath, and say, "Speaking of Jake," while looking at Cara. She turns her body to face me, the phone still in her hand, and waits for more.

"He asked me out on a date for tonight," I share, still unsure of what I'm actually saying.

"He what?!" she gasps.

"He kinda asked me out on a date tonight," I repeat, shaking my head a little as I pull my phone from my bag. "After he saved his number under 'Future Husband.'"

Cara's eyes widen in disbelief, exactly how I expected. "I didn't even know you guys talked, and now you're going on a date?!"

I let out a nervous laugh, running a hand through my hair. "I know. I was surprised, too. He was all, like, 'I can still make you my future wife and shit.'"

She opens her mouth, her finger already swiping to call someone—probably Natalie or Tasha—but I stop her with a quick, "Wait."

When she pauses, I sigh. "I don't even know if I'm going," I admit, my voice faltering. "I mean, I said yes, but it was so random. Totally out of the blue. And now, I'm second-guessing it." I pause, looking down at my lap while trying to collect my thoughts. "I thought he was into Tasha."

Cara stops mid-swipe and just looks at me, soft and steady. "Allie," she urges, her voice gentler now, "Why would he ask you out if he was interested in someone else?"

I shrug, unsure of the answer myself. "I don't know... Why me?"

Her eyes narrow slightly, like she's seeing right through me. "Why not you? You're a catch. Guys have just been too blind to see it. Maybe he sees you, now."

I stare at her, chewing on the thought, but before I can reply, my phone buzzes. I glance down and see a new message pop up, the sudden interruption pulling my attention away from the conversation.

FUTURE HUSBAND:

At the risk of sounding like a stalker, are we still on for tonight? I know you must be awake after seeing Cara's story.

I show the text to Cara, and she chuckles as she clicks through her phone and turns it around for me to see her Insta story. It was me taking a sip of the Venti Salted Caramel Mocha she brought me with my eyes closed. My hair is wet and ringlets are falling around my face. I look calm and entirely too lost in the coffee. We both laugh, and then I let out a sigh.

"Give him a chance. You need to put yourself out there. You guys aren't moving any time soon, and it's not like he's asking you to marry him. Entertain it for a bit," she says, pointing to my phone.

Rolling my eyes, I grab the phone to reply.

ME:

Hey! Yes, I'm awake.

FUTURE HUSBAND:

Good. Did you sleep ok?

ME:

Like trash

FUTURE HUSBAND:

Sorry

ME:

Not your fault.

I see the three dots that show he's typing pop up and then disappear. This happens a few times before I finally sigh and type.

Me: And yeah. I'm still good for tonight, if you are.

Future Husband: Is 7 okay?

Me: Sounds good. Where are we going?

Future Husband: Dinner and maybe for a walk?

Future husband: Or would you rather go to a movie?

Me: Either sounds good. Just wondering what to wear.

Future husband: Whatever you decide to wear will be perfect. See you tonight, Allison.

Cara is smiling at me and lifting her eyebrows as she opens up her hand, signaling to me to hand her my phone. I smack her on her hand, and we both chuckle.

"Jerk," I say.

"You know you love me," she says while she winks.

She reads all the texts and gives me back my phone, smiling, and hopping off the bed quicker than lightning. She rushes to my closet opening both doors. She does a shimmy dance, and whispers, "It's showtime."

7

NOW

MEANWHILE BACK AT MAMA'S, TIM MCGRAW

Allie

WE ARRIVE at Jake's house about forty minutes later, and it's like stepping back through time. He still lives in the same house we used to spend all of our time in so long ago.

The house is a beautiful, Southern-style, brick home, sitting in the middle of six acres of land. The front yard is surrounded by pine trees and canopies of oak trees that shade most of it. There's a gravel driveway leading to the front porch that still looks exactly the same. Quaint and charming. Wind chimes are hanging up, a small fountain with fish sits to the right, and two white rocking chairs to the left. The wooden door has wear and tear marks from years of hosting busy boys and their friends, and the same "Welcome to Gma and Pop Pop's House" sign on the door from way back when.

Back when his Gma would host the best Friday night dinners. Back when we would all hang out in his huge backyard with chickens, cows, and goats walking around. He used to have a fire going most weekends, and people would just show up and hang out while we all talked about our hopes and dreams. Back when we used to sneak into his grandma's extra bedroom in the garage and he would touch me the way only he ever has.

"Allie," I hear his voice from the front door, cutting through the quiet as I stand on the porch, still taking it all in. The weight of everything, of this place, wraps around me like a memory I can't shake off. I snap out of it quickly, turning toward him, offering a quick apology and a shake of my head before stepping inside.

And then—then—my breath catches in my throat. The house looks exactly the same. I almost expected it to be different, but it hasn't changed at all. The smell, the feel of the air, even the creak of the floorboards—everything is the same. The only new addition is the smart TV on the stand, gleaming in the corner like it doesn't belong.

Pop Pop's old recliner is still there, tucked into its familiar corner, facing the TV at the back end of the living room. I can almost hear the soft, rhythmic hum of him rocking in it, the echo of old stories and laughter filling the space. The emerald green carpet beneath my feet, worn in places, is still there. It's like stepping back in time.

The walls are covered in snapshots of Jake and Derek growing up—racing karts, grinning in football uniforms, standing beside trophies that used to feel like the world's biggest achievements. And then, there are the porcelain dolls, lined up in a glass cabinet, their lifeless eyes somehow watching me as if they know all the secrets I've kept hidden.

I glance at the L-shaped couch in front of me, its fabric faded, worn from years of use. It's still holding its shape, though, stubbornly defying time, just like everything else in this house. Every crease, every indent, is a memory. I touch my fingers to the armrest, feeling the marks from years of sitting, of living.

"Nothing has changed," I whisper, the words tasting strange in my mouth.

Jake steps closer, and his voice is soft, barely above a murmur. "Except that she's gone now." His words hang heavy in the air, like they belong to a different time, a different life. He doesn't look at me when he says it, his eyes tracing the edges of the room as if he's afraid to meet mine. "Come on," he says, his voice more steady now. "I'll show you where you can sleep."

Who's gone? Gma is gone? I can't even wrap my head around that statement as I follow him to one of the rooms that used to have all his pictures and things for when he decided to spend the night here. Except now, it's a very standard guest bedroom without any personal touches. The bed still sits in the middle, but the once-dark comforter with football print is replaced by a plain gray one. The desk that used to hold all the shirts he always needed to fold and put away is replaced by a smaller one with a wooden chair and an empty flower vase. There are a couple of towels by the door on a small nightstand that he places my bags next to.

"The bathroom is—" he starts, but I interrupt him that *way* as I point to the hallway that leads to what used to be the main bedroom.

"I remember," I add, giving him a guarded smile. He smiles back and tells me to make myself comfortable and that he will be taking a shower.

He closes the door behind him as I sit on the bed and take a deep breath. How did I find myself in this place again? I'm a little overwhelmed right now and low-key still shocked at the turn of events. I open my bag, grab some house clothes and go take a shower.

After the shower, I wander to the living room with my laptop in hand, where I find Jake sitting, watching TV. I look at him and wave my hand softly as I whisper a *thank you* for letting me crash here. I ask for the Wi-Fi password and start to walk back to the room when I hear him speak.

"You can come sit out here, Allie."

"I don't want to be a bother," I murmur, hesitating by the door. "I've already inconvenienced you enough."

Jake looks up, his gaze steady, and there's a quiet sincerity in his voice. "You're not a bother. Please, come sit out here. Unless you want to be alone, which I'd understand."

The words feel like a weight in my chest. "I don't love being alone, Jake. Never have and probably never will."

I say it so quietly, like it's a confession I've never admitted to anyone before. Slowly, I walk toward the spot next to him—the spot I used to sit in so many years ago, back when everything felt easier, simpler. It's strange how some places can feel like home even after so much time.

Jake doesn't respond at first, but I hear the soft clink of his beer bottle as he takes a sip. "I know," he says after a moment.

I glance at him, confused. "You know what?"

"That you don't like being alone," he says, his voice soft, but there's a knowingness in it that catches me off guard.

For a second, the weight of the past settles in between us, and I just nod. I shift my focus to his beer, trying to break the quiet. "I see old habits die hard."

Jake chuckles, the sound low and warm. "You want one?"

I shake my head, but before I can protest further, he's already getting up, heading for the kitchen. His jeans fit him just right, hugging the muscles of his thighs, and I can't help but notice how his shirt spreads across his back, highlighting the defined muscles there. It's such a subtle thing, but it captures my attention in a way I don't want to acknowledge.

I pull my computer closer, trying to distract myself. I need to send an email to the help desk at my company about the B&B situation—explain everything and figure out what comes next.

My fingers tap the keys, but my mind keeps wandering, sliding back to the way Jake moves through the house, like he's been here all along, as if nothing's changed.

When he returns, he's holding a glass of white wine, the condensation pooling around the rim. I reach for it, and as I take my first sip, the taste hits me—sweet, crisp, with a hint of peach. Moscato. My favorite.

I look up at Jake, surprised. "You remembered?" I don't mean for it to sound as soft as it does, but I can't help it. It's... nice.

Jake raises an eyebrow, like it's no big deal. "You've always been easy to remember," he says, and there's that quiet warmth in his voice again, as if he's not just talking about the wine. "Impossible to forget, actually."

I sip again, the cool wine sliding down my throat, and I can't help but smile. It's perfect. And for the first time since I walked through that door, I feel like maybe—just maybe—I'm not so lost after all.

"I'm sorry about Gma," I say.

"Yeah, me too," he adds.

"I didn't know she passed. I know how much she meant to you. How did Pop Pop take it?"

"Brutally. It's still hard for him. He lives here part-time. The garage room is his now when he's here, but he's in Jupiter with my brother for a while."

Why is his brother living so far away? And why is Pop Pop not living with his parents? There are so many things I want to know, but I don't think it's my place to ask anymore.

"Do you know which school is your first assignment?" he adds, changing the topic.

"Yeah, I'm going to an elementary school on the west side of Jacksonville first, but I won't know the next school until I'm almost done there. I'll be there for the whole of next week."

"What are you teaching them?"

"Small group reading intervention," I say with a smile, hoping it doesn't sound as trivial as it feels.

He glances over at me, a small, knowing smile tugging at the corners of his lips. "You always loved reading, so it doesn't surprise me."

I shake my head slightly, feeling a warmth in my chest. "Correction: Love. Present tense. Books are still my lifeline."

"Noted," he replies, his attention already drifting back to the TV, but there's something in his tone—something soft and understanding—that lingers in the air between us.

My heart twists at the simplicity of it all. The way we fall into this easy, effortless conversation, like no time has passed at all, like we haven't both lived entire lives apart. And it's too much. The connection feels so familiar, so comforting, and yet it hurts because I don't deserve it. I don't deserve his kindness, his thoughtfulness, not after everything.

I set my glass down, the cool wine still clinging to my fingertips. The weight in my chest grows heavier, and I know I need to go before I crumble.

"I should probably head to bed," I say, my voice quieter than I mean for it to be.

Jake looks up from the TV, his brow furrowed slightly. "You sure?"

"Yeah, just... tired," I mumble, already gathering my things —my phone, my bag. I don't look back at him, not even a glance. I can't.

I make my way to the room, each step feeling like it takes me farther away from something I've just realized I might want, and maybe even need, but can never have. The second I cross the threshold, I let the tears fall. I don't try to hold them back this time. The floodgates open as I walk to the bed, and I collapse onto it, my body shaking with the quiet sobs I've been holding in all day.

I hide these tears from him. I don't want him to see the cracks in me, the part of me that is still broken and unraveling, still clinging to things I can never reach again.

The tears feel deserved, as much as they hurt. They're for me. For what I've lost. For everything I've been too afraid to face. And I'll face it alone, because no one else should have to carry it. Certainly not Jake.

8

———

THEN

BICICLETA, CARLOS VIVES Y SHAKIRA

Allie

I SPENT the day styling my hair, painting my nails, and hanging out with Cara. No matter how much I see her now, I still feel like time is running away from me, so I try to soak in all the minutes we have together. I am always afraid I will never get the chance to do all the things I want to do with her, no matter how much time we spend together. I guess that's what happens when you grow up in different cities and countries than your best friend all your life. After spending the rest of the day together getting me ready, I find myself alone with a book. It's about 6:40 p.m., and I'm dressed, lying in bed reading, when my mom comes in.

"Hola, amorcito[1]," she says as she steps through the door and sits on my bed, kissing my forehead and tucking my hair behind my ear.

"What are you reading now?"

———

1. Little love

"Just *The Hunger Games*," I say, and I look at her smirk as I add, "Again."

"Are you ever going to get tired of rereading that book?"

I touch my chest like she stabbed me and say, "Never." Ha, I just did the same thing Jake did last night. Maybe we are more alike than I thought.

We both laugh and chat books for a bit. My mom is amazing and a huge bookworm, too. My love for reading grew because of her sharing so many things about the books she was reading. She read *The Hunger Games* once a couple of years ago so we could talk about it, but dystopian is not her thing. We usually read the same book once a month and have our own little book club.

"Are you going somewhere?" she asks, looking at my eyes once she notices the mascara I have on. I usually don't wear makeup unless it is a special event or game night, so it makes sense why she is curious.

"I, um, yeah. If you're okay with it," I tell her.

She raises her eyebrows and says, "Cuéntame[2]."

I tell her about Jake asking me out to dinner and maybe a movie tonight. She knows who Jake is because in this small town, everybody knows everybody, and I am cheering at almost every varsity game. I tell her I'm a little nervous and I don't even know where we are going. She reminds me I am seventeen and a fun person and that no matter where we go, as long as I keep an open mind and a good spirit, I will have fun. As always, she reminds me of my curfew, too.

I'm not shy by any means. Actually quite the opposite, but I have never had a boyfriend before. I kinda dated a guy named Ryder a couple of years ago, but it didn't go anywhere because we moved. It's already hard enough to make new friends without the added stress of a long-distance boyfriend. So, the

---

2. Tell me

idea of going on a date still terrifies me a little bit. She tells me to turn on my location and to call her once I know where we're going and whether we will be watching a movie or not. She kisses my head again and leaves me to read a little bit more.

The cool evening air hits me as I step outside, the sky still holding onto its bruised purple from the fading sunset. The clock on my phone reads 6:55 p.m. I hear the rumble of an engine before I see it, a low growl in the distance, growing louder. Then, around the corner, his truck appears—an old pickup, its paint faded and chipped like it's been through more than a few storms. It's a relic, something that couldn't be newer than '95 or '96, its body creaking with every bump in the road.

He drives with the window down, his arm hanging loosely out the side, his fingers drumming against the door as he glides forward. For a second, it looks like the truck's somehow out of place here, as if it doesn't belong in the neighborhood with its pristine lawns and freshly paved roads. It's almost like something from a different time—gritty, rough, unpolished but damn nice too.

The truck pulls to a stop in front of the house with a quiet sigh of the engine. I make my way down the driveway, my steps a little unsteady, and climb into the front seat. My hand grips the edge of the door, and as I slide into the seat, the first thing I notice is how off everything feels. The smell of oil and leather hits me in a way that feels familiar but wrong, like I'm stepping into a memory that doesn't belong to me.

Then, I see it—his door is cracked halfway open, and his foot is already out, ready to hit the ground. It's like he's in motion, even before I've fully settled in. I swallow, unsure if I should ask or if it even matters. The silence stretches between us, thicker than it should be.

"Hi!" I greet him with a smile.

He looks at me for a minute and pulls his foot inside. Closing the door, he says, "Hi, Allie."

He looks absolutely dreamy with a black fitted T-shirt that highlights his arms and shows the hint of a tattoo peeking out. He is also wearing dark jeans, and I realize I don't think I've ever seen him in anything other than shorts before. I quickly look up at his face and find him looking at me with a show-stopper smile, and he says, "You look beautiful."

I chuckle and look at my jeans and the flowy, teal top I decided to wear. I look casual; just as if I was going to school. "Likewise," I say, and quickly face forward.

We are both sitting there in silence, so I look back at him while pointing at the road. "So, are we gonna get going?"

He smirks and nods without saying anything else. The truck starts slowly rolling forward, and he turns the volume up just a little. Enough for me to tell that the song is *Son of a Song of a Sailor* but still low enough that it would be comfortable to have a conversation.

"For the record, you should let a guy open the door for you when he's picking you up for a date," he says in a low husky voice while he quickly looks at me then back at the road. Goose-bumps rise on my arms as I am left almost speechless by his comment. I clear my throat and say, "Sorry, a habit I guess," shrugging and biting on my lip.

"You are in the habit of going out with jerks who won't even open the door for you?"

I almost choke as I cough and laugh at the same time. "I'm in the habit of getting my own door. I don't really date."

The light turns red, and he slowly stops while raising an eyebrow and turning slightly to look at me. "Like in Baker?"

"No, like in general. We move so much that I don't think people even notice me. I meet new people all the time, but I think I'm more of the fascinating new girl than anything else."

Jeez, that sounds depressing, so I continue, "It's fine. This is the life we live, and it truly isn't a big deal. I love traveling and meeting new people, it just doesn't go hand in hand with relationships."

He stares for a second, then looks forward so he can keep driving. "Allie, if you really think people don't notice you, you're wrong."

"Then maybe I come on too strong and scare guys away. Either way, I have only been on a handful of dates, and this is my first time getting picked up for one, for sure."

"If they are too scared to ask you out, that's on them. Not you. You are just too strong for people who are too weak. For the right person...you're exactly what they want. Exactly what they need."

And with that, I die a little. What do I even say to that? I have no idea, so I don't say anything and keep looking forward.

We pass the time talking about random things, food mostly, and some things we like. I tell him how much I love starchy food: all forms of potato, bread, pasta, and chips. He makes me laugh when he shares that he is not a favorite kind of person and he enjoys it all. Food, music, hobbies. He says the only thing he doesn't love is reading because he can't shut his brain off long enough to enjoy it, which opens the door for me to talk about all the things I love about reading, especially being able to shut my brain off and wander into new worlds with every book I pick up. We keep talking, and all of a sudden I remember I don't even know where we are going. We are on the highway now, so he might be taking me to Jax.

My heart starts beating fast, like palpitations, as I start imagining a worst-case scenario. I don't want to be rude and grab my phone, but if I don't do something soon, we might need to pull over for me to go on a walk.

Breathe, Allie. Breathe.

I decide to just ask and stop freaking out when he takes the exit to Roosevelt and keeps driving. He looks at me and smiles and says, "We're almost there. I hope you're hungry."

Hungry? More like *starving,* but I need to calm down if I'm going to enjoy dinner at all. Until now, being with him has been so easy. He's easy to talk to, and the ride has been smooth. He is friends with all of my friends, so there's no reason for me not to trust him. This is not a psychological thriller, and he is not a serial killer. Maybe if I were upfront with him about my anxiety issues, he would have realized that the unknown would drive me up the wall.

In the middle of my freakout, I completely zone ou,t and before I know it, he's parked and is walking toward my door. I grab my purse, but before I open the door, he beats me to it. He holds my hand as a step out of his truck, and smiles at me, reaching over my head to close it. He guides me with his hand on my lower back while we walk. "I hope you like Mexican food," he says.

I could practically squeal with excitement when I say, "I fucking love Mexican."

We go in and get seated almost immediately in a booth by the back of the restaurant. It's a small mom-and-pop place with colorful decorations. There are booths and tall tables. Ranchera is playing in the background, and it smells incredible.

The waitress comes and asks in Spanish what we want to drink, and to my surprise, he says, "Agua, por favor."

I look at her, smile, and say the same thing. She leaves us to look at the menu, and while I'm reading it, I ask him, "Do you speak Spanish, or do you just come here a lot?"

He smiles and says, "Both and neither. I speak a little bit but not as much as I would like. And I love this place, but I also don't come here as often as I would like since it's outside of Baker Oaks."

"And here I was thinking you were trying to impress me with your Spanish," I sass while putting my hands under my chin and fluttering my eyelashes.

"What if I was?" he says smirking, not taking his eyes off me for one second.

We both laugh softly and go back to the menu. The waitress comes back with our water and takes our orders. A chimichanga, queso, and chips for me and fajitas for Jake.

We fall into comfortable conversation as I eat my weight in chips and queso, and not once does he say anything about it. He tells me about his plan to go to UF next fall to study history or business and continue playing football. I tell him that University of Florida is my top choice too, but I haven't gotten my acceptance letter, yet. I talk about why I want to go into education and how I hope someday to share my passion for learning with children. I learn his favorite color is green and he loves being outside almost more than anything else. He loves animals and his Gma. He promises to take me over to have dinner with her so I can hear all the stories she has to tell.

We continue talking and eating as our food comes out. His plate is sizzling right in front of him, and it smells amazing. Even better than my mouth-watering chimichanga. I don't want to stare, but it smells fantastic; like someone's grandma cut the peppers and onions herself after picking them from the garden. He hands me a small plate with a fork, and I look at him with a puzzled look.

"Do you want some?" I ask while taking the plate from him.

"No, that's for you to grab some fajitas," he says.

Shaking my head, I reply with, "No, no. I couldn't."

He smiles the biggest smile and says, "You know you want to. Go ahead. It would be an honor to share my fajitas with you." He hasn't even tried them yet, and he is still letting me have some first. Looking at his eyes—I swear he is smiling with them too—I whisper a *thank you* and dig right in.

He laughs softly, so I look up and say, "I know, I'm ridiculous," brushing him off.

"More like adorable," he adds and laughs some more as I lower my head.

I don't know how long we've been at the restaurant, but it must be late because when he asks for the check, I look around and notice we're the only people left. I offer to pay for half, and he doesn't even entertain the thought.

We walk side by side toward the truck, the quiet of the evening wrapping around us like a soft blanket. As we reach it, Jake opens the door for me with a smooth gesture, offering his hand to help me up. His fingers curl around mine, strong and steady, guiding me as I hop up into the truck. It feels effortless, like we've done this a thousand times before.

I settle into the seat, thinking about this night and how perfect it has been—better than I ever expected—and now, I feel a strange pull, like I don't want it to end, but at the same time, I'm so full, so content, I could fall asleep right here.

Jake slides into the driver's seat, his movements smooth as he adjusts himself and starts the engine. He glances at me, his expression softening with concern. "Are you too tired from last night? I can take you home."

"Or?" I ask, my voice light, teasing.

"Or we can drive around and keep talking for a while," he says, sheepishly, like he's unsure if I'll go for it

I lean back, letting out a comfortable sigh, already knowing my answer. "Option two, please."

"Attagirl." His grin is wide, and I can't help but return it. He winks at me, and the small, playful gesture has my stomach doing flips and my smile widening. He places the truck in reverse, and we pull out of the parking lot. The night feels endless as the road stretches out ahead of us. I don't want it to end. Not yet. I'm in no rush to go anywhere, just... to be here, in this moment with him.

9

———

NOW

BACK TO DECEMBER (TAYLOR'S VERSION),
TAYLOR SWIFT

Allie

I WAKE up to the smell of coffee and something irresistibly fried, and I instantly know Jake is probably in the kitchen, working his magic with one of his mom's recipes. The scent brings me back to another time, to when he used to cook for me all the time. I remember the first time he made me country fried steak. I had no idea what I was getting myself into, but the moment that crispy, golden piece of heaven hit my tongue, I was unraveling. It was unreal—better than anything I'd ever had. He loved seeing the way I lit up when I tried something new, and it made him cook for me even more.

I roll out of bed and slip into the bathroom, quickly brushing my teeth and splashing water on my face. I check the messy bun I'd thrown together last night in a half-hearted attempt to keep my curls under control, and thankfully, it's still holding up, though the mess of curls around my hairline tells a different story.

Grabbing my laptop, I head toward the kitchen, already looking forward to whatever he's making.

"Good morning," I say, my voice thick and groggy, still too far from caffeinated to sound anything resembling human. I'm cheerful, sure, but not before coffee. Everyone who knows me well—even my coworkers—understands this.

Jake looks up, his voice rough with sleep, but his smile is warm. "Hey," he responds, his eyes crinkling in that way that makes me feel like everything is right in the world.

"It smells fantastic," I say, inhaling deeply. "What are you making?"

"Biscuits and gravy," he replies, turning back to the stove. The words alone make my stomach rumble, and I glance over at the bubbling sausage gravy, thick and rich with just the right amount of seasoning.

I stare at it for a second, the excitement bubbling up in my chest. I don't even need to say anything. The man knows his way around food, and his sausage gravy is, hands down, the best I've ever had.

"Want to help?" he asks, a hint of uncertainty in his voice, like he's not sure if I'll want to jump in.

I look at him, that warmth from earlier spreading through me again. He's asking because he wants me to be a part of it, and for a second, it makes me want to pause everything and just soak in this moment.

I flash him a smile. "I'm pretty sure you don't need my help," I tease, leaning against the counter. "But I'd love to help taste-test."

He chuckles, shaking his head, but I see a playful glint in his eye. "Alright, deal," he says, turning his attention back to the stove.

"Sure. How can I help?"

He instructs me to crack some eggs and whisk them, and to

set the little table for two. He also offers coffee, so I grab a mug that is sitting out.

"Thanks. Coffee is great." It's warm and creamy but not too creamy. It's just right. I wonder how many times he saw me adding the same amount of sugar and cream to make this so long ago; it is still as perfect as it could be.

"I'm glad," he says smiling at me and stirring the pot in front of him. "What are your plans for today?"

"I am waiting for the office to answer my email about the B&B, but it might be tomorrow before I hear anything, so I'm considering just getting a hotel in Jax until they can figure it out."

He doesn't say anything while he mixes the gravy. He looks up at me and then back at his pot. He drags his hand over his face and says, "Or you can stay here until they figure it out."

"Jake, you couldn't even look me in the eyes when you said that. I'm not staying here. You have been so kind already, and I appreciate it, but I can't."

"Why are you being so difficult?"

"I'm not being difficult. I'm being respectful. You have a whole life that I'm not a part of, and I won't intrude." He winces at my words and instantly scowls. "I didn't mean it like that. You do have a life though, and I don't want to be a burden."

"You will never be a burden, and I'm offering," he says.

"I don't know anything about your life anymore, Jake. I don't even know if you're dating someone, and the worst thing that could happen to me is having to explain to your girlfriend who I am, how we know each other, and why I am staying here."

He moves the pot of gravy off of the hot stove and places the mitten on the countertop. He's moving methodically in the kitchen and not keeping eye contact with me. He turns around silently, but the change in his demeanor is immediate. He opens the fridge, and with one hand on the door, he bends down to grab something from inside. His knuckles turn white from his grip on the door, and the tips of his ears are red. He's either completely mad or, at least, very annoyed right now. The ears were always his first tell.

He gets the orange juice out, places it on the countertop, and while leaning against it, he looks at me and says, "Do you really think if I were dating someone you would be here without me checking with her first?"

No, I don't think so. "I don't know, Jake."

"Allie, you know me better than that. Time has passed, but values don't just go away."

His words hit me like a sharp stab to the chest, and suddenly, all the air feels like it's been sucked out of the room. Regret floods in, sharp and suffocating. What is wrong with me? Why did I doubt him?

His next words slice through the silence, and I feel the weight of them deep in my stomach. "And besides, every single person I have been with since you, eventually gets to know who you are. Whether I want them to or not."

I freeze, confusion clouding my thoughts. I stare at him, trying to process what he's saying, but I can't quite grasp it. Before I can ask, he adds, "Either from me calling your name in my sleep, or when they realize that the ghost of the girlfriend of the past will haunt me forever, no matter how hard I try to move on."

A shudder runs through me, the pain in his voice so raw I almost can't stand it. His words hang in the air, heavy and real, and I have no idea how to respond. Tears threaten again, burning the back of my throat, and I take a deep breath to steady myself. No. Not now.

"Jake," I say, my voice trembling with the weight of everything unsaid between us, "We're either going to have this conversation right now, or you need to stop throwing little jabs my way. I can just leave."

The words feel like they're coming from someone else, someone who isn't this vulnerable. But the sting of his casually cruel comments—honest, for sure, but teetering between telling me flat out he hates me or just letting me know right under the surface—are too much to ignore anymore. He's not the only one with a cage around his heart. I've built a wall around mine—high and tight, brick by brick, and every time I look at him, I feel like I'm being pulled back in time—to who we were, to how it felt to be his.

But I can't keep letting him make these little digs at me. I can't keep pretending it doesn't hurt, even if he doesn't mean to wound me every time. He needs to know it does. We need to talk about it now.

He turns his body to face me completely, and in a soft whisper, says, "I don't want you to leave."

"Then, let's talk. You want to talk? Go ahead," I snap back. I sound like the biggest bitch, but I am on the verge of tear,s and I can't break down in front of him. *Get a grip.*

He doesn't say anything, or at least nothing my ears can hear. He makes a low noise that sounds a lot like a mix between a mumble and a grunt, while he rubs his beard with his eyes closed.

"We were children, Jake," I add, swallowing hard and stopping briefly. "I said sorry then, and I've said sorry now. I can't do anything to change the past, and I can't sit around while you keep making comments like that. Like, I don't even know you anymore, and I refuse to let you treat me like this." I can't tolerate this again, so he can get it together, or I can leave.

That catches his attention, and he turns around slowly and looks me in the eyes. His eyes are glossy from either sadness or rage. *Maybe both.* "We were not kids. Nothing we felt was childish. Nothing we did was either," he sighs and continues, "but I can agree to let it rest and try to have a fresh start. It will take time to get used to it, though. To get used to seeing you back here."

"I'm not back, Jake. I'm here for work and honestly, I might be back in Jacksonville for six months and then on to the next place."

"A guy can dream."

We stare at each other for what feels like an eternity but also not long enough, and then he says, "I miss you. No matter how much time has passed. I miss you so much but more than anything, I miss my friend. You were my favorite person, Allie, and I miss that."

Please. It was hard enough knowing I broke his heart and mine, but the weight of knowing that our friendship ended that night, too? It doesn't just keep breaking my heart—it shatters it. Every single time I think about it, every time I remember how we used to be, it feels like I'm losing him all over again.

The words burn at the back of my throat as they escape, sounding hollow even to my own ears. "We can definitely try to be friends again."

It's not a promise. Hell, it's barely even a hope. It's just the only thing I can say, the only thing that doesn't feel like a complete lie. But I'm not sure if I believe it. And I'm not sure if he believes it either.

He looks at me, his eyes softening for a split second, like he sees the cracks in my voice, in the way I said it. Then, he smiles. It's small but genuine, and it hits me harder than it should. "I'd like that."

And for a moment, there's this strange, almost peaceful silence between us, like we've both agreed to start over, even if we don't really know what that looks like.

10

THEN

ROBARTE UN BESO, CARLOS VIVES & SEBASTIAN YATRA

Allie

FUTURE HUSBAND:

Good morning, Allison.

ME:

Right back at you, Jacob,

FUTURE HUSBAND:

Nobody calls me that.

ME:

Nobody calls me Allison, either.

FUTURE HUSBAND:

But it suits you.

ME:

Blah

FUTURE HUSBAND:

I kinda like being the only one who calls you Allison.

ME:

My parents do, so if you want me to relate you with them, then go ahead. Maybe I can call you Daddy.

CALL YOU DADDY? *Who the fuck says that? Well, it's too late to take it back now, but I can try to change the subject.*

ME:

I had fun last night, thank you!

FUTURE HUSBAND:

You don't have to thank me for taking you out on a date. But I had a good time, too. Would love to hang out today too if you are free.

ME:

Sundays are spent with my family.

FUTURE HUSBAND:

No problem :)

ME:

But you could come?

FUTURE HUSBAND:

To your house?

ME:

Yeah, there's always people here, and there will be food, too.

FUTURE HUSBAND:

I don't want to impose.

ME:

You're not! My family is a lot though, so be warned,

FUTURE HUSBAND:

What should I bring?

Squeeeeee. Did I really? Did I ask him to come over? What??

"Mami!" I shout, hoping she can hear me wherever she is in the house.

"Yes?" she says back, standing right by my door. She must have been close, which works for me because I don't want to get up.

"Can you tell Rosalia to add an extra plate for a friend please?"

"Sure thing, mi niña. Anything else?"

"Nope, that's all. Gracias!" She closes the door, leaving me alone again. I grab my phone and shoot Jake another text.

ME:

> Nothing, just come prepared to deal with the loudest people you have ever met.

FUTURE HUSBAND:

> Not a problem.

WE ARE SITTING on the porch talking and snacking, enjoying our traditional Sunday shenanigans. My mom comes from a huge family of ten children and parents who lived their whole lives to make sure their children grew up to be friends more than family. It's very important for her that, although we have lived in so many places and moved so much, we still stay in touch with this part of her. Hence, why *Family Sunday* was born. We eat and talk and dance. Sometimes my twin brothers' friends join, sometimes Cara and her family join, and sometimes it's just us. Cara is an usual add-on here on Sundays. My brothers get along with her fine, well, at least one of them does. Manny seems to always pick on her, but she takes no shit, which makes all of us laugh even more. Her little sister, Nellie, comes sometimes but not always. She's younger than all of us but also wicked smart, so she spends her free time with her nose buried in a book.

The weather, in typical Florida fashion, is hotter than hell and more humid than a steam room. However, the sun is out, and the skies are clear, making it a beautiful day. There's a table set out, full of snacks and drinks, and my mom's famous Sangria that we are allowed to indulge in as long as we stay home.

The bell rings, and we all stop and look at each other when mom says, "Why is Cara ringing the bell? She knows the door stays open."

"I can go get the door," Manny adds quickly.

At the same time I say, "Cara? She's not coming today."

"Oh, I thought you said someone was coming."

"Yeah, my friend, Jake." Everyone stops and looks at me like I have three heads.

"Wepa, un novio![1]" Gus teases.

"Then, you can go get the door yourself," Manny says.

"Stop it right now!" I say as I feel heat rising to my cheeks. I swear if I had fair skin, I would 100% be blushing right now. If these people make a big deal out of it, I may just die of embarrassment today. I do, however, not blame them for wondering what is happening, considering this would be the first time I invited a guy friend here.

My mom clears her throat, looks at everyone else, and then looks at me. "Well, are you going to let Jake in?" she asks, pointing toward the front door.

I sigh and turn around. I hear them giggling as I speed walk back into the house. I reach the door, close my eyes, and take a

---

1. Oh, a boyfriend!

deep breath in. I open it and try to smile, but my breath catches, and it sounds more like a hiss at the sight of Jake.

He's wearing a dark T-shirt with cargo shorts and flip-flops. I'm pretty sure this is his typical attire, but it's almost like I was blind and I can now suddenly notice every detail about him. How his T-shirt hugs his arms in all the right places. How tall he is as he towers over me, holding a dish and smiling. How his dark hazelnut eyes shine when he smiles and looks at me. How his lips are the perfect shade of kissable pink. He smirks, and I know I've been caught ogling him. I chuckle and try to brush it off. I clear my throat and say, "Hi, sorry about the wait."

"No need to apologize. I will happily wait for you." He winks.

¡Dios mio! I might die today.

"Come on in. We have to walk out back, everyone's outside."

He steps in and turns around to look at the living area as he says, "I've never seen this part of your house before. The couple of parties I've been here for, I come in through the back door. It's beautiful."

The first room after you walk into the house is dreamy. Beautiful, white marble floors with mahogany accents lead the way to an open-concept living room with floor-to-ceiling windows overlooking the Spanish garden. There are two sets of staircases that wrap around on each side of the room and lead to the second floor of the house where our bedrooms are. There's a large beige sectional with plants at the corners and a coffee table full of photo albums. And across from it, there's a forest green accent wall with safari illustrations from my mom's favorite artist. There's also a recliner that matches the accents on the staircases, holding a burnt orange blanket and a copy of the book I'm currently reading. The room is light and airy but also mini-malist. It says *stay a while but maybe not too long if you're plan-*

ning on partying, which is exactly why my mom had it decorated like this. It gives cozy vibes.

"Thank you. I love this room. It's my second favorite in the house."

"What's your first?" he asks, truly wondering.

"Maybe I'll show you one day," and then it's my turn to wink at him. He smiles at me, and I giggle a little and start walking toward the backyard.

I try to warn him about my family's teasing him and how everyone would be drinking and laughing, and he just says he's fine and he's got it. I introduce my mom, brothers, and their friends to Jake, but they already know him, so they shake hands and whatnot. My mom kisses him on the cheek and hugs him as if she already loves him, and I really want to crawl under the floor.

We sit next to each other and quickly fall into conversation with everyone else. I am learning more about him this afternoon than I did last night, and it's great to see how easily he fits in with everyone. My mom is laughing at something he says. One of my brothers is dancing while the other one scrolls on his phone. It is almost like we have done this a thousand times before.

It starts to get dark and my mom sends us all on our way with a reminder that there's school tomorrow and we need to get in bed soon. We all say our goodbyes, and I walk Jake back to the front door. "Thank you for hanging out with my family today. I'm sure you had better things to do," I say as I stand by the door.

He holds my eyes and says, "There's nothing better than getting to know you, Allie, and that includes your family. Plus, I had fun." This boy is leaving me speechless and without air to breathe.

"I like getting to know you too," I say because what else do you say after he comes out with something like that?

"Does your mom always kiss people on the cheeks? Or is that part of your culture?"

"Definitely part of the culture. Sorry if that was weird."

"It wasn't. I was just wondering if I should kiss your cheek right now, too. You know, since we're saying goodbye and all."

I smile and nod. He dips down and kisses me on the right cheek. He then whispers in my ear, "Goodnight, Honey. See you at school tomorrow."

"Honey? That's new." I shiver after hearing the name come out of his lips in that raspy voice that makes my insides turn.

"I told you, I wanted a name for you that only I use, and clearly Allison wasn't it." He walks backwards not dropping his eyes from mine, until he reaches his truck.

I watch him drive away as my cheeks burn with heat. I turn around, go back inside, and close the door behind me. *Honey,* I whisper in the hallway, to no one in particular. I do a little leap and let a squeak out as I walk to my room holding my face like the dork I am.

Not washing my face ever again.

11

———

NOW

CONEY ISLAND, TAYLOR SWIFT FT. THE
NATIONAL

Allie

"THIS IS me calling you now, Cara," I tell her for the eighth time since I picked up the phone to Facetime her and explain the last twenty-four hours of hell.

"I just don't understand how you go from not even wanting to hear anything about Jake for ten years to staying at his house and not fucking telling me. I already have to worry about Nellie all the damn time with not answering texts or telling me shit about her unless I pry it out of her. Don't be this person, too. A text would've been nice!" She's upset, and I don't blame her. Especially after I've told her so many times *not* to tell me anything about Jake, even when I knew she had stuff she wanted to share with me. I hear her heavy breathing and practically see her fuming.

"I needed to wrap my head around this, too, girl. I'm still in shock, and a lot is going on in my head. I'm sorry, though."

I let out a slow breath, feeling the weight of her words. I knew she'd be upset. Hell, I'm upset, too, but right now, the last thing I can focus on is Cara. She's been my rock for so long, but this... this feels like too much. "I should've called you last night. Maybe you would've slapped some sense into me through the phone."

Silence stretches out, thick and uncomfortable. I hate talking on the phone, especially when I'm not sure what I'm feeling. But with Cara, it's always been different. Even when I'm a mess, even when I feel like I'm losing my mind, her voice always calms me. Always. I can almost see her now, pacing around or maybe sitting down somewhere to listen. Then, I hear it—the sound of ice cubes clinking in a glass, the soft scrape of them as they tumble.

She takes a deep sip, and I know she's thinking, processing. Trying to keep it together, just like I am. "What are you going to do?" she asks, her voice cool but still wrapped in that thread of concern.

I can practically hear the annoyance in her tone. Multi-tasking—talking to me and pouring herself ice-cold water. She does it when she's trying to settle herself, and after knowing her for as long as I have, I can tell. She's probably fighting the urge to shout at me right now, but she's being patient, waiting for me to figure it out. So I speak up, laying it all out, even though it feels like too much.

"I have no fucking clue. I'm still waiting for them to email me back. I have to show up at work tomorrow though, so I guess I will be leaving from here."

Her voice is quiet for a second, then comes that sharp, practical edge I know so well. "A ride share from there will cost half a kidney. Isn't your first job in Jax?"

"It is. It'll be fine. They can reimburse me."

I don't really know if it'll be fine. I don't know how any of this is going to go, but I'm telling her what she wants to hear, what I want to hear, even if it doesn't feel real. The uncertainty is gnawing at me, but Cara's always been the one who knows how to handle things. If I can keep it together for one more day... maybe things will start making sense. Or maybe they won't.

"You know, you can also call your dad. He'll put you in the nicest hotel ever," she says. "You also have your trust fund, babe, if you wanted to you could use that to do whatever you want. To stay wherever you want."

I shake my head and stare at her.

She stares back and shrugs.

"I am not calling him. I don't even know where he's at now, and I am not touching that money. I have made it this far without it, I can keep going."

My relationship with my dad got all kinds of messed up ten years ago, and I promised myself I would never ask for anything else from him. I still talk to my mom and see her often but not him. His 'help' always comes with consequences, and I have worked too hard to understand my value in life to let him make me feel like a failure.

"I can practically hear your thoughts. What else is going through that beautiful head of yours right now?" She smiles fondly at me. She's not mad anymore, she's worried.

"How are you feeling after all that shit went down with Cole?" Her boyfriend of ten years broke up with her, and the asshole deserves to burn in hell. I actually hope I see him while I'm here so I can smack in on the head.

"Don't change the topic, Allie. Answer the question."

"I just don't want to mess this up."

"What 'this'? The job? Or Jake?" Her eyebrows raise as she smirks nonchalantly.

"The job." *Jake. Both.* I quickly look away so she can't see right through me and say, "I need to go."

"I need to go, too. Meal prepping is calling my name. I'll talk to you later, and please call me the next time something like this happens. I would rather not murder you next time I see you. Ok?" She sticks her tongue out and then smiles at me. She can be a pain in the butt, but Cara is seriously like the sister I never had but always needed.

"Love you, bye!"

I put the phone on the nightstand and start going through my suitcase to find something to wear now, and tomorrow. I get dressed quickly and start working on my plan for tomorrow on my laptop.

Taylor Swift is playing, and I'm deep into my work when I hear a soft knock and the door opening. I look up through my lashes and whisper a soft, "Yes?" I need to finish doing this to be ready for tomorrow, so I really don't want to spend time arguing with Jake again.

"I'm just checking on you. I'm about to head to town and wanted to know if you needed anything or if you wanted to come?" he says.

He is looking at me with a shy smile while he stands there, leaning against the door frame. *God, he's gorgeous.* I feel my heart skip a beat just like it did back in high school, and I really can't allow myself to go back there.

I close my computer and set it next to me. "I need to go grocery shopping, but with where I'm staying still up in the air, I don't want to get too many things."

"Just come with and you can grab some snacks. For as long as you are here, you can eat anything that I have."

"I appreciate that, but you are already doing enough." I look down because staring at his eyes for too long makes me think of things I want to do but shouldn't. He's still leaning against the door frame, waiting for an answer, so I say, "Do you mind if I go with you?"

He rubs his thick beard with his hand but simply says, "If I did, I wouldn't have asked you to come, Allie." He stops to look at me and quietly says, "Come on, let's go."

He walks out, giving me space to get ready. I already have on a black, beige, and soft pink maxi dress with tiny flowers. Flowers are my favorite print for dresses, and maxi dresses have become a staple in my wardrobe because they can be dressed up or down, and they are so comfortable. I put my sandals on, wrap my hair in a messy bun, and grab my purse. I walk out the door, and he's already waiting in his truck.

He has always loved trucks, but this is nothing like the one he had before. He drives a black Silverado that is so shiny, almost like he just washed it. As soon as I step inside, I marvel at how beautiful it is. The inside is black leather, and it smells just like him. How did I miss all these details last night? *Oh right, you were freaking out last night, Allie.*

I snap my seat belt in place and look at him with a soft smile. He looks at me and asks if I'm ready. I nod and we start to roll.

The windows are down, the warm breeze blowing as we drive by. "Will this be awkward? You and me, at a store?"

"For who?" he replies while still looking forward.

"For us. For any people there. I don't know." I look back out the window.

"I think the more we hang out, the less awkward it will be for us. And as for people there, who in particular are you worried about?" He peers at me through his eyelashes. He has dark eyes, but his lashes are practically black. They are full and long, framing his eyes and making them look even more beautiful. I know women who would kill to have lashes like his.

"I don't know, past girlfriends? Cashiers who are secretly in love with you? People who may remember me? Who may remember us?" I keep looking out the window because that was a ballsy thing to say. *Great job, Allie. Keep making it weird.*

He chuckles, "Allie, people will talk regardless. I haven't dated anybody who works there nor are there any cashiers who are secretly in love with me. If it makes you feel better, we can go into Jacksonville or Lake City."

"Nah, nope. No need. I'm fine."

He laughs and turns the music up. Joji is playing, and he is singing the lyrics like it's his favorite song, and I start to relax. I can't continue to be this tense around him, but it's so hard. I'm either so obsessed with him it makes my body tingle, or I hurt all over and I don't want to let my guard down. I'll find a hotel or another B&B tomorrow and call it a day.

We arrive at the grocery store and grab a basket. I turn to go our separate ways, but he grabs me by the elbow and turns me toward him. "Let's walk this way," he says as he grabs my basket and sets it in the cart.

We wander in the store adding things to the cart. He grabs meats and vegetables, but I opt for premade lunches, chips, and fruit. He chuckles next to me but then just shrugs when I look at him. He always thought I had the cravings of a three-year-old, and it's still the case. I could survive on deli meat, crackers, and fruit. It feels so natural to just walk the aisles and talk about random things with him. We catch up on the usual topics and joke about our snack choices some more. Being with him is refreshing, like second nature.

WE MAKE it back to his house, unload the truck, and put things where they go. We snack on some chips and fruit as we put everything away, and I start packing things to bring with me tomorrow so it's ready to go.

I want to ask more about his life, what he's been up to, but I don't want to pry. I don't feel like I have the right to anymore. After everything, it seems... intrusive, even though I'm curious. So, I finish putting my things away and start to turn, ready to walk off, when I feel him gently take my hand and tap it against the counter. The warmth of his touch lingers there, and I glance at him, unsure of what he's asking with just that little gesture.

I used to love sitting on kitchen counters when we were together. He'd cook, and I'd just keep him company, my legs swinging under the countertop, the space between us feeling like home. I look at the counter, then back at him, and before I even realize it, I'm pulling myself up onto the cool surface.

I think about it for a moment, weighing the decision. But honestly, what's the harm? What's the worst that can happen? There's no script for this, and I might not know what I'm doing, but I know what I feel.

I hear him say, almost like a whisper, "That's my girl," and I freeze. It hits me harder than it should, and I see it in his eyes, the sudden realization of what he just said. Neither of us really wanted to go there, not now. I don't want to make it awkward, so I scramble for something lighthearted.

I plaster a smile on my face, forcing my tone to be playful, "You have me on the counter, what are you cooking for me?" I open my palm and gesture across the countertop space, adding with a wink, "Chop chop, time's a wastin'."

It works. The tension cracks, and he laughs, his shoulders relaxing. He turns around, grabbing ingredients, setting the rhythm of the kitchen back to the familiar hum of comfort. The smell in the air is intoxicating, something savory and delicious, filling the entire house. My eyes drift closed for a moment as the scent envelopes me, but when I open them again, I'm smiling.

The country music playing softly in the background somehow adds to the magic, making it feel like we've slipped into this little bubble—just us, just like we used to be, where everything feels simple and possible. I sip my wine, pass him condiments when he needs them, and it all feels so easy. Like no time has passed. Like we're not caught in a mess of the past. Like we're just two people, existing together in a moment where nothing else matters.

I can't remember the last time I felt this... grounded.

Dinner's ready, and he's bringing everything to the table. I start scooting forward to get down from the counter, but he shakes his head as he holds my gaze. He walks toward me without looking away and comes to stand in front of me. Then he grabs me by the waist, whispering in a hoarse voice, "Let me help you down, don't need you getting hurt under my watch."

My skin prickles, and I shiver while I slowly reply, "I weigh a lot, Jake. You don't need to put strain on your knee by picking me up. I can hop down."

He leans closer, picks me up like I'm weightless, and places me on the ground, but he doesn't move away. He is so close to me; his lips are almost touching my ear, and my chest is practically flush against his. I feel his chest moving quickly and his breath picking up, so I don't move. I close my eyes and mentally count to try to keep my breathing even.

His warm breath caresses my neck as he says, "You're not heavy, Allie. I can bench press 455 pounds. You are as light as a feather in comparison, I can pick you up no problem, no matter how many curves you have." He lets go of my waist and slowly walks back, giving me some space, but all of a sudden I feel like I might lose my footing and just melt into a puddle right here. *Puddle, I am a puddle.*

He is still looking, turmoil reflecting in his eyes. He lets out a breath and shakes his head. He looks back up and says, "And for the record, the curves suit you."

12

THEN

KISS ME, ED SHEERAN

Allie

THERE'S AN AWAY GAME TOMORROW, and it's so far away we won't have much warm up time before the game, so we're having an extra long practice. It's almost 7:00 p.m., and I'm exhausted and ready to go home. I start walking out of the locker room and see that football practice isn't over. I head to the bleachers to watch them.

Jake and I have been talking nonstop since this weekend. He also finds me at school every chance he gets, even though we don't have any classes together. And every day, he walks me to my car, even if he's not going home yet. He has been so attentive and overall the opposite of what I thought a football player would be. He hasn't kissed me, yet, and it's fine if he wants to take this slow. But with the amount of time that we have spent together or just talking this week, you would think we have been dating for months.

Practice is still going, so I grab a book from my bag, get comfortable and start reading. The humidity in the air makes the pages feel almost wet, which is fitting, given the sinking feeling I'm getting while reading this chapter. The boys keep playing, and I keep reading, wondering if I'm maybe overstepping waiting for him.

"Allie. Allie, wake up," I hear a voice in the distance. Suddenly, I feel like I'm falling, and I jerk, but strong arms hold me in a tight hug, and I start floating. I flutter my eyes open and see Jake smirking and when I try to move he softly adds, "Shh, it's ok. I got you."

Is he carrying me? What happened? I must have fallen asleep. Oh God, so embarrassing. "Jake, put me down." I'm mortified. Please let this be a dream.

He smiles and says, "I already got you up, might as well let me finish this."

Why is this so sexy and mortifying at the same time? I squirm, trying to loosen the hold he has on me, but he just shakes his head slightly. He's amused by this. At the fact that he is built of stones, and no matter how curvy I am, I can't make him budge. "You are going to get hurt, put me down."

"Who's going to get hurt, me?" he says.

"My weight."

He scoffs and says, "You're not even heavy."

I'm the biggest cheerleader on the squad because I'm built like a thick gymnast, as opposed to a petite cheerleader. It's not an issue. I have worked hard to love my body the way it is, but love doesn't take away the fact that I'm heavy.

"Your eyebrows are speaking. I promise you, you are not heavy, Allison. I warm up with twice your weight. Let me take care of you." He keeps walking like I'm not dead weight.

We're almost to the parking lot when he asks if I drove today. I shake my head and he keeps walking to his truck. He puts me down briefly to open the door and places me in the passenger seat. He leans in to buckle me up, and I can smell him even more now. He smells like wood, mixed with sweat, and a hint of something minty, and it should gross me out, but instead, it sparks something in me. He closes the door and walks around to his side.

As he starts driving, he asks if I'm hungry, to which I nod. We go back and forth with what to get but we end up going for smoothies and wraps. We're waiting at the drive-thru, and I yawn, trying to curl up on his seat. I'm so tired from the week and practice, I could sleep for a week.

"Why did you wait for me?" he asks, his voice trembling slightly. "Don't get me wrong, I loved seeing you there when I got done, but you're clearly exhausted."

He starts to reach for me, his hand hovering in the air for just a second, before he pulls it back, almost like he's afraid of what I might say or do. I see the uncertainty flicker in his eyes, and my heart tightens a little.

I smile at him. "Because I wanted to. Isn't that a good enough reason?"

"Yes, it is." He smiles back and places his hand on top of mine. It feels nice, like it belongs there. My skin flushes immediately, and I have never been more thankful for having tanned skin than right now. *Seriously? My heart racing over a hand on mine?* Maybe it is not just the hand, but whose hand it is.

We make it to my house a while later, and I don't think I'll ever get tired of his company. He's so funny, kind, and interesting. It seems like he has his shit together, too. "Do you want me to pick you up in the morning?" he asks as we reach the front door. He looks nervous, like he's unsure of what he wants to do, or like he wants to say more than what he's actually saying.

I look up at him and smile, trying to ease whatever nerves he has. "You don't have to, but if you want to, I'm good with that." He smiles and reaches for my hand. He steps closer and holds it in his, and my whole arm is suddenly aware of his touch. Like he ignited a fire within me with just a mere touch. "5:oo a.m. good?"

"Great, just don't judge when I look like a raccoon."

He snickers and tucks a piece of hair behind my ear, "Not a morning person are we, Honey?"

"Nope, not at all."

"I bet you are the cutest looking raccoon in all of Baker." He takes a step closer.

"Oh, is that so? Not in the whole country?" I close our distance a little bit more.

"Oh baby, in the whole universe." He is so close all of my senses are on alert. That woodsy, sweaty smell will be the death of me. It reminds me of camping and good memories. The hand he used to tuck my hair stays on my shoulder and his other hand still holds mine. He is so close that if I were to go up on my tippy toes and lean forward just a little bit, his lips would be on mine. *And I want that, oh so bad.*

"You can't take it back when you see me in the morning." I peer at him through my thin lashes.

"Don't you get it? Nothing can stand against you, Honey." He raises both hands to grab my face. We are sharing the same breath, and the air is thick with intention. He lowers his face to mine. Our noses touch lightly, and right when I think he won't do anything, he closes the inch between us and kisses me.

His kiss feels like my lips landed on a pillow made just for them. So soft and tender. He kisses me gently, his lips lingering a bit longer with every move on every curve. He takes his time, teasing and slowly exploring as if I were a subject he's studying and he wants to be an expert in the matter. He doesn't use his tongue, but it's not just a peck either. I don't know what to do with my hands, so I keep them next to me awkwardly because I'm floating. He tastes like peppermint and good choices. My own little peppermint kiss I never want to let go of. After what feels like ten minutes, but also not long enough all the same, he breaks the kiss and traces my bottom lip with his thumb. "Sorry, but I had to," he says, a little out of breath. "I couldn't go one more day without tasting you."

And that, my friends, is how a girl dies a swooning death. "You don't have to apologize. I wanted it, too." He takes my words as permission to do it again. He's still soft and gentle, so I bite his lower lip, and he smirks against my mouth. He pulls away, but our noses are touching, the air we breathe is mingling, and my heart is racing.

With his eyes closed, his hands holding my face to his as he whispers, "Easy, baby." If this man calls me baby one more time, I might change my name because I've never been more excited about being called anything other than Allie before. "Easy with my heart. If you do that, I won't be able to leave this porch, and we both have a busy day tomorrow." He kisses me one more time and then walks back. Leaving me breathless and lost in him. "Good night, Allie." He smiles tenderly walking back toward his truck.

"Good night, Jake."

I walk into my house, close the door, and lean against it. I feel like my heart is soaring and my legs are jello. What is happening to me? It's been less than a week, but I feel like I've known him longer, and that kiss was as if we've been practicing for years. It was absolutely perfect. I have read books that describe this feeling of belonging to someone, and I always thought it was fiction. But the way that one kiss made me feel, it's making me rethink everything I thought I knew.

PART 2

WHEN THE SUN GOES DOWN IN GEORGIA, COREY SMITH

Falling in love with her was like a sudden blitz on the field—fast, powerful, and unavoidable.
I didn't see it coming, but once it hit, it knocked the wind out of me.
She left me there, on the sidelines, the game clock ticking down, waiting for the next play.
I didn't know if I was waiting for a touchdown or for the whistle to blow—caught in that split-second, when anything could happen, but nothing did.
She didn't pull me back into the game, and she didn't leave me in the dust either. She just... let the clock run out.

$$13$$

NOW

CORNELIA STREET (LIVE FROM PARIS), TAYLOR SWIFT

Jake

IT'S 5:00 A.M., and the noises coming from Allie's room sound like she's at war. *Allie's room.* She's been here a couple of days, and my stupid heart is already claiming her. I know, logically, that this weekend was an alternate reality in which wishful thinking played a big part, but how could I not take anything she was willing to give me? Even if it was just letting me help her.

Pathetic. Anyone paying attention would see how I'm being a fool and acting like I'm eighteen again. Allie came into my life ten years ago like a force of nature; touching everything in sight with magic and leaving devastation behind when she left.

I was finally at a point where I'd accepted it—she was it for me. We were the right people, just in the wrong place, at the wrong time. So, I had settled into my routine, focused on teaching, coaching, and keeping my life in order. And then—just like that—she falls right back into my world.

A second chance? A gift? Or just a cruel tease from fate?

She looks at me the same way I look at her, but I can't ever tell what's really going on in that head of hers. Maybe she's just as lost as I am.

I hear her from behind the door, cursing under her breath. "Coño, why is it so hard to just find something the first time?" I smile, knowing exactly what she's doing. Trying to get dressed, no doubt, already frustrated with herself. "Shit, shit, shit," she mutters, the rustle of clothes following each curse.

I could offer to help, but what would I even do? It's better if I just stay the hell out of it, let her sort herself out. She used to be the worst in the mornings, barely able to function without coffee. Her mood was a whole separate subject that I had to navigate. But today? Today, I've got the coffee brewing, and I'm scrambling eggs on the stove. She loved food—still does, I bet— and feeding her was always something I enjoyed. Hell, I still do. It's the only thing I've wanted to do since the second I saw her again at the airport. Corey Smith's smooth voice hums through the speakers while the sizzle of bacon fills the air. The scent of grease, salt, and coffee mingles and wraps the house in warmth. I hear the door open. I turn, expecting to see a half-awake, caffeine-deprived version of Allie, but instead, I freeze.

She's standing in the doorway, walking toward me with that soft, shy smile. It's not like her at all. I'd almost forgotten how it felt to see her smile like that—guilty, maybe, but still so damn endearing. She must still be feeling the sting of her morning outburst, but somehow, I find it charming. She always had a way of making the smallest things seem important. And, for some goddamn reason, I still find myself completely captivated by it.

She is wearing what I assume is her business attire. She has on a blue dress that touches every single curve of her body down to her hips, where it gets wider. It stops right above the knees which shouldn't be that sexy, but she makes everything look like it was made for her. She is wearing heels that hug her beautiful feet and give her a nice height. Her legs look incredible in that outfit. My eyes keep roaming over her body, and I notice the top of her dress. It shows some cleavage but not too much; leaving a lot to the imagination. Her hair is half up and pulled behind her perfect ears, which are adorned by earrings that say "teacher" on them. She is perfect. She was perfect then, and she's perfect now.

Her lips move, but I don't hear anything. "Mm, sorry, what?" I say stupidly like I wasn't just caught ogling her.

"I said, you're up early."

"Oh, yeah. I have to be at school early. How did you sleep?" *Smooth, Jake, smooth.*

"Great. The bed is great." Her cheeks darken. I always liked that about her. She always says that because she has dark skin, you can't see when she's blushing. Little does she know her cheeks get a darker glow to them when she's embarrassed or when she says something she doesn't mean. It's adorable.

"I'm glad. There's coffee in the pot and creamer in the fridge." She thanks me and grabs a mug. Two teaspoons of sugar and a splash of creamer later, she sits at the breakfast table. She takes a sip of her coffee, closes her eyes and hums. The little sounds she makes will be my undoing, they always have been, and apparently, they always will be. The worst part? She doesn't even know she makes them.

Giving her the plate I made for her, her eyes widen. Two eggs over medium, a couple pieces of bread, some bacon, a piece of avocado, and everything but the bagel seasoning. That used to be her breakfast of choice, and maybe I should have asked if she wanted anything because she's just staring at it in silence. *Fantastic, Jake. Way to go.* "You don't have to eat it. I can put it in a to-go box or something."

"It's... ummmm... it's perfect, Jake. Thank you," she says in a tender tone. "How did you know?"

"How did I know what?" I ask, wiping the countertop to make sure things are clean before we head out. I try to keep my focus on her, though, but it is so hard to look at her and not want to kiss that sweet pout off her face.

She looks at her plate and then at me. "That this is my comfort meal," she says quickly.

Because I know you, Allie. "You used to say breakfast was the most important meal, and I know you have a big day today. It's not a big deal."

"Thank you. This is so kind." Then she starts eating.

I grab a few things to put in my bag. We have practice after school today, so I make sure to grab snacks for the long day. I set my bag on top of the table and see her standing, but I grab the plate from her hands. "Let me take this for you."

"Thanks. Did you eat before I got up?"

"Nah, I don't eat in the mornings. I have planning mid-morning, so I usually eat then—" I point at my big duffle bag on the table, "—that's why my bag is so big. Full of snacks."

"You didn't have to cook for me, I'm already messing up your routine enough. I'll be out of your hair today."

Please don't leave is all I want to say, but instead I say, "I don't mind cooking at all, and you aren't messing anything up. You can stay for as long as you need to." I'd take any time I can spend with her and get to know the woman she has grown into. I had a feeling the reason I was never able to completely move on is because she holds my heart, but seeing her again confirmed it in ways I can't even begin to explain. I just wish it was the same for her. She looks so mature and grown up. And happy. So happy. Still a little erratic and skittish, but she wouldn't be her without that.

"How are you getting to work today?" I ask, knowing full well there's no way she'll get an Uber out here this early.

"Well, that's part of the reason for my screaming this morning," she huffs, "Sorry about that. The first Uber available won't get here until like eight, and I need to be at work at seven forty-five. I was going to ask if you could drop me off at the rideshare stop on your way in."

She looks at me with a mix of embarrassment and guilt. It probably took everything in her to ask for that. She used to hate asking for help and when things don't go according to plan. Right now, both of those things are happening. *I wish she knew I would give her the world if she just asked.*

She swivels in the chair, slightly turning her legs as I walk toward her. There's a small wall right behind her with a metal basket that holds my keys and some mail. I stand in front of her, and I see her eyes look up from under her eyelashes. She is wearing these oversized glasses that don't let you see her beautiful hazel eyes from far away, but from right here, they look every bit the perfection that they are. Her eyes have a brown ring around them with speckles of green and gold inside of her honey-colored irises.

I reach behind her, and her body stiffens. *So responsive to me still.* I grab the keys and put some space between us. I need it to think. She can deny it all she wants, but her body doesn't lie, so I smile softly at her. I grab her hand, and I feel her warm skin prickle under my touch. I open her palm gently and place the keys into it. "Here, you can take my truck." Over my dead body will she get a rideshare when I have a vehicle she can use. "You can drop me off at school on your way out. I have practice, so I won't need to be back until later. If they solve your B&B issue, then I can take you tonight."

"Jake, I can't take this. You are already doing so much," she looks miserable as she shakes her head, and her entire body says no.

"It's not a big deal. Please just take it. You'd be doing me a favor since I won't be worrying about you all day." She doesn't need to know I've been worrying about her since the day I met her. "Come on, let's go. We need to leave so neither of us are late."

While she drives, she looks at the streets we pass as if sh's seeing ghosts. Her knuckles are gripping the steering wheel so hard it's almost like she is holding on for dear life. I turn the music up to try and ease her jitters, and Taylor Swift fills my truck with her voice. I know it's her because I can't listen to a single song of hers without it reminding me of Allie.

Allie scoffs and whispers, "Of course this would be the song to play." She is not really talking to me, and I don't think she realizes it either. *God, she's adorable.* I stare at her little pouty lip as she tries so hard not to sing the lyrics, but her memory betrays her as she mouths the words. Something about a heartbreak that time can't heal.

I swear I hear her voice shake as she tries to stop herself from singing, but then she whispers, *"Cornelia Street,"* as she stares at the road in front of us. Center Street is right in front of us. The same street where we sat so many times to eat, talk, and kiss. Something in the song says she wouldn't be able to walk the street again because it would remind her of something else.

Then everything clicks. This is her *Cornelia Street.* Her eyes are watering while the song keeps playing in the background. She blinks and keeps staring in front of her. Seeing her like this now, it breaks my heart. If she truly loved me, to the point that a street is bringing back all those memories and bringing tears to her eyes, why did she leave? Why did she leave me? If she truly didn't care about us, then why is she having this reaction?

We pull up in front of the high school, and she takes it all in. Her eyes are wide, full of emotion, "It still looks the same."

"Yeah," I sigh, "They've added some portables in the back, and the rooms have been painted, but everything else is the same," I add. "Coach Blake is still the cheer coach, and Principal Parker is still here."

She looks at me like I just brought her back in time. I squeeze her hand and smile at her.

"You'll have to come in and say hi to them before you leave." *She's leaving again.*

She nods as I open the door. I hand her a post-it note with my phone number, she looks at it and grabs it, her fingertips touching my hand. Goosebumps spread up my arm but humid air slips into the cabin from the open door, and it brings us back to reality.

"See you later, Allie."

14

———

NOW

STAY, ZEDD & ALESSIA CARA

Allie

TODAY HAS BEEN HELL! I spent the day trapped in meetings to learn the needs of this school. I will be working there for the next two weeks, and then I'm being transferred to another school. Their principal was so nice, but they have a lot of new teachers in need of training and so little time to do so. I will be recording lessons for them to watch and doing professional development sessions with them. Those are my favorite! I call them Make and Take. They come in ready to learn, but we also make things they can take and use in the classroom. I always leave those meetings giddy and proud of all their hard work and efforts to make learning more fun for their students. But the endless meetings are not my favorite part at all.

Also, my company is struggling to find me a decent B&B, so they suggested I go to a hotel. I hate them though, so I am not entirely sure what to do. Hotels make me feel lifeless, like I'm in a cardboard box. I have never liked them, so staying in one for six months is not appealing at all. I will stay at Jake's tonight and then transfer to the hotel tomorrow. I have one more night with him, and I really want to get to know him more. Not the boy I loved once but the man he has turned into. He still has the heart of gold that made me love him the first time. *The first time.* Like I ever stopped loving him. My mom once said the most important people you are with in your life are the first and the last. The first one because they show you how to love, and the last one because they love you through it all. I truly think Jake was both, even if he won't love me forever, I know I will always love him.

The company was able to provide a rental car for me, though, and they will have it available tomorrow morning. My plan is to drive to Baker now, and hopefully catch Jake at practice then head back to his house to pack. I already requested an Uber for tomorrow morning, so the whole taking-him-to-work deal won't happen again. It can't be comfortable for him to have me staying at his house after everything that happened, especially without any notice; he is just too much of a gentleman to admit it or kick me out. Anyone else would have.

I make it to the school just in time to see the players walk off the field. It brings me back to all the Thursday nights we walked off of the field, hand in hand, after practice. Of the Friday Night Lights that we shared. Memories of happiness and comfort. I park the truck and grab my phone to text him to tell him I'm here, when I realize I still have his number blocked on my phone, but the name is still the same *Future Husband*. I sigh, unblock him and message him.

ME:

Hey, It's Allie. I'm here.

ME:

I mean, Allie Zabana, not sure how many more Allies you have saved.

ME:

Not that it's an issue! You can have all the Allies you want.

ME:

You don't need my permission or anything.

Jesus.

ME:

Anyways, I'm here.

I see the three dots dancing and disappearing and dancing, again. I'm staring at the phone in my hand judging my own life choices when the driver side door opens, scaring me half to death.

"Por Dios!" I whisper, half in a gasp and half in a scream, dropping the phone and covering my ears, as if not hearing whoever is at the door will save me. I slowly turn and see Jake standing there with a panty-dropping smile. *Kill me now, please.* Then, I get a text, FROM HIM, while he's standing right there.

FUTURE HUSBAND:

Hey Allie, Allie Zabana, not my only Allie and not the one that needs to give me permission.

I look up from my phone to find him looking at me with the smuggest grin. *Please, tierra, swallow me whole, now.* "I was rambling, you know," I say with a sigh.

"Yes, Allie, I do know. Want me to drive? You're probably exhausted."

I climb through to the passenger side, struggling a little to get my butt over to the other side and finally making it in the least sexy way possible. He looks at me and smiles, but it doesn't reach his eyes. His eyes are tired and heavy as he holds my gaze and puts his bag in the back. He doesn't say anything else as he swiftly gets behind the steering wheel, closes the door and blasts the AC on high. He has drops of sweat running down the side of his face, and I can tell he's exhausted, too. He's not wearing the same clothes he was wearing this morning, probably changed for practice. He has dry-fit shorts and a long-sleeved shirt that says Coach Clarke on the right side.

"Where are we going?" I ask.

"To get something to eat. I had a long day, and I really don't want to deal with anything right now," he sighs, "and I think the feeling is mutual. So, let's go eat."

"You don't have—" I don't even finish my sentence when he gives me his I-mean-business stare. It's both terrifying and compelling, looking into his eyes when he's 100% serious about something.

We don't say anything for a bit until he adds, "Please don't fight me on this, I don't have the energy today to try to convince you to just be with me. Just—let's eat, and then we can go home."

He turns his focus back to driving, and we fall into an uncomfortable silence. It's never been like this between us, but he just said *we can go home*. But it's not ours, it's his. I'm just crashing into his life and blurring all the lines. Ha, *lines*? More like years of walls built up by the pain I inflicted ten years ago. I look out the passenger side window and silently wipe away a tear from my eye.

"Chinese?" he asks.

"Always," I whisper.

We grab our food and head back to his place, the silence in the car thickening with every mile. The only sound is the low hum of the engine, and my own breath, a little faster than usual, like I'm not sure what to do with myself around him.

When we get to his place, we set the bags of food down on the table, the crinkle of paper loud in the quiet. He doesn't look at me. I don't look at him. We both know this routine by now, the small rituals of eating together without needing to speak, but tonight it feels different—heavier, like the air is waiting for something to break it.

The soft strumming of country music fills the space between us, the lyrics slow and aching, like they know exactly what we're not saying. I don't know why I'm suddenly so aware of him—the way his fingers grip his fork, the tension in his jaw, the way his shirt clings to his chest, like he's holding himself together.

I want to say something, anything, but the words stick in my throat, tangled up with all the things I'm afraid to say. All the things I want to ask. His gaze flickers to mine for a second, but it's fleeting.

"Do you want to talk about it?" I ask in between bites of my crab Rangoon.

He drinks some water, lays his elbows on the table, and looks at me. I can tell he's thinking about speaking, but it's almost as if something is holding him back. I can't blame him, not entirely. I may be sitting in his house, but I'm practically a stranger, so I say exactly that, "You don't have to talk to me, Jake. I know I'm practically a stranger to you, but you're upset, and I hate to see you like this."

"You could never be a stranger, Allie," he sighs. "No matter the time that passes or distance between us. It was just a long day, and some of the boys are struggling with a specific class, and I feel like they're being punished for something they didn't do. One of them has a really tough home life, and I can't get through to him. I need to mention it to Nick, and see if he can help him outside of the field, too.." He closes his eyes and shakes his head, "I'm just trying to figure it out, and I didn't have the energy to worry about dinner, you know? It has nothing to do with not wanting to open up to you," he finishes and takes a sip of his beer.

"I understand. My offer still stands." I reach to hold his hand. He lets me, and I swear sparks fly where we touch. I squeeze his hand while holding his gaze for what feels like an eternity. The song changes, and it's a more upbeat rhythm bringing me back to reality. I pull my hand back from him and clear my throat. "So, my company can't seem to find me a B&B, so they are placing me in a hotel. I didn't want to take a taxi back to the city tonight, so I scheduled an Uber for tomorrow morning. I will head to school, and then from there check into the hotel. If it's ok with you that I stay an extra night."

"Allie," he says softly.

I catch the flicker of regret in his eyes just before he opens his mouth, but before he can say anything, I cut him off. "It's okay, really. I'll repack, and I'll leave tonight. I'm so sorry for barging in like this. You've been nothing but kind, and I... I took advantage of it." My hands tremble as I grab what's left of my food, shoving it into the container, but my grip falters. The cup of water slips from my fingers, crashing to the table with a slap and spilling everywhere.

"Shit, I'm sorry," I mutter, scrambling for paper towels, my heart racing as I blot up the spill, my movements frantic, unco-ordinated. Everything's a blur, a mess. I'm a mess.

Jake's hand—warm, rough, steady—wraps around my fore-arm, stopping me mid-cleanup. His voice is low, almost sooth-ing, but I can't bring myself to stop. "Allie, stop for a second."

I don't. I can't. The urgency pulses in my chest, like if I just keep moving, maybe I'll somehow fix everything. I can't look at him, not now, because the more I do, the more everything unravels inside me. I want to vanish. I want to shrink into the floor and disappear.

"I can't stop, Jake. I'm ruining everything. This whole table.

Your whole life. I never meant to—" My voice cracks, the words too tight to hold. The weight of everything presses down, thick and suffocating, and it feels like if I don't leave right now, I'm going to break wide open.

"You're not ruining anything," he says, his voice steady, but the way he says it makes my heart stutter. The simple certainty in his tone doesn't match the chaos swirling inside me. His hand lingers on my arm, warm and grounding, but I pull away.

"I can't seem to get anything right. This... this is all I can do." My voice shakes as I swipe at the table again, my hands moving faster now, desperate to fix the mess I've made of every-thing. "I can clean this up. I'll be gone in no time. You won't even have to—"

"Stop!" His voice cuts through my rambling like a blade, sharp and deep, the kind I only heard him use when he was frustrated, when his patience was frayed beyond repair, and it seems to still be the case. The sudden force of it makes me freeze, my breath hitching in my throat.

"Can you just stop for a second and let me talk?"

I snap my head up, startled, and find him standing there, his eyes—those warm, familiar chestnut eyes—darkened and stormy. His gaze is so intense, I feel it like a physical weight on my skin.

I try to read his face, but it's like trying to decipher a puzzle with half the pieces missing. Troubled, yes. Angry, maybe? But... is that concern I see buried in there, too?

I inhale, slow, shaky, trying to steady myself, trying to calm the hurricane of thoughts swirling in my head. I place the wet paper towel on top of my bag and snap my eyes up to him.

"Can I be honest with you?" he asks, and I hear the vulnera-bility in his voice. I nod my head, and he continues, "I don't think you should go. If I remember correctly, you hate hotels because of how much you guys moved when you were growing up. Jacksonville is not that far from here, and you can borrow my truck for as long as you need it. I have an extra room that isn't being used, and I would love to have your company, even if it's only for six months. I meant what I said the other day about me losing my best friend when I lost you, and having you back is bringing back a lot of memories—not all happy, I will admit—but most of them are. I'd be willing to push the sad ones aside for a chance to make new, happy ones with you."

He stops, and I think he's done talking but he keeps going, "I don't know much about you right now, but something tells me you're still the amazing person you used to be, and I'd be honored to spend some time with you until you move again."

Tears blur my vision as I stare at him, the weight of everything crashing down around me. My chest tightens, but I force the words out anyway, even though they feel like rocks in my throat. "Jake, I don't think I can."

He doesn't hesitate, doesn't blink. His eyes are steady, unwavering, like he's already made up his mind. "I'm sure you can." His voice is quiet, but firm, like he's saying it to both of us, as if he's trying to convince me—and maybe himself—of something neither of us fully believes. "Now, if you don't want to, that's a different story. But... I never asked anything from you, Allie, and it's one of my biggest regrets in life. So, this is me asking you to stay here. I'm not asking you to stay forever—God knows you wouldn't—but I'm asking you to stay, for now."

His words hit me like a tidal wave, crashing through my defenses, and suddenly, I'm drowning in them. I can't breathe. I can't think. I just stand there, frozen, as they sink deep into my chest, into places I thought I'd closed off years ago. I don't have the words to match his, but his plea lands somewhere deeper than just my ears—it tugs at something inside me, something that's been buried and broken for a decade.

The ache in my chest tightens when I realize the depth of

what he's saying. He's asking me to stay now, but more than that —he's admitting, with raw honesty, that his biggest regret is not asking me to stay ten years ago. And despite knowing this moment will be fleeting, temporary, he's still asking, still hoping.

It breaks me. And maybe it should. I don't know. But what I do know is this: my feelings for Jake never really went away, not in the way I told myself they did. I've lied to myself for years, pretending the scars didn't ache. But they do. They always have.

And so, I nod, barely able to breathe, my voice a fragile whisper. "Okay. I'll stay."

The moment the words leave my lips, he's there—his arms around me, pulling me into him with such force, as though he's afraid that if he lets go for even a second, I might slip away again. I bury my face in his chest, breathing him in, letting myself be swallowed by the warmth and strength of him. And for the first time in what feels like forever, I let myself believe that maybe—just maybe— I can stay.

My arms are at my side, and I am holding on tight to all my emotions when he whispers a broken *thank you* that makes me lose all my bearings. Tears fall down my face, I let out my breath, and hug him back. My arms wrap around him, and for the first time in so long, he feels like the one thing I have never found before: *home*.

15

———

THEN

STEAL THE SHOW, LAUV

Jake

Touchdown!

The crowd goes wild! We've won our first game in the play-offs. We all gather together clapping our hands, and smacking each other's backs for a game well played. The Commanders didn't come to play fair tonight, and for a minute there I thought we weren't going to make it. The offensive line was on fire, and I have never been more proud of being a part of it. Our quarterback played his best game of the season, and everyone knows it. His girl, Kate, ran to him. and all the cheerleaders turned to look at them while shaking their sparkling poms. I'm sure they were all shouting something about winning. but I can't focus on anything but *her*.

I have been secretly watching her for months. I don't get how nobody else is. Her caramel skin glows under the moonlight and droplets of sweat give her a shimmery look that shouldn't be legal. She has curves that make her skirt seem shorter than it is. Red is definitely her color, but I am sure that all colors would look good on her because she is stunning. She has a high ponytail with one of those big obnoxious bows cheerleaders wear, making her look like a doll, and she is shaking her poms in front of her, but her eyes are on me. I have never felt like the luckiest man alive until now. I take my helmet off and run to her, slowing down when I'm close to reaching her. Her smile grows wider when she sees that it was *her* I was running to. I make it to her and whisper a *hi* between my toothy grin. With sparks in her eyes, she tells me *congratulations*. Her poms stop shaking the same way my heart stops beating. I can tell she doesn't know how to handle us in this moment, but I do the one thing I know will erase every doubt in her mind. I drop my helmet, close the distance between us, grab her face, and kiss her like she's never been kissed before. I kiss her like she's mine and I don't care who sees it because if it were up to me, I would scream it at the top of my lungs. I feel the poms on my chest, and I can't tell if she's pushing me away or holding on to me, so I break the kiss and look at her beautiful honey eyes. *Honey.* If she only knew all the reasons I call her Honey. Her eyes, her skin, her hair. Sweet honey that has me sticky with lust and wanting to come back for more.

"Thanks," I say.

"For what?" she asks sheepishly.

"For letting me show everyone who wants to see that you are taken."

"Oh, am I now? Since when?" she says with a smirk and biting her lower lip.

"Honey, since the moment your eyes met mine for the first time, I've been yours. It's just been a matter of you letting me show you that you can be mine, too." And with that, she rises to the tips of her toes, drops her poms and tries to kiss me, but she can't reach me, so she pulls down on my jersey, bringing me to her for another kiss. This one with more intent than the first and leaving no doubt in my mind that I will forever belong to her.

THE RIDE back into town is smooth. The bus is loud with laughter, and everyone talks about the game. We usually meet on Saturdays to watch the replay and talk strategy, but the coach is letting us sleep in and meet on Sunday instead. I'm sitting alone when Nick sits next to me with a loud "bro" like he can't believe what just happened.

"So, Allie, huh?" he asks.

"Yeah, man," I say with a smile on my face.

"I thought you weren't into being in a serious relationship, and she doesn't strike me as the one-night-stand type of girl."

"I know I said that, but, man, I don't know, there's something about her that I just couldn't stay away from. Have you ever even looked at her? Nevermind, don't answer that." I sigh. "I think she might be the one."

"Bro, you've been seeing her for how long? A week? How can you even say that?"

"I know, but I think she's it."

"You're so fucked dude. I hope she feels the same way because this is a trainwreck waiting to happen."

I look at him, punch him in the arm, and nod.

"Later." He goes back to his seat in the back with the other guys, all talking about the party tonight and the girls they're gonna get with. In the meantime, there's only one girl on my mind, and she has honey eyes and the perfect smile. God, her smile. I grab my phone from my bag and text her.

ME:

Hola, beautiful :)

FUTURE WIFE:

Hey, Handsome. ♥

ME:

How's the bus ride? Full of glitter and screams?

FUTURE WIFE:

More like full of make-up talk and gossip about you and me.

ME:

Oh, really?

FUTURE WIFE:

Yeah, I've been asked by so many of them when we became exclusive. I'm really close to making an announcement so they can leave me alone.

ME:

Oh, now I'm intrigued. What would said announcement be?

FUTURE WIFE:

That we are not exclusive.

What a way of breaking someone's heart.

ME:

We're not? I didn't know you were seeing other guys. I know I'm not seeing anyone else.

FUTURE WIFE:

What? No! I'm not seeing anyone else but we've never had the official talk, so I just assumed.

ME:

Allison, we have been together every single day since our first date. I kissed you in front of everyone today, and for the record you kissed me back.

ME:

I think that's pretty exclusive, no?

I watch the three dots floating and disappearing, floating and disappearing.

ME:

Do you want to see other people?

FUTURE WIFE:

What? No! I just …. I don't know, I thought the guy was supposed to ask if I wanted to be his girlfriend, you know?

ME:

Oh! I mean, I can if that's what you want me to do.

ME:

Would you do me the honor of being my girlfriend, Allison Zabana?

ME:

Do you want me to ask your father, too? ;)

FUTURE WIFE:

You are insufferable. Stop mocking me. I've never done this before, so I didn't know. And stop calling me Allison.

ME:

So, is that a yes?

FUTURE WIFE:

Yes, Jacob. I guess you can be my boyfriend.

Smiling, I look at the text and screenshot this conversation. I save it in my favorite pictures and go back to my texts.

ME:

Luckiest man alive.

FUTURE WIFE:

Goodbye, Jake ♥

ME:

Goodbye, Honey

I close my eyes with my phone in hand and a smile on my face. The way I would give what I don't have to be sitting next to her right now. Maybe it makes me whipped or whatever, but she's worth that and more. I can't believe she's giving us a chance, now officially, too. I can't believe I get to call her mine.

16

———

NOW

YOU ARE THE REASON (DUET VERSION), CALUM SCOTT FT. LEONA LEWIS

Jake

ALLIE'S BEEN HERE for a couple of weeks, and we've fallen into this comfortable routine that has my brain in a fog. Other than not being able to touch her or kiss her whenever I want, it feels like we're in a relationship again. We come home every night after work; sometimes we cook together, sometimes we pick up takeout, but we always sit at the table to have dinner together. We laugh and tell each other about our day, and it feels so good to have her here.

Today, she finds out what her next assignment is, and we've discussed that if it's on the other side of Jax, she might need to leave here and stay somewhere closer to her job. The logical part of my brain understands it, but my mixed-up emotions don't. I selfishly want her to stay here. I'm secretly hoping she realizes the same thing I did through the years; that we are IT, and nothing will ever compare. I hope she realizes it soon since long ago, we weren't enough. I see the way she looks at me though, and I keep hoping it means whatI've been wanting it to mean for so long.

Walking toward my truck in the school parking lot, I get a text from Allie saying she's ordering pizza since I had practice tonight and it's already late. I smile while looking at my phone just at the thought of seeing her. I'm so fucked.

"Jake, wait up," I hear Nick shout behind me. Nick has been my friend since middle school and is currently another football coach, too. He teaches mechanics for the home economics department, and like me, Baker is where his life is. He has lived here his whole life, and he's not planning on going anywhere. Unlike me though, he married his high school sweetheart, and they have a beautiful daughter together. He approaches me with a smack on the back and asks what I'm up to tonight since it's Friday. He knows I usually don't do much and often, he asks me to spend the night with them at his place. Fridays are his nights to hang out with Bella—his daughter—when there are no football games, so his wife Natalie can spend some time by herself. I haven't seen them in a while, so I try my best to let him down gently.

"Just going home. Allie ordered some pizza, and I'm sure we'll either watch a movie or play a game or something."

His face transforms from shock into something that resembles disbelief and disappointment, but he tries to hide it with a tight lip smile, and he nods.

"What?" I ask.

"Nothing man, have a good night." His mouth closes back into a straight line.

"Just say it, Nick," I say, crossing my arms.

"Are you sure this is a good idea, man? Do I need to remind you what happened last time she left? Your whole life was fucked up. You're in a good place now. Is it worth it to mess with that?"

He was by my side when I had to venture into adult life without her after I thought we would share so many firsts together. First day of college. First college football game. First graduation. First time moving in together. I could keep going, but I just sigh, and rubbing my face, add, "She will always be worth it, and you know it."

"Where do you two stand? Huh? Have you had that conversation or are you still just wishing she realizes that you were the one for her?"

I stare at him, but before I can say anything he continues, "Does she even know you would give up your entire life for another chance with her? Does she know that you *did* lose yourself and your entire life because of her? Probably not, right?"

He isn't wrong, but hearing someone else say it stings more than it should.

"I let her go once, I'm not doing it again. End of conversation."

He stares at me for a moment, shakes his head, and adjusts his red and blue baseball cap.

"Just be careful, man. We're not eighteen anymore, and at the very least you deserve an explanation."

He walks toward his jeep, leaving me and my thoughts stranded. He is right, but the thought of saying something to her, her not feeling the same, and fucking this up is even worse than letting her go completely. I know she's not seeing anyone, but could I even survive a fling with her, just for her to leave me again?

I DRIVE HOME FEELING UNEASY. Nick's words replay in my head. My knuckles are white from holding the steering wheel so tight, and sweat is running down my back. I pull into my driveway and see the little black sedan she's renting while she's here. She's home already which means I have no time to calm the fuck down, so I better get my shit together out here. Do I tell her that these last two weeks with her here have been better than ten years without her? Do I tell her that every time I see her and can't touch her, I feel like my blood is going to pour out of me? Or do I just walk up to her and kiss her senseless? Touch her like I know she hasn't been touched in years because nobody knows her like I do, even after all this time?

I walk into the house and do none of those things because when I see her, she is twirling around the house with her wild wet curls bouncing, her eyes closed and a broom in her hand using it as a microphone.

I know at this moment that I would rather have her here as only a friend than be without her in any other way.

Closing the door, I lean against it quietly, setting my bag down and hanging my keys on their peg. Arms folded over my chest, my smile grows as I keep watching her dance, oblivious to the fact that I'm here.

She is absolutely precious; there is no other word to describe her. I used to think she was perfect, but nobody truly is, and that's okay. But she was perfect for me and seeing this twirling ball of energy in my living room, I think she might still be. She's mouthing the words to some song, and I would bet money it's either Taylor Swift or some reggaeton, but I can't pinpoint what it is. She never sings the right lyrics to anything, and it sounds like a mixture of mumbled words and heavy breathing from the dancing and singing. I'm smiling, surely like an idiot, when she lifts her gaze and jumps back after she sees me.

"Dios mio, Jake, you scared the sparkles out of me," she says, holding her chest and grabbing her phone from the side pocket of her tiny shorts.

I snicker. "I didn't want to interrupt your little dance party."

She laughs and shakes her head, and that's the Allie that steals all of my breath. The 'unapologetically her' Allie.

"What are you doing with that broom? Do you even know how to use one?" Allie grew up very differently than I did. Where I grew up having chores and having to do my part, Allie never had to lift a finger a day in her life, or at least she didn't back when we dated.

She squints her eyes, "Ha ha, so funny. Of course I know how to use a broom, thank you very much. And I'm cleaning your house, that's what I'm doing."

"Why?"

"Because it needed to be done."

"But you're a guest here, I was going to clean tomorrow."

She takes a deep breath, while holding the broom in her right hand and stares at me with her ridiculously gorgeous hazel eyes, "You can't expect me to live here and not help. You already don't want me to cook."

"I just don't want you burning the house down," I say, smirking.

"Ha ha, again, very funny. I have grown up, Jake, and I am self-sufficient, so if I say I'm cleaning the house, I'm cleaning the house."

"Whoa, whoa, ceasefire," I say, lifting my hands in defeat. "I just hate seeing you doing so much after a week at work." Changing the topic I ask, "How was your Friday?"

"It was fine, I have one more week at this school, and then I will be given a new assignment." She continues sweeping and uses the dustpan to collect whatever junk she got from the floor. She quickly walks past me to throw it in the trash can, and the scent of warm vanilla with passion fruit hits me straight in my core. I clear my throat as she looks around at the space she still has to clean and looks back at me expectantly.

"Don't let me stop you, then," I say, trying to control my smirk. The little sassy thing rolls her eyes, takes her earbud out of her ear, places it on the counter top, and reaches in her back pocket for her phone. She does something on her phone, and then Zac Brown Band starts blasting from her phone as she places it on the countertop next to her earbud.

She's bouncing up and down, swinging side to side, and carrying on like nobody's watching. But I'm watching alright. She looks so carefree and happy. So happy. My heart tugs as I reminisce about all the times she looked just like that with me, blissfully lost in happiness.

I'm still standing by the door, lost in her presence when she says, "You know you can join me if you want. Stop being a grouchy pants."

"You know I don't dance, Allie."

"That never stopped you from dancing with me before," she says, opening her hazel eyes, and it feels like she stares straight into my soul. She stops dancing and just keeps looking at me with a soft smile, challenging me to move to her. She sways her hips slowly, side to side, like a siren ready to enthrall a sailor, and I am so utterly fucked if I think I'm getting out of this one unscathed.

She reaches behind her back and takes out the hair tie she had holding back half of her brown curls. She shakes her head like a puppy and the rest of her hair falls around her face.

Fucked, Jake, you are so fucked.

As if she knows what she's doing to me, she looks at me again as she sways, mouthing the lyrics. She lifts her hand, palm up, and motions for me to join her. And I do because how can I ever say no to her?

I walk to her, and she squeals and picks up the tempo of her dancing. She's still holding the broom like a microphone, so I just stand across from her and move awkwardly. I have two left feet, so I hate dancing, but for her, I always will.

Her smile is big and bright as she holds my hand and twirls under me. I take the broom from her hand and place it against the wall. I grab both her hands and dance with her. She closes her eyes and bounces while holding my hands, and I try to keep up but fail miserably and end up almost stepping on her. She laughs and looks at me but keeps on moving as much as she can without dragging me to the ground. I'm lost in her eyes, in her moves, in her scent, in her soft hands on mine. Completely lost in her.

She stops dancing, and I look at her, but I don't even notice the change in song until then. It's a slow song, something about being the reason for the heart beating and it's like the stars are aligning because, yes, Allie, you will always be my reason.

Her breaths are picking up, even though she stopped moving, and she keeps looking at me. Her lips part slowly as she breathes through her mouth and says, "Jake," barely as a whisper.

Holding her gaze, I say, "Allison, no thinking, just dancing." I smile knowing how much she hates it when I call her that, but it has always been our thing. She drops her gaze immediately and bites those full lips I am dying to taste; I want to know if they still taste like everything I have always wanted in life. I tuck my index finger under her chin and lift her face as I say, "Look at me." And she does.

I notice the tears falling down her face and the turmoil hiding behind her eyes. I hold her face with both hands, letting my forehead drop to hers. I wipe her tears softly with my thumbs and drop my hands to her back, bringing her flush against my chest.

She's so nervous, I can almost feel her heartbeat about to

match mine which is beating erratically fast. My hand is so close to her face, so I do just what I've been wanting to do since the day she crashed into me in the airport, and cup her cheek with my right hand. She leans against the touch as I say, "Hi, Honey."

Her hands, which were loosely at her side, slowly come up to lay flat against my chest, and she lifts her gaze back to me.

We stare at each other for a second. Then another one. It's taking everything in my power to hold up my end of the deal and be her friend. Just her friend. The music stops, breaking the spell we've been under and immediately grounding us again. Or maybe I'm so transfixed by her eyes and her hands on my body that everything else ceases to exist.

I can't hold it in anymore; I release a breath as she catches hers and growl, "Fuck it," while dipping my face and closing the space between us with a kiss. She releases the air she's holding as her lips dance with mine. Her lips still taste like fruity heaven. They still feel as soft as they used to, and they still fit perfectly in mine. *Mine*, I repeat in my head as we get lost in the kiss. It's not urgent or rough, but you can taste the desperation in us both.

I let go of her lips, foreheads still together. Our breathing is in sync, and our touch is electric. I'm trying to find words to describe everything going through my mind right now when Allie beats me to it, whispering, "I've missed you," completely shattering the only pieces of my heart left.

17

——————

THEN

HO HEY, NASHVILLE CAST

Allie

JAKE and I are laying on my bed watching Friday Night Lights. It's been a whirlwind these past few weeks, what with us dating and our hectic schedules. With the team making it to the playoffs—which are next week—he has had crazy hours of practice, making it harder to see him, but he still makes sure we spend time together every day. If they win this game, they go to the state playoffs, and our school's team hasn't been in ten years.

The people at school are still teasing us, and Cara is always hounding me for details. Our relationship feels both too fast and not fast enough. Like my heart has been waiting for him all my life, and now that he's finally here, I don't want to waste any time being apart from him. Which is crazy, right? Because it sounds a little crazy, considering we're only in high school.

My parents are out of town for work, and my brothers are camping with friends, so I have the house to myself and decided to invite him over. We've been binge-watching this show, cuddling and kissing for hours now. We ate pizza, popcorn and peanut M&M's while chatting about anything and everything. Some important topics and some just absolutely not. It's so easy to just be with him. And I hope it is as easy for him to just be with me, too.

My head lays on his chest, and his fingers trail across my arm. I yawn, and he pulls the blanket higher to cover me more.

"I don't want to go to sleep, yet," I say.

"You're tired, Allie. It's ok if you do," he answers.

"I'm not ready for you to leave, yet."

"Well, I don't have to if you don't want me to," he adds.

I lift myself up from my comfortable position to look at him. We have kissed plenty before and even felt each other up a little, but we haven't done anything else. Part of the reason is because of lack of privacy, but also partly because I have never done anything like that before, and I don't even know how to bring it up.

"Jake, I—" He interrupts me.

"I can leave, too. I don't have to if you don't want me to. I just thought I'd offer. I don't have anywhere to be early tomorrow, and honestly, being with you calms my nerves about the game next week."

"It's not that, it's just..." I trail off, and he keeps looking at me, waiting for a reply. "I've never slept with anyone before."

"I already know you snore, baby, it's not a big deal. I kinda like it." He laughs a little.

"I mean, I've never had sex before," I flat out say, covering my face in embarrassment. I'm sure I would look very flushed if he was able to see my face right now.

"Allie," he says. "Allie, look at me please." He pulls my hands off my face. I look at him and take a deep breath before opening my mouth, but he covers my lips with his index finger and says, "When I said I could stay, I didn't mean we had to have sex for me to stay. I would never want you to feel pressured into doing anything you don't want to. I would be happy just staying here and being your giant human pillow."

Before I can speak, he continues, "If you want me to stay, I can even sleep on the floor if that'd make you feel more comfortable, but I can also go home. You tell me, baby."

I knew he was a gentleman, but I thought he wanted to have sex with me, and that's why he said that he could stay here. This is all so confusing.

"You don't want to have sex with me?" I ask shyly.

"Oh, Honey," he says smirking as he puts a curl behind my ear. "It's not that I don't want to, trust me. I can't wait to be with you in every way I can. In any way you'd let me. There's not a moment that goes by with you that I don't think about it. Not a single second that I don't think about your body underneath mine, and about the kind of sounds you'd make when I drive you crazy with my hands, my mouth, my whole body. Wanting you is not an issue, but we have our whole lives, Allie. I'm not in a rush."

Our whole lives? All of a sudden the room is twenty degrees hotter, and my whole body feels like it's on fire. The mental image of him doing things to me with his hands and mouth has me tingling with anticipation, and we're not even touching. He says he's not in a rush, but after hearing him say that, I might be.

"That was a good answer, Jake."

"I mean it."

And I believe him, and, God, if I wasn't already gone for this boy, I am now. But there's no denying my brain what my heart already knows. I'm in love with Jake, and I wouldn't love anything more than letting him take me completely. Take every part of me. I sit up all the way and straddle his lap coming face to face with him.

"Allie, I—" I put my finger on his lips.

"It's my turn to talk now." I start slowly grinding on him as I say, "I didn't think I was ready, but hearing you say that, has my body all sorts of hot, and I would very much like to find out some of the things you've thought about with me under you." I bring my hands to each side of his face and kiss him like I've never kissed him before. We're all tongue and teeth. Moans and hands everywhere while I move in slow circles on top of him. He puts pressure on my back slowing me down, so I break our kiss and look at him. Our breaths are frantic and labored. His chest is rising and falling, and my nipples hard against the fabric of my top.

"Allie, are you sure?" he asks with concern in his eyes, and this is the moment I know for sure that I love him. The look in his eyes is one of pure adoration, and his patient words and hands are making my heart skip a beat, even though I'm ready to devour him. I don't say anything, just stare at him, biting my lips when he adds, "We can stop right now. I'm in no rush. Like I said, we have a lifetime, baby." I lay my whole body against him and hug him tight because I never want to let go. I inhale deeply, and he says, "It's okay, Allie, it truly is. I'm sorry if I rushed you or if you felt pressure in any way," and, God, can he be any more perfect?

"Jake," it comes out more like a moan than a whisper, and he tightens his grip on my back. My chest is flush against his, and our breaths are dancing against each others' lips.

"I want to, I'm just scared. Would you be gentle?" I don't even know why I ask because I know he will, but I sense his hesitation. He is using every ounce of control he has not to touch me right now.

"Please, Jake, I want to." I close the little distance between us and kiss him. I kiss him tenderly but with purpose. "Please, make love to me." I kiss him again. He responds to my kiss, immediately deepening it and bringing his hands to my hair.

I nip at his bottom lip, and he tightens his grip even more, so

I chuckle, and in what feels like a second, he has me flat against the bed with my hands above my head, and he's pinning my hips down with his.

He lifts himself up slowly and whispers, "I love you" right against my face. When I'm about to reply, he says, "Shh, you don't have to say it back. It's ok. I just couldn't go another minute without letting you know," and he starts kissing me again. "I love you, sweet girl, and that won't change if we stop this now. I don't think it will ever change. Know that at any moment you can say stop, and we stop."

I respond with the only thing I can think of, "Please don't make me ask again." To be honest, I'm ready to beg.

I am lost to the kissing, the nipping, and the licking. He teases as he moves lower on my neck, to my chest. His hands slide up under my shirt, and when he feels the edge of my very thin bra, I arch against him with a soft moan, and he hisses. He looks at me and says, "If at any point you want me to stop, you just say it, okay? No questions asked, I'll stop." I nod, and he says, "I need words, Allie, words."

"Yes, Jake. Yes."

That one word unleashes a beast. In a fraction of a minute, he pulls my shirt over my head. He's lowering the straps of my bra and nipping at my neck. It makes me wonder how experienced he is because there's no way he's a rookie when he kisses and touches me like this.

My feet are pushing against the mattress, trying to find some friction, but he keeps teasing me. His hand grabs my breast, and he touches my nipple with gentle fingers, and it feels so good I moan. He lowers his mouth over my other nipple, twirling his tongue around it, and I may just come from this alone. My back is arching, and he uses his other hand to pin me down while he's holding himself off of me with the other one.

His mouth is over my nipple, nipping, licking, twirling. My

panties feel damp against me, and I hope that's normal because this feels entirely too good.

I. Need. More.

I lift my leg up and pull his hip against mine, and he lets out a sound like a groan. Keeping his eyes on me, he slowly pulls down my leggings, with tender hands, calming my nerves. He kisses my neck, and my chest, and keeps going, reaching my nipple, letting his hands explore down, right in between my folds. "You are soaked for me, Honey," he says.

And I whisper, "I'm sorry."

That has him looking up at me. "Baby, that's nothing to be sorry about. That's a good thing. It just means you're responsive to my touch." He smirks and adds, "I love it." He drops back down to my nipple. With his hand still teasing, he works a finger in, and it feels like heaven on earth when he curves it inside of me. He lifts my leg as he lowers his head right on top of my mound and places my foot on his shoulder.

"This might feel too intense, and you're going to want me to stop, but trust the process," he adds confidently, and I feel myself tighten against his finger in anticipation. He lowers his mouth to my clit while slipping another finger in me. With my foot on his shoulder, I can't satisfy my urge to lift myself up every time he licks me. I feel like my belly is full of water, and I get goosebumps all over my skin. He curls his fingers inside of me at the same time he sucks on my clit, and I see stars. My insides clench against him. My legs shiver. My toes curl, and I scream his name.

He kisses my thigh, my hip, my belly, and I flinch. "So beautiful. So perfect," he whispers in between kisses, and I am on a high I never want to come down from. He removes his shirt over his head in one smooth sweep. Seeing the move in movies and in real life are two very different things. Holy hotness. He pulls his pants down, and I'm sure he can see all over my face, exactly how I feel about the way his naked body looks right in front of me. I can't believe he's mine.

My body is still coming down from the orgasm, but I instantly feel the tingle on my skin again as he climbs up my body. I'm squirming under him. He brings his hands next to my face and peppers kisses along my chin and my jaw.

"Hey, hey, it's okay. I've got you," he says in the sweetest tone. He holds my gaze as he lifts my leg again holding it under my knee. He looks straight at me, never dropping my gaze, wrapping me in this moment. He gently says, "Breathe," as he slowly thrusts inside. I hold my breath and close my eyes.

"Breathe, baby, breathe."

So I do, following his command and trying to relax.

"So pretty, so perfect," he coos, and slowly, I start to stretch around him. It's a burning sensation, but with his praise and slow gentleness, it turns into a good feeling.

His hands are everywhere but not in a frenetic manner. His moves are purposeful and tender. I feel him everywhere. On top of me, around me, and in me. It's too much and not enough at the same time.

His hand makes it to the top of my clit again, and he circles it with slow motions as he pumps in and out of me. I feel that tingly wet pool again and then straight to fireworks everywhere. "So perfect," he whispers to my ear, and then he shivers with his body tensing.

I feel him everywhere still. His skin slick with sweat. His smell is slowly becoming my favorite thing in the world. His presence. His everything. I'm sure I'm never going to be the same again.

He falls next to me on the bed with his eyes closed and his hand on my leg. I turn my body to face him, but I stay quiet because what do you say? I feel like telling him that I love him, but it would be cliché, so I don't. I just keep looking at his face as he smiles. He starts getting up, and I try to stop him, when he says, "I have to go throw this away." I look down to see the condom I didn't even notice he'd put on. And silly me because I didn't even think about it.

He comes back, and we continue to snuggle until I surely drift to sleep because the next thing I know, it's morning time, and there's a note next to my pillow that says,

getting coffee, be right back.

143,
    J.

18

———

NOW

AM I WRONG, NICO & VINZ

Allie

JAKE KISSED ME. Holy shit, he just kissed me.

The music keeps playing in the background, and our bodies are still close, but nothing is happening. My breathing is slowing, my tears are dried now, and I don't even know why I was crying in the first place. A mix of longing and hope. Longing for what I lost and hope that I can find it again. I find the courage to finally look up at him, and to my surprise, he is looking down, right at me. His eyes full of feeling, something I can't quite pinpoint because it certainly can't be love.

Suddenly, it's too much. I've let my guard down, and we're both about to pay the price. I pull away from him, saying, "I can't do this." I turn my body around trying to walk as far away from him as possible and lock myself behind the safety of the bedroom door.

I hear his steps quickly behind me, and then his hand is on my wrist, stopping me as he says, "Wait!" I stop dead in my tracks but don't dare to turn around to face him. He has a man's hands, I notice; not a boy anymore, a whole-ass man. His grip is strong, without hurting, and he whispers for me to stop so softly I almost miss it.

I turn around to look at him, but I can't, so I keep my gaze down. "Look at me, Honey," he says, and I do because right now, I don't think I could deny this man anything. He loosens his grip on my wrist, pulling me closer to him. My chest is practically on his, and I try to look up at him through my lashes.

He brings my hand to his chest and places it right on his left side. "Can you feel that?" he asks and then continues, "That's my fucking heart about to leap out of my chest. That happens every single time I look at you. Every. Single. Time. It happened then, and it keeps happening now. It never changed, and I don't think it ever will."

I gasp and open my mouth to speak, but he lets go of the hand on his chest and covers my mouth with his finger.

"Please, let me finish talking. Ten years ago, my whole world crumbled down, and you were the last pebble that made the landslide final. I have done a lot to try to forget you. To erase you from my memories, but fuck, Allie, you came into my life once like a wrecking ball, and you have never left. No matter what I try, my heart knows it belongs with you. My mind knows it, too. Whether that's what's best for me or not." He rubs his eyes and pulls me to him for a hug.

His hand drags over my head and tears start to fall on my cheeks. "Nothing I do will ever erase you, and to be honest, I was finally resigned to the fact I was never going to be able to move on when you came into my life and hit me like a hurricane, again."

He kisses my forehead and pulls me tighter then says, "What if I'm ready to embrace you in my life again? What if I'm willing to take this natural disaster that is everything I feel for you and turn it into a natural wonder? Because that's exactly what you are. Pure, natural perfection."

I continue crying on his chest, and I know he can feel it because he rubs gentle circles on my back while saying soothing words that reach the deepest parts of my soul. "Shh, it's okay. I'm not mad you left, not anymore at least. If you let me, I would love to let you into my life completely again, even if it's for six months or however long you're here."

To that, I have nothing to say, so my body stiffens. I pull back and look into his beautiful chocolate eyes. With his thick dark eyelashes and his eyes wet from tears, I realize I'm not the only one with the hundreds of what-ifs. I realize this sweet man, who has taken a huge part of my heart that will never be filled by anyone else, might still love me. Even if it took ten years for me to come back.

That's when I realize I might still love him, too. I reach up to his lips on my tippy toes and kiss him. And we kiss until we are all hands, teeth, tongue, and moans. Oh God, moans! I stop before this goes too far for both of us. I take an abrupt step back and nod. I reach and grab the broom from the wall next to him and ask him if he wants to get cleaned up and we can watch a movie after he settles for the night. He nods and disappears into his room, but before he turns, I catch him rubbing his lip with a smile on his face.

WE'RE WATCHING some sort of Adam Sandler movie, but I have not been paying attention; I can't stop thinking about his words, replaying them over and over again in my head.

Nothing I do will ever erase you.

We're sitting side by side, barely touching, and the air is thick with anticipation. Every now and then, he looks my way and smiles, but turns back toward the T.V. again. I know he's being respectful and giving me space, but I have a knot in my throat, and I feel the urge to say something.

"Hey, Jake?" I say softly.

"Allison," he replies with a smirk.

"Mm, how would this work? You know I'm only here for a short amount of time. I would hate for us to start something that would just end suddenly."

"We already started something, and we hit pause abruptly. Can you look me in the eyes and say that it was ever truly over?"

Did he just say that? Okay, so I guess we're going with the absolute truth, so I say, "I'm sure you've been around plenty in the last ten years. It's not like you have been here waiting for me."

"I'm sure you have, too, and yet, here we are again," he deadpans, not knowing it couldn't be further from the truth. I've been attracted to many other people before, but I've had zero desire to make it past a couple of dates. Even the kisses have been uninteresting. I thought I was broken until I learned in therapy that some people just need an emotional connection before they can have a physical connection with anyone, and that's definitely me. Although I've tried to have a connection with someone, deep down my heart has been shut since Jake, making it impossible for me to truly connect with anyone.

We stare at each other before he adds, "What are you afraid of? Of falling in love with me again?"

"Jake," I whisper.

"Honey," he says with conviction.

"Oh, don't *honey* me. That's playing dirty."

"I'm not going to push you to do something you don't want to, but the way your body reacts to me tells me more than your words ever will." As if on cue, I get goosebumps all over my arms. He's not wrong. We both know it.

"Tell me I'm wrong," he says as he pulls my feet off the ground and across his legs.

"Tell me you don't want me, don't want us, and I'll walk away. I'll just be your friend, Allie." When I don't say anything, he grabs my hand and pulls me to him. Wrapping his hand behind my thigh he places me on top of him so I straddle him, and he raises his hand to cup my cheek. I lean into his touch, and it's electric, magnetic, and the way my body wants to be as close to him as possible is absolutely unavoidable.

"Tell me I'm wrong, baby," he adds.

He looks at my lips, so I bite them slightly, and then he looks straight into my eyes and says, "Or better yet, show me I'm right."

I lose all the control I have left and let myself kiss him deeply as I melt into his body.

19

———

NOW

WHEN THE PARTY'S OVER, BILLIE EILISH

Allie

JAKE and I have been *a thing* for two weeks now. We fell easily into a domestic routine that gives me a taste of what could've been if we had stayed together back then. He's still the sweet, kind, goofy, honest boy I fell in love with once, but now, he has aged like fine wine into the man of everyone's dreams. And that's what he is, truly. He has all the qualities that a good man, boyfriend, or husband should have, and somehow, he's still hung up on me.

He wakes up an hour earlier than I do to tend to his garden and chickens, makes me coffee, and he always has something for me to eat even though he usually doesn't even have breakfast. He's patient with my morning grumpiness and comes back to the house with the biggest smile when he sees me. He's the easiest person to like and love, and yet, he's still giving *me* his time. Regardless of what happened then.

Two weeks of sweet kisses, holding hands, and texts throughout the day. Two weeks of him respecting me to the point that he hasn't tried to do anything more than just kiss and hug me, because I pull back every time. Two weeks of him showing me his unending patience and understanding my feelings.

Two weeks of me daydreaming about spending more time with him but not wanting to share him, so we stay in. Two weeks of him showing me how to do some things in the garden and letting me love on his chicks. Those are some salty ladies, and it took them a bit to warm up to me, but just like Jake, they are so easy to love.

We walk hand in hand to gather eggs at night and share the kitchen to cook when possible. He has football practice almost every day, so I do some work on my computer until he gets home every night. *Home.* A word I didn't know the meaning of until I found him. A word that left my vocabulary for years and I never thought I'd find again. A word that pops into my mind when I think of him.

I'm driving back to his place, thinking about what I'll wear tonight. He asked me last night if he could take me with him to the football game. He needs to be there early with the players, but he's letting me come to the field, and then we'll go out to dinner afterwards. A date. A date with Jake. My Jake. I never thought that would ever happen again. Yet here we are.

The road is wet from the rain earlier, so I'm being extra careful and staying in the middle lane but the I-10 is still an interstate and the minimum speed is still pretty fast for these conditions. Taylor Swift is playing, and I'm singing along when the car in front of me swerves into the other lane, and I hit my brakes in response, just not fast or hard enough.

"MISS, MISS, CAN YOU HEAR ME?"

I cough and open my eyes to bright lights in front of me.

"There you are. Try not to move," the voice says.

"Can you follow the light?"

I squint my eyes but follow it as the voice behind it praises me for following directions.

"Can you tell us your name, sweetie?"

"Allie," I try to say, but it comes out as a whisper.

So, I clear my throat and say it again, "Allie."

"Good, can you give me your full name?"

"Allison Marie Zabana Orozia, but please call me Allie," I say.

The guy moves away from the light, and I can finally see him. He looks like he could be twenty-two years old. He is smiling at me kindly, and it's then I notice he's wearing an EMT uniform. EMT. *Oh shit, where am I?* I look around and see I'm in the car still, but I'm on the side of the road. Oh God, I hit that car in front of me. I start to panic and look around when he adds gently, "You're okay. Can you tell me what happened?"

"I was driving, and then the car in front of me moved suddenly to the other lane. I hit the breaks, but I think I hit something else, too."

"Yeah, sounds about right. There was a truck stopped in the middle of the road and you managed to hit it. You hit it at the right angle, so your car just swerved into the side of the road. Nobody else was hurt, but you hit your head pretty badly."

I sigh with relief.

"You were unconscious for a while, but you seem to be doing better. Do you know what year this is?"

"Yes, 2023."

"That's correct," he says. "The fire department will help us get you out, so hang tight."

A few minutes later, they stabilize my neck and get me out

into a gurney. They put me in the back of an ambulance, and we head to the hospital.

On the ride there, they ask me more questions, take my vitals, and do another assessment. We make it to the hospital, and I get wheeled into an exam room. After what feels like hours later, I'm back in a room, waiting. They give me my phone, and I text Jake to tell him I won't make it to the game and that I will text him when I get back. My mind is spinning, so I hit send without reading any of his previous texts or anything else on the phone.

The door creaks open, and the doctor steps in, his shoes squeaking softly on the tile. He looks down at my chart, his expression neutral, and then meets my eyes. "Everything seems fine," he says, voice too calm, like the storm inside me doesn't matter. "You've got some mild concussion symptoms, but you should be fine to go home—if you're not alone."

His words swirl in my head. "I won't be," I say, but the weight of it feels too heavy for a simple answer. I haven't even thought about the time, haven't looked at the clock. I feel... off, like I'm trapped in a moment that won't let go.

He nods, scribbling something on the chart. "Take some Motrin. Rest. You're good to go."

I sign the release papers without even thinking. The pen feels strange in my hand, like it doesn't belong to me. Then I shuffle into my clothes, each movement slow and heavy, like I'm pulling myself through water. I don't remember the last time I felt like this—disconnected, dizzy, unsure if the ground is even steady beneath me.

I walk out into the lobby, my phone buzzing weakly in my pocket. The screen lights up for a second before dimming, and I fumble to unlock it. The battery's almost dead. I swipe through the apps. No taxis, no rideshares. Nothing. My stomach tightens.

It's not even the idea of waiting that bothers me—it's the feeling of being stuck.

I grab my bag, its strap digging into my shoulder, and step toward the door. My feet move before I can stop them. There's no one to talk to, no one to help. I don't want to ask for help. I just want to get out. I start walking.

The GPS says I'm about an hour walk away from his house, so I choose to continue walking instead of waiting for an available taxi. My body aches, but I just want a shower and to lay down. It would be fine if it wasn't for the fact it is starting to rain again, and the sidewalks are still muddy from the rain earlier. I keep walking, and after a while it's almost therapeutic, and tears start falling from my eyes. I don't even realize it until my lips taste the difference between the rain and the tears.

I feel a vehicle slow down behind me, and when I look, it's a dark Chevy truck. The truck stops by me, the door opens, and I hear a familiar voice say, "Get in the truck, Allie."

I hop in and continue crying. Jake says nothing and just lets me cry next to him. He takes his shirt off and passes it to me as he turns the heat on in his truck. He gives me gentle squeezes on my knee and asks, "Are you ready to talk about it?" When I don't say anything, he just turns the radio on and drives. The world around me kept moving while I was suspended in time between the accident, the hospital, and now.

We make it to his place and after walking in, I immediately hug him. I am covered in dirt and soaking wet, but somehow, he doesn't care and squeezes me tighter. "I don't want to talk about it," I whisper in between sobs. "I'm okay, but I don't want to think anymore. I just want to forget it all."

"Shh. Let me take care of you, Allie," he whispers in my ear as he holds my trembling body. He smells like mint, wood, and comfort. He caresses my hair and continues to whisper, alternating between soft shushes and gently asking me to let him take care of me. My sobs get lost between his tight hug and the rain pouring outside. I feel filthy and unworthy of his kindness, especially after not telling him the whole truth, yet. How does this man continue to put me first? How does he choose to take care of me?

He pulls away from me, and while grabbing my face, he looks deeply into my eyes. I look down, unable to contain my tears and hating to see the pity in his eyes. "I am such a wreck, Jake. Everything I touch dies or ends. Please just let me go to bed. You don't have to take care of me."

"I want to." He kisses my forehead. Gently. Lovingly. Like I'm fragile and even the slightest push will break me.

"I don't deserve you. I don't want you to pity me. I can do it. Let me forget on my own." I break into sobs.

"It's not pity, it's sympathy. And if anything it's selfishness." He lifts my chin and holds my gaze. "Seeing you like this kills me. I'm looking out for myself here. Let me take care of you, baby."

Baby. I will never get tired of hearing that after I thought I never would again. Not from the only person I wanted to hear it from the most. From the only one who matters. *Him.*

I close the gap between us and crash my mouth against his with a kiss. He tastes like honey and mint. His lips are soft mounds against mine, but nothing about the way he's kissing me is soft. It is ravenous. Like he has been in the desert and finally found water.

He bends down and grabs me by the butt as he lifts me. I gasp and shake my head rapidly, and he groans against my throat, "Honey, so help me God, if you make a comment about your weight right now. I don't care how crappy you feel, the only words coming out of your mouth about your body should be to say how fucking fantastic each inch of you is. Just wrap your legs around me." He guides me up with a squeeze. I look into his eyes that are darkening with desire and kiss him.

We are a mess of whimpers, kisses, and lust. Of years of words unspoken into this rush of desire without control. He keeps walking us into the bathroom without breaking the kiss. He turns the water on and shuts the door without even flinching. My hands are all over him, and he finally puts me down. We break apart for a moment that feels like an eternity. Our chests are rising, and he looks at me asking for my approval before this goes any further. I nod, and he smoothly takes his shirt off in one quick movement and charges toward me.

I am completely dirty after today, but it doesn't stop me. He kisses my lips, traces my jaw with his tongue, and sucks on my neck. My entire body is tingling with anticipation. He unbuttons my dress as he continues to kiss me. I pull at his thick soft hair, slowly making my way to grab his neck. My dress falls to the ground around my feet, and I remove my panties stepping out of each side, one leg at a time.

"Fuck. Get in the shower," he commands and opens the curtains. I get in right under the hot stream of water, letting it run all over me. I don't want to cry, but the weight of the day comes crashing down, and my tears start falling once again. He steps into the shower too and grabs my ponytail gently. "May I?" he asks, and I nod. I don't even know what he's asking, but for him it will always be yes.

He lets my hair down and pushes my head gently back. He massages my head under the water, and I let a soft moan free. He tightens his hold on my head, and I can't help but gasp and let out another moan.

"I want to do the right thing here and just help you get cleaned up. But if you keep making those sweet little noises, I won't be able to do that. I can't promise you I won't do all the things I want to do to you."

His voice is hoarse, and I shiver at the promise. He turns me around and starts rubbing soap on my back, pushing into my skin with his calloused fingers, giving me a delicious mix of softness and pain.

My head tilts back as he pushes me closer to the wall, massaging the knots around my neck and upper back. He grabs my hair and moves it out of the way, and immediately my skin breaks into goosebumps. *Everywhere.* He gives me a quick kiss on the nape of my neck, and a shiver goes down my spine.

My nipples harden against the cold tile, and the more he massages my back, the more turned on I am. I can't help the sounds coming out of me as he intensifies the massage. The more he touches me, the more he pushes me against the wall, and I am already a sloppy mess. I arch my back almost involuntarily, and my ass touches the tip of his hard cock, and he hisses.

"Is the wall too cold? I'm sorry if I'm pushing too hard." He lowers his mouth to my neck and places a gentle kiss.

I shiver again. "Oh yes. Please keep pushing." I try to sound normal, but the words come out like a gasp. This is ridiculous, he's not even touching anything besides my back, and my whole body is responding to him like this.

He gets closer and lowers his mouth right next to my ear. "Push you? Like this?" His voice is raspy and full of desire as he shoves my whole body against the wall to the point I have to tilt my head to the side. He grabs my hair and twists it in his hand without moving his mouth from my ear. "Against the wall like this?" He asks, and when I shiver and gasp, he growls and adds, "You want me to fuck you, don't you?"

"Please," I beg.

"My sweet girl grew up, and she likes it a little rough now?" His voice has a hint of darkness and softness all mixed together.

I gather the strength need to say, "I wouldn't know how I like it now."

"Now, don't be shy, Honey, tell me what you want. How do you want it?" He tugs at my hair making my head move back more.

With a soft moan, I add, "It's not shyness, it's just been ten years."

His whole body tenses, and he moves backward. He slowly turns me around and lifts my face by the chin. "What do you mean?" His body went from *all fucking,* to *all business* in three seconds flat. *Jake, forever the gentleman.* He holds my gaze, and I take a deep breath but don't say anything. "Allie," he whispers, "Please, tell me what you mean."

"Exactly what it sounds like, there was you, and then there was nobody else."

His breath catches; his wandering eyes roam over my face, looking for a tell, ready to call my bluff. I thought sharing this with him would make me feel pathetic, but what it makes me feel is *seen.* He is looking at me with an emotion I don't see often. A mix of sadness and guilt. I see his inner turmoil, but he still asks the question I was hoping he wouldn't as the steam from the shower keeps rising and water falls all around us. "Why? Why didn't you?"

This is it, now or never. I reach for his face, moving his dark hair from his face and softly touching his beard before I whisper, "Honestly? My heart belonged to you then, and nobody came even close enough to earning it back. So, I chose to keep my heart and my body forever yours."

"Allie," he whispers, his eyes on mine searching for the lie, but it doesn't come because it's true. I know sex is just sex for most people, but not for me. My heart, my body, and my brain are all in sync. Can't turn it off, and I don't want to.

We stare at each other, and I open my mouth to say, "I knew —" but his mouth is on mine instantly. His body, flushed against mine, pinning me against the cold tile wall again. His hands are in my hair, and he's pulling and grabbing as he kisses me as if his life depends on it. He continues to kiss my jaw and my neck, his hands roaming my back, then my arms, and my breasts. My breath catches, and he lowers his mouth to catch one of my nipples. His tongue swirls, hardening it, and immediately his other hand reaches for the other.

My hands find his hair, and I pull him closer to me. I gasp. This feels so good. Too good. I might just come from this. *Get it together.* "Jake."

He takes his mouth off my nipple and looks up while still touching the other. "Please don't ask me to stop, Honey—because I will—but fuck, I don't want to."

My chest is moving up and down. How do I even say anything but, "Yes, please."

He drops to one knee, leaving his left leg up. He grabs one of my ankles and sets my foot on his thigh. He traces kisses from my belly button to the top of my mound. He drags his nose against my folds. "God, you still smell the same." Opening me with his fingers, he flattens his tongue and strokes from my entrance to my clit. He doesn't just lick, he devours. Like he has been starving and this is his first meal.

He moves his hand from my leg and traces my thigh, climbing toward my pussy, and the noises coming out of me are anything but decent. My skin prickles, the feeling of the water from the shower on my chest and the stiff wall behind me. His hands roaming and his tongue working me have my body on a high I can't describe. And I don't ever want to come down.

He works a finger in and smirks against me. "So wet for me, baby." He's moving his finger in and out while licking me.

"More, please," I beg, gasping for a release I'm chasing but don't want to reach yet.

"There's nothing I wouldn't give you, Honey." He adds

another finger. And as wet as I am, it should slide right in, but he takes his time, and suddenly I feel so full.

"Fuck, you're so tight." He licks, sucks, and flicks his tongue around my clit.

"Oh God, I'm so close." His fingers pump in and out, and I'm tightening around them. The flush against my skin feels as if I am in front of fire, and liquid pleasure fills my lower belly and then explodes.

He pumps his fingers to the rhythm of his tongue chasing my high with them. My pussy is tightening more and more around his fingers, and everything throbs. He slows down, letting me catch my breath. He moves back, taking his fingers out of me and rubs them against his lips. He licks his lips, holding my gaze and grunting, "So sweet." He sucks on his fingers still looking at me. "Just like passion fruit."

He smirks and stands up. His cock is hard and precum glistens on the tip. "Come on, let me clean you up."

I grasp his dick, and he hisses and adds, "Oh, Honey, we'll have time for all of that, but this moment is about you. I'm taking care of you, so hands off."

I do just that. Take my hands off and let him show me how well he can take care of me, again and again.

20

———

THEN

GOLD RUSH, TAYLOR SWIFT

Jake

ME:

Pick you up before school?

I WAIT a few minutes but she never replies. I wonder if she's even awake, and I'd hate for her to be late to school because I know how much *she* hates it. Yesterday, after I got back to her house, we spent half the morning in bed with me, whispering sweet praises right into her ear while making her body shatter under my hands. I could have spent all day just making her feel good. The truth is that she's perfect, and my heart and whole body realized it, too. Eventually, we got out of bed, and then I spent more time caressing her and showing her how much I love her in the shower. I helped her wash her beautiful hair, even though she had to guide me little by little on how to brush and detangle those wild curls I love so much.

We left the house briefly around lunch time and came back just in time for Family Sunday. I met her dad this time, and that guy is a scary motherfucker. He towers over me by a few inches, and he's so broad I asked if he ever played football. The guy is solid, and he kept looking at me like I was an unwelcome sight in his home. I don't blame him, I don't fit in her beautiful three-story home full of marble floors and hardwood accents. Complete with a garden tended to every day by professionals and where her Titi Rosalia, who I found out is not her aunt but more like a governess, makes sure the house is running smoothly. I have never experienced so much luxury before in a home, and I think everyone could tell.

I stayed next to Allie through the afternoon, but eventually, I felt way too out of place with him looking at me like that, speaking mostly in Spanish. It annoyed me when Allie would translate for me, so I excused myself and left. Her mom is the complete opposite, and so are her brothers, but I have a feeling that her dad doesn't approve of his princess dating a country boy like me. She messaged me last night, checking on me, but I let her know I needed some rest, and she needed to spend time with her family.

Now that she's not replying to my text, I'm worried she might still be asleep, so I head to her door to ask someone about her. I park in the driveway, careful not to block any of the vehicles, and walk to the side door where the kitchen is. I hear people talking, so I start to walk toward the door but then stop when I hear the conversation.

Allie is talking to someone mostly in Spanish. She sounds annoyed, and there's no hiding it, but I can't tell what they're saying. *Oh, how I wish I had paid more attention in Spanish class.* I can't hear the other voice, but Allie is getting more and more agitated. Her tone is clipped, and her usual confidence isn't there. I shouldn't be eavesdropping, but I don't know what to do. Suddenly, I hear something being smacked on the table and her dad saying, "I told you to take the damn jersey off, Allison, now." *Allison.* She said nobody calls her by her full name, and if that's how her dad talks to her when he does, then I don't want her to associate me with *that.*

"Papi, Jake *is* my boyfriend, so whether you like it or not, I am wearing the jersey to school," she says with the sassiest tone I have ever heard coming out of her mouth. I'm starting to worry, and my instincts are screaming that I need to help her. To get her out of whatever is making her this uncomfortable.

What happens next stops time. It feels like an eternity is happening in a split second. I hear a slap and a soft sob asking him to stop. That's the moment all my senses go on high alert. Like every cell in my body is screaming at me, "Go to her!" Completely unraveled by the thought of someone, *anyone,* hurting her, I push through the door and ask what the hell is going on.

Her dad is standing tall right in front of her, and she looks scared as shit. I walk to stand in front of her, and he raises his hand motioning for me to stop.

"This is between me and my disrespectful daughter," he says without looking at me. "You can go back to the farm you came from."

I walk around his hand and add, "Respectfully, sir, I'm not comfortable with you laying hands on Allie. Your daughter or not."

"If you don't walk away from my house, I will have you escorted out in five seconds flat." His tone is dry and harsh, but all I focus on is the small sobs behind my back and Allie asking me to go. I turn around to face her, grab her bag from the floor, and hold her hand. Not looking at her dad once, I pull Allie out of the house and keep walking. Her dad says something like *this isn't over,* but I can't stand there and let him degrade her like that. Nobody lays a finger on her, especially not her dad.

We speed walk to the truck without saying a word. It's a beautiful sunny day outside, even with the light fog, I can see that it will be perfect. I start driving away from the house, the opposite way from school. Allie isn't crying anymore, but she's just looking out the window, with her back turned to me.

"Sorry if I was out of line," I say with concern in my voice.

"It's complicated," she says without looking my way.

"Allie, nobody should lay a hand on you. It's that simple."

She sighs and says, "In my family, and how my Dad grew up, the way I talked to him was not acceptable. The slap was his way of reminding me who he is and who I am. That I'm his child, and I should have not raised my voice at him."

"It doesn't matter. He shouldn't have done that. I'm sorry. Does this happen often?" My knuckles are white from holding the steering wheel so tight. I could hurt him for just talking to her like that, let alone hurting her.

"Long story short, no, it doesn't. He travels a lot, so we don't see each other often, and I usually don't talk back to him, like ever. The last time I said 'no' to him, I was twelve and he wanted me to continue music classes, but the schedule was killing me, so I said no. That was the last time I got in trouble."

She'd rather not talk to him or express her opinions than risk him being offended and doing something like that. Call me an idealist if you want, but I don't think that should be the relationship you have with a parent. Your parents should be the people who believe in you the most. Even if you are not close to them, you should not fear them. They should be your safe space.

I'm sure her mom is that for her, but is it enough? Aside from Cara, does she have anyone who she can be unapologetically herself with? Or is she constantly walking on eggshells around the people she loves?

"Where are we going by the way?" she asks.

"I figured you needed some time, and school didn't sound like the place for it. So we're going to the river."

"The river? For what?"

"To relax, baby. We don't have to swim, but some fresh air will do you good. This may be as good for me as it will be for you."

MOMENTS LATER, we make it to a grassy area where we park, and I guide her down the path to the river. This is one of my favorite spots because of how quiet it is. The St. Mary's River has some deep and perfect for swimming areas, but this part under The Twin Bridges is a great thinking spot. She walks beside me, but I can see she doesn't love the sand on her feet, so with one quick sweep I pick her up and carry her.

She yelps and wiggles in my arms, but I just kiss her forehead and keep walking. Her eyes are so light right now. Like they're reflecting the light and the shades of green, yellow, and brown dance in them. Now that I look at it, her hair also has golden, brown, and reddish tones to it. It's beautiful, just like her. "You are stunning, Honey."

She looks down after the compliment, surely a little embarrassed from the attention. How did this beautiful and magical girl ever begin to feel like she didn't deserve all the attention in the world?

Once we make it to the river bank, I put her down. I take my shoes off, and she does the same. Then, we walk hand in hand to the water. I stick my feet in, but she's hesitant. I raise an eyebrow at her.

"Doesn't it scare you? This water is so brown."

Laughing, I say, "It's clean, I promise. Look." I squat down to scoop some water on my hands and she can see how clear it is so I explain, "Tannins make it look this dark. The roots from the trees around here release the color, and it acts as a dye in the water. Almost like when you steep tea."

Her eyes widen, and she nods. She walks closer and lets her feet touch the water. She closes her eyes and takes a deep breath. She whispers something so softly that, if I wasn't focusing solely on her, I would have missed it. Smirking, I say, "Can you say that louder so my brain knows I didn't make it up?"

She opens her golden eyes and looks up at me with a soft smile. She has my jersey on and some tiny shorts that show her thick legs, and she looks like an absolute mirage with her toes in the water and her wild hair in the air.

"Allie, can you say that again, baby?" I press.

She turns her body toward me, places both hands next to my face, and says as clear as day, "I love you, Jake Clarke." Then, she kisses me. This is it. This is the kiss that ruins me for everyone else. And at eighteen, I know at this moment, this girl holds my whole future in her hands.

21

____

NOW

IF THE WORLD WAS ENDING, JP SAXE AND EVA LUNA MONTANER

Jake

AFTER THE SHOWER, I take Allie to my room. Get her all dried off and into one of my shirts. She's still in shock. I can tell because she hasn't said much after the shower. She is sitting on the couch right now watching the rain fall outside while I am making her some tea.

When I got her message that she wasn't going to make it to the game, I knew something was wrong. It's not like her to not give details. The game had ended when I heard about the crash on the highway, and I started to panic when she wouldn't answer my calls. I was on my way home when I saw her walking on the side of the road, and if it wasn't for her explaining that she was in a crash, I would have never guessed that she was in it.

I thought my heart was being ripped out of my chest seeing her walking and crying in the rain. I could recognize her body from feet away, but it took self-control not to jump out of my truck the second I knew it was her. She was defeated and physically spent. Her sagging shoulders and swollen eyes told me more than words could ever say. She needed me, that was clear. I don't want to pressure her into telling me more about what happened because I swear, I will kill whoever did this to her. The kettle whistles, pulling me from my daze. I add a bag of chamomile tea, a splash of cream, and two teaspoons of sugar. Assuming she'd take her tea just like her coffee.

I walk back to the couch and hand her the cup. I sit right behind her, and she crawls up to sit right between my legs with her head on my chest. She sighs and takes a sip before she turns her head around and asks for some painkillers. I push her forward a little to get out from under her, grab her some medicine, and sit back down. She takes the pills, swallows them, closes her eyes, and places her head back on my chest.

"I'm sorry I made you get up after you were already comfortable," she says. The sadness in her voice making me feel like the world's biggest asshole for being intimate with her after the day she had. "I'm sorry to be such a burden."

I notice how she uses her hands to wipe her eyes. "Shh," I say. "You're not a burden." She takes a sip of her tea, but sobs impede her from drinking more as she continues to cry.

"Please don't cry, Honey. I promise you I like taking care of you. You were never a burden, and you never will be, but I do need you to talk to me and tell me what happened."

She takes another sip of her tea, puts the mug down, and turns her body so she can look at me. She starts talking about her day and ends with the recollection of the events, and I feel like an even bigger asshole after she tells me she lost consciousness. All I could think about was making her feel good without even knowing the magnitude of the crash. I hug her tight and apologize for that. She just giggles and reassures me it was exactly what she needed. She finishes telling me how she told the doctors she wouldn't be alone, but then she wouldn't even call me to tell me to pick her up.

"Why didn't you call, baby? You shouldn't have left the hospital walking after a concussion. That was reckless."

"I didn't even know what time it was, and I knew you had a game tonight. I didn't want you to worry—" she says nonchalantly like she's not the thing that matters most to me right now, "—and I didn't want to see you at the hospital again."

"I'm always worrying about you, especially now. I can definitely be at a hospital. I'm a grown man." I don't need her worrying about me to the point where she is putting herself in danger. I'm supposed to be the one protecting her. I can take care of myself.

"I didn't want you to leave the game," she says, sounding completely hurt. Like the thought of asking me to be with her, at the fucking hospital nonetheless, would cause issues for me. Little does she know I would leave it all just to be what she needs.

"I would have left my own wedding to find you," I add.

"The roads were dangerous," she rebuttals.

"Even if the world was ending, I would have gone out to find you. Also, you're sleeping in my room tonight." I look straight into her eyes and hold her stare so she doesn't think for a second that I was asking her a question.

"That's your space, Jake, I don't want to intrude," she says.

Silly, silly girl. This whole place means nothing without her. Having her here proved what I knew all along. I want her here with me, always. I always did, and I'm sure I always will. I am tired of living with the ghost of her here.

"Please invade my space. I want you everywhere. I want to see every corner of this house and remember how you looked sitting, standing, or lying there. Go ahead and take over. You already live in my thoughts all the time, might as well be a physical part of me too." I kiss her forehead before continuing. "I am not letting you out of my sight, so if you don't sleep in my room, I will sit right on that chair watching you sleep in your room."

"You will be sore."

"Happily sore," I add, still comforting her with my touch.

"Why are you so good to me?" she asks with a soft sigh. I can tell she's completely done. Emotionally and mentally done. She needs a break, she needs to be taken care of.

Because I love you, I want to say, but it seems frivolous; too soon. Instead, I say, "You deserve it." I rub her arms. Right here, with her head on my chest in the dim light of my room, is where I want to be for the rest of my life. I knew it at eighteen ,and I sure as hell know it now, too.

"I have to call the company tomorrow and figure out the car situation, too. This is just a nightmare," she sighs with hopelessness in her voice.

"The most important thing is you're alive and you're okay. I think you should give yourself grace and a few days to rest. The world can wait."

"I need to send an email at least." She tries to grab her phone from the table, but I grab it first,open her email app, and start composing an email instead. I am very familiar with concussion protocol, and she should not be looking at screens right now.

"Who should I send this email to?" I say showing her that I'm typing.

She frowns and adds, "To Lindsey, she is my direct supervisor."

"Sent." I place the phone back down on the table and return my hands to her arms.

"Thank you," she says, resting her head back down.

I caress her arms and place gentle kisses on her head until her breathing slows and I hear soft snores. She cuddles deeper into my chest as she continues to sleep peacefully. *This right here is heaven*, I think as I stare at the most beautiful girl I have ever seen, sleeping soundly on me.

22
———

THEN

HEY THERE DELILAH, PLAIN WHITE T'S

Allie

I STAND in front of my locker trying to get the things I need while waiting for Jake to show up, as he does every morning before class. We have been spending more time together this week, and he has picked me up or dropped me off practically every day. I drove today because I have to run a few errands after cheer practice and can't wait for him to get out of his.

We have been together every free minute these past few days, but I try to avoid the *my dad slapped me in front of you* topic. Things at home are not great, even though I haven't seen my dad since that day. My mom is trying to play peacekeeper. My brothers are trying to get me to chill and maybe apologize, but I refuse. I am almost eighteen, and in less than a year, I will be moving away for college, so why should I apologize for loving this boy? Jake has done nothing wrong, and the thing he has done right from the start is putting me first. Even when we got caught skipping class on Monday, he took the blame. I only got detention, but he got community service, too.

Dad comes from a family where you marry 'up.' You marry someone who can give you a better life. But for him, a better life is not someone who will necessarily treat you right. It's not someone who will be good company. It's someone who can provide you with more money than what you have now, and I don't agree with him at all. I already have more money that I want. I don't care about the trust fund or the black card Dad lets me use. Money comes and goes, but at the end of the day, I want to grow old with someone who understands me. With someone who's kind, funny, and respectful. I don't care about the things he does, and that's what the whole conversation was about. I don't even know why he's so stressed about marriage right now. Nobody's thinking about it but him.

I'm placing things back inside my locker when I hear a squeal coming from who I'm sure is Cara. She starts bouncing next to me and hands me her college acceptance letter. I know what it is before I even open it because I also received mine this morning. Deep red letters on an envelope with the name Stanford University front and center confirm what I already know; she got in too. I hug her and whisper a congratulations. I kiss her cheek, and I can't help but jump with her. For years, we have been talking about going to Stanford together, even when we were miles apart, and now that we get to spend our senior year together and go to college together, I don't blame her excitement. I would be feeling the same way if it wasn't for the tall, handsome, sweet boy with chestnut eyes staring right at me with furrowed brows.

He walks toward us, and as I stop bouncing, he says, "Don't stop on my account, beautiful," placing a quick kiss on my head.

"You are looking at two girls who got accepted into their top choice of college, boys," Cara says, referring to Jake and Cole who are both standing next to us.

"Congrats, babe," Cole says and picks Cara up from the

ground. They walk in a tight embrace back to class without even looking back.

I close the distance between Jake and me and give him a tight hug without uttering a word about college. I turn back and close the locker as I ask him about the game tomorrow. "Are you nervous about playing the Commanders?"

"No, but don't change the subject, baby. You got into your top choice?" he asks with pride in his eyes, but if only he knew that my top choice was not UF like I had told him. What if he won't be as supportive? When we had the college conversation, I always talked about UF because it was my second choice, and the chances of me getting into Stanford were slim.

"I did."

"Congratulations! I'm so proud of you!" he adds with a huge smile.

"Thank you," I say in a clipped tone. I am trying to keep this conversation moving quickly so I don't make a scene this early in the morning, which I know is about to happen at any moment. I don't want to think about the lies I've told about school or the fact that I want to pick Stanford but I also want Jake.

"I guess now we won't have to find out what long-distance relationships are like, huh?" he says, pulling me closer to him and grabbing my backpack.

I guess we *will* have the conversation now. *Tierra trágame.* "Yeah, about that," I say, and he stops abruptly, turning his body to face me and losing all the light he had in his eyes. As soon as he looks in my eyes he knows there's something wrong, and I don't know how to approach this with the five minutes we have before the bell rings. I take a deep breath and keep talking, "I haven't heard from UF. This acceptance letter was from somewhere else."

"Oh, I thought UF was your top choice. I must have remembered wrong. Where were you accepted?"

I stare at him and bite my lip slightly. Concern floats in his eyes as he says "Allie, where did you get in?"

"Stanford," I say.

"Like California, Stanford?"

"Yep, that's the one."

"What's up, Jake?" I hear someone shout from behind us, but Jake pays no attention to them. His eyes are only on me when he drops our bags, picks me up by the back of my legs, and spins me around like I am made of feathers and not flesh and bones.

"Aah, put me down," I squeal.

"Freaking Stanford! My girl is going to Stanford!" he shouts, and people around us stop and clap.

He finally sets me down but won't let me go. Noticing my inner turmoil, he whispers in my ear, "We will figure it out, Honey. You and me. I have no doubt, but please let me celebrate with you right now." Then, the bell rings.

"Saved by the bell," I whisper hoping he won't hear me, but he gives me that look. The one that asks me to trust him,to breathe, and to not let all my negative thoughts swarm me quicker than lightning.

"I love you, Allie," he says and walks into class leaving me in the hallway both speechless and breathless.

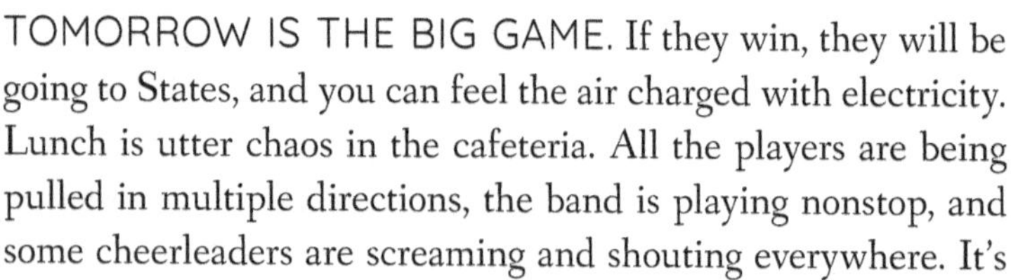

TOMORROW IS THE BIG GAME. If they win, they will be going to States, and you can feel the air charged with electricity. Lunch is utter chaos in the cafeteria. All the players are being pulled in multiple directions, the band is playing nonstop, and some cheerleaders are screaming and shouting everywhere. It's overwhelming. Tin trays smack on the table. The instruments play. There's clapping, stomping, and shouting. A sea of red, white, and black. Everyone is up on their feet participating in some way or another, and I'm just standing in awe of how this small town is coming together for its own. Even the quiet kids are smiling and looking around. Some cheerleaders are practically being thrown in the air, and the cafeteria monitors are looking down as if nothing is happening.

I see Jake surrounded by his offensive linemen, and it's easy to see they are a close group. They have their inside jokes. They have each others' backs.

They are gathering together in what looks like a huddle, and these huge six-foot-plus seniors are all trying to pick up Alex, their quarterback and captain. He's fighting them, but eventually, he loses the battle, and they lift him. They shout, "Cap! Cap! Cap!" and "Hoo, Hoo, Hoo!" as they move him around. Finally, they place him on top of a table, and this is when one of the teachers looks up. The whole room goes quiet and looks back at Mr. Porter. It feels like the longest three seconds. Mr. Porter and the crowd are in a staring contest with Alex standing on top of the table, then Mr. Porter smiles at everyone and turns his body around like nothing is happening.

The crowd goes wild, and in no time, they're shouting, "SPEECH! SPEECH! SPEECH!" I know tomorrow they will be more focused and reserved, so they are allowing all the silliness and chaos to happen today, and it's intoxicating.

I feel an electric pull somewhere near, so I look around, and I find Jake looking at me from across the cafeteria. As soon as our eyes meet, he smiles. And gosh, if that smile doesn't make me feel like both putty and the shittiest person alive for not telling him about Stanford.

The room is quiet, and Alex starts giving the people what they want; a speech. He talks about sportsmanship, but more than that, he talks about brotherhood and how this might be the last chance they all get to play together. He talks about how proud he is of all of them, that whatever happens tomorrow won't change how he feels about them, and that everyone should just enjoy the game. He talks about being a Shark no matter where they go and no matter what tomorrow brings. The crowd goes wild.

Everyone is clapping, cheering, screaming. Some of the freshman girls are swooning over this soon-to-be man, and I don't blame them because that was pretty impressive. In the meantime, I can't focus on anything really because Jake keeps his intense gaze on me, and I feel like a million bucks. Alex keeps talking, but everything is fading to the outside because Jake is walking toward me. I smile at him and give him my attention like I have a choice. Like him looking at me that way is not making me question everything.

"*Hola*, beautiful," he says.

"Hey, handsome, I love when you talk Spanish to me even if it's just an *hola*," I add with a smile, wrapping my arms around his neck and stretching on my tiptoes to reach him.

"I'm trying to use some Spanish every day. I figured starting with greetings would be ideal."

His sweet smile, his hands around my hips, and his fresh mint scent invade all my senses, and I have no other choice than to close the space between us and kiss him. The kiss starts soft and tentative, like all of our school kisses, but it turns quickly into a heavy and passionate kiss. The type of kiss that erases all previous memories and ruins you for the future. I am pretty sure there was a before Jake, but there won't be an after. I can feel it in my bones.

Someone coughs, and we stop immediately. I feel like we were just caught. When I turn my face, Alex, Nick, and Cole are all whistling, clapping, and grabbing Jake. I just want to kill them all. "You're all insufferable," I say.

"But you love us," Cole says with a wink as they walk back, dragging Jake with them.

"See you later, love bug," Alex adds, blowing pretend kisses my way.

I roll my eyes and catch up to them so I'm not left behind.

I WENT STRAIGHT HOME INSTEAD of waiting for Jake today. Since I'm avoiding my dad like the plague, I've been locked in my room all afternoon. This week has felt like it was a whole month in between spending the weekend with Jake, dealing with my dad's outburst, end of the quarter tests, and getting ready for the game tomorrow.

There's a soft knock on my door, and when I look up, I find my mom and Jake both standing there. I look at them astonished, but before I can say anything, my mom opens the door wider saying, "Don't make me regret this. In bed by ten, Allie." She lets Jake inside and closes the door behind him.

"What are you doing here?" I ask sheepishly. He grabs my hands and lifts me up from the bed, straight into his arms.

His arms are an immediate comfort, giving me reassurance that whatever funk I thought we were in might just be in my head. But I really do have to talk to him about my dreams so he doesn't freak out about us. I say nothing though, and he knows something is up, because Jake knows me to my core. We are in tune. One heart beating in two bodies.

"Words, Allie, I need words." I let out a sigh and sit on the edge of my bed with him following beside me. I breathe again, and then let it all out.

"When we first started dating, I told you my top school was UF, and before you ask, no, not because you were going there but because their education program is fantastic, and I never thought in a million years I would have a chance at Stanford. So, imagine my surprise when that letter came in the mail. I was worried about how you would react, and a thousand scenarios went through my head, so I hid it from you." I stop, breathe, and swallow. I look into his eyes and see nothing but warmth, so I continue, "I know we have talked about dating through college and then coming back here, and I still think it's a great plan, Jake. I love you so much, and even though we're young, I think there will never be anything as special as this ever again."

"But?" he asks, and I swear I see the light dim in his eyes.

Ah, I hate this, "I know when we talked about this, we were both going to be at the same college or at the very least, close by since my other choices were less than five hours away. But Jake, now I'm going to be 2,000 miles away in a different time zone, and I don't want to be the reason you miss out on living your best college life. I know how men are, and I would rather let this go than worry about you being miserable or regretting making a promise to me when you didn't have all the facts."

He looks at me with eyes wide and grabs my hands. He takes a deep breath, almost like he's mustering the courage to tell me we are about to be over, so I beat him to it and put him out of his misery.

"Jake, it's okay, I understand. I'm not going to lie to you, I will be heartbroken, but it will be okay."

"Allie, stop," he says, and I hear the pain in his words as he continues, "Is this what you want, or is this what you think *I* want?" He waits, and when I don't say anything, he continues, "Because if this is what you want, I will fight it. I will prove to you how much I *don't need* to be single to enjoy my college life. I won't ever look at another woman after you regardless of how many miles exist between us. I would wait a decade for you if it meant I get to have you. You are it. I mean it, and I won't let this go." He smiles at me and keeps going, "And if this is what you think *I* want, let me show you right now how wrong you are." With that, he closes the distance between us with a kiss.

His hand is in my hair, and the other is on my lower back pulling me flush against him. The kiss is frantic. It's rushed, deep, and slightly rough. His tongue invades my space with purpose, without one doubt in the world. *Mine* is what it feels like he's telling me with his lips, his hands, and his breaths. I moan into his lips, and he swallows the sound by deepening the kiss. When my hands go up to pull on his hair, he lets go of my lips, and whispers exactly what I need to hear. "You're mine, Honey. I only want you, and I will only ever want you." We are a mess of heavy breathing, fast heart rates, and pent-up want, but with my parents in the house, we won't take this further.

He brings both hands to hold my face and says into my lips, "Two thousand miles or twenty thousand, if that's where your dreams are, you go chase them. I will wait for you. And we can do long-distance. You love flying, so you can come to me as often as you want. There will be a spot on the right side of my bed for you."

Tears fall, and I smile, saying, "I actually hate flying. I just love traveling, and flying comes with the territory. I love you, Jake, and if you truly mean that, I would love nothing more than to continue this."

As he hugs me, he whispers, "It was never an option, Honey. I'm never letting you go."

23

THEN

WITHOUT YOU, DAVID GUETTA FT. USHER

Jake

THIS IS the game we've all been waiting for since last year. *Last year,* we lost right before State, and it won't happen again . I can't keep my head focused because of the whiplash I'm getting from Allie. She says she'll be fine going to Stanford and coming back to this small town, but for some reason I don't believe her. She seemed torn about telling me she got accepted, and I think it's because she is thinking of letting me go.

She said she wanted to still be together and come back here to continue our lives together. But she said it when she thought she had no chance at going to Stanford. And now that she got accepted, who am I to clip her wings? Will I miss her? Absofuckinglutely. Will I pout and make a big deal out of this? No. She deserves to be celebrated even if I am scared shitless she will leave here and never look back. She will leave us and never look back.

There is some chatter on the bus, but mostly, we're all quiet. Some of us are listening to music, others are snoring. I hear Alex and Coach talking about the game, and Nick is sitting next to me, completely out. We play the Commanders tonight, and although we beat them already this season, they won this round of last year's playoffs. We really need to work together and try not to be predictable if we are going to be able to win and go to State. I'm pretty sure everyone in Baker is going to this game tonight. Businesses closed, the school had an early release scheduled, and the parents were carpooling so they could make the hour drive.

We're pulling up to the Commanders' parking lot when the coach tells us to grab our gear, get off the bus, and get set up. As we quietly walk down to the locker room in a line, we look around and see all the families and fans from the Commanders. Green and tan fill the space, and we have to walk through the masses to make it to the locker room. You could hear a pin drop with how quiet the crowd is as we walked by. Everyone is staring at us, and we keep our heads forward. The only sound is the pads bumping against our bags and helmets and the cleats click-clacking on the sidewalk.

The cheerleaders, band, and flag team should be here soon, and that sense of dread comes back to my stomach just thinking about Allie. I wish she would just talk to me, instead of hiding whatever she's trying her damnedest not to tell me. But I need to get my head in the game and push it aside, as hard as it is.

We get in the locker room to get dressed. We can hear the people outside, and there's music playing, too, but we are focused on getting ready. Coach gets up, and we face him waiting to hear what he has to say.

"Today, we are here not only to play a game but to win it. Last year we almost had them, and then, we crumbled at the end and lost. I could tell you that we play football for the fun of it, but we all know that in a game, you play to win even if it doesn't pay off. Last year, we lost big against this same team on our field. It was hard, but we learned from it. I look around this locker room, and I see players who took that loss and worked on their weaknesses from that game to the point where I now find strengths. I see players who worked twice as hard to be better. To make it to this game y'all are about to play tonight. And you better show it. I want this win more than anything, but I can't be the one to get it for you. You have to want it badly enough to go out there and show them WHO. YOU. ARE. I know who you are, but sometimes you forget. So, before we go out there, let me remind you. You are the kings of this game. You are the best team I have ever coached and probably ever will. You work together as a team COME WHAT MAY, and it shows. You are leaders. You are beasts. Don't go out there and act all fragile. Go out there and dominate the field. Show them you are the mighty Sharks, and nobody goes up against a shark and comes out without battle scars. Let's show them what we are made of."

We're all clapping, stomping our feet, hitting the lockers, and ready to go. Alex gets up and shouts, "Sharks on three," and we all get up and follow along. "One! Two! Three! SHARKS!"

Claps sound all around until Coach settles us down before we get out onto the field.

LIGHTS ARE BRIGHT AND BURNING. We are tied in the last quarter, the ball is in our hands, and we just made our first down. We are on yard fifty with a ways to go, but we are making it count. Coach calls a time-out to bring us all in, and he looks furious. The offensive line has played like shit today; letting too many players by, making it harder to score when we should have been ahead by the way their offense is playing. Our defense is solid, but theirs is a different beast.

"What on earth are y'all doing out there?" he screams at us. "I have never been more disappointed IN MY LIFE of my offensive line like I am right now."

We all stare at him in the dead silence, nobody willing to speak up. Those questions were rhetorical, and even though we are tired as shit, our self-preservation stays strong. We just say *yes sir* as he speaks. "Blake, stop fucking up out there. Clarke, I don't know where your head is tonight, but I need it BACK IN HERE RIGHT FUCKING NOW. Go play like you want to go to State, NOW!"

"Yes, sir," we all shout, military style, and get back on the field. The cheerleaders are doing some chants, and my eyes quickly try to find curves for days and tan legs to see if she'll look at me and give me some reassurance. She doesn't, and I still kind of like it because she is so immersed in what she's doing that not much can make her lose focus. I need to do the same and get my head in the game.

I take my position, and Alex calls the play. I take a step back immediately after we break and cover him with my whole body so he can run the ball. James and I are basically his human shields, and where he goes, we go. This is the one play in the game in which I have to run, and I'm ready. The play starts, and we follow in position quickly. They're coming at us, but the rest of the line is pushing and shoving them away as we advance with our QB. A big Commander is running this way, so I get ready to block him when I feel something big and hard hit me into the ground from the right, and everything goes black.

PART 3

UNSTEADY, X AMBASSADORS

Hold on
Hold on to me
Don't let me go
Be the thread of gold
I need to hold on to.

____

24

THEN

HOLD ON, CHORD OVERSTREET

Allie

THE CROWD IS BOUNCING and screaming about whatever play is happening. Then, a big gasp falls among them. Instantly, everything goes eerily quiet, and with all eyes on the field, it's clear something happened. I turn around to see a player on the ground. I frantically scan the field looking for Jake, but I can't see him. I keep looking, trying to remain calm, but I can't see his broad frame. I can't find his eyes on me like they usually are, or the shiny number fifty from his jersey. The medics are running to whoever is on the ground, and when they clear the area, I can see what I have been worried about since we started dating. Jake is on the ground surrounded by the medics, and he's not moving.

I drop my poms, and run to him, ignoring everyone shouting my name. Telling me to come back or stop. Fuck that and fuck them, I need to see what's happening. I finally make it there, and he is unconscious. Eyes closed, helmet still on, they're checking so many things at the same time.

"Jake," I let out a sob, covering my mouth. Nick comes toward me quickly. I'm crying, it feels like everything is in slow motion but going so fast at the same time. And I'm completely useless. I just stand here sobbing and silently praying. *Open your eyes, baby, just open them.* I hear the ambulance pulling up, and in seconds, two EMTs run in.

They check his vitals, remove his helmet after securing the neck brace, and tilt him to put him on the gurney. He opens his eyes and screams. An earth-shattering scream. It's then I pay attention to more than just his face, and see what's making him scream like this, and I notice he is grabbing his leg. He keeps trying to get up to look at it before the EMTs force him down.

He won't stop twitching and pulling on the neck brace. He won't stop moving, and he's not letting them do what they need to do. I try to get close to see if I can get through to him, but they won't let me, so I just watch as he desperately tries to figure out what happened and is completely overwhelmed by pain. The female EMT, a little blonde who couldn't be more than 100 pounds, basically climbs on top of him to keep him from moving while the male EMT gives him a shot of something, and finally, he's back down with his eyes closed and calm. *Did they sedate him? Holy shit.*

They're wheeling him out, and I run behind them, begging them to please let me go with them. Coach looks at me with pity in his eyes, but when the EMTs say it's his call, he nods and says, "I'm calling his parents, and I will be right behind you."

I run behind them, trying to keep up. Tasha follows and brings me my bag and my phone before going back to formation. She looks destroyed, too, just like how I feel. And that's when it hits me that Jake is so loved by everyone, and nobody knows what's happening. I catch up with the paramedics, and as soon as they put him in the ambulance, I hop in, too, trying to stay out of their way to the best of my ability.

It smells sterile here, just like a hospital would, and I hate it. There are very bright white lights over where Jake is lying down, and the male paramedic, *Smith*, according to his badge, hooks Jake up to an IV. Suddenly, we're moving, and he keeps working on Jake. He puts some medicine in the IV, and then he moves on to stabilize Jake's leg, prepping as best as they can. That has to hurt like hell, but I keep my comments to myself and try to calm my breathing. I shoot my mom a text, letting her know what happened, but I don't have Jake's family's number to message them. *God, please be okay.* I keep repeating on a loop in my mind.

"Could you answer some questions for us about his medical history?" he says.

"Sure, I can try to answer as much as I know. I don't have his mom's phone number," I say.

"Can you give me his full name, date of birth, and his address?"

I answer the questions dumbfounded and control my breathing so I don't have a panic attack. He asks how old I am, and I lie and say I'm eighteen because I don't want to be in trouble for being in here with him as a minor. However, there was no way in hell I was going to let him ride by himself. He explained that he gave him a sedative as well as some pretty strong painkillers. He says the doctors will have to confirm, but he thinks Jake tore something in his knee, which is why his leg looks like that. He also has some bruising in his abdomen. The EMT is worried about internal bleeding, and he's going to keep Jake sedated until we get to the hospital and they can triage him properly, especially since he freaked out before.

In the blink of an eye, we make it to the hospital, and he's taken inside. If this doesn't look like a scene from Grey's Anatomy, I don't know what does. He's brought in quickly, and I'm trying to follow along with them, but they're faster than I am. The hospital feels even colder than usual, and the chaos that usually surrounds an emergency room is even worse. I feel as if I am twirling inside a tornado from hell.

They bring Jake into an exam room and are running all sorts of tests on him. They're talking about how they need to wake him up to test his brain functions and assess his ability to answer questions. Nobody is talking to me, they're just going around, passing along information, and I have never felt more alone than this moment. I want answers, but above all, I want to wake up from this fucking nightmare and see Jake smile again.

I speak up and explain what I was told happened since I didn't see the hit. I tell them he was not hit in the head, but he was slammed into the ground. They explain to me that sometimes you can get head trauma from hitting the ground.

They step away for a second, and I sit right next to him and hold his hand. I start whispering how much I love him and that he can't leave me. "You are the love of my life, and I can tell there will only always be you. Please hold onto that. I will be so lost without you. Please." I repeat my pleas over and over while trying not to cry more than I have. My heart beats faster. My hands are sweating, and I swear to God, if I am about to have a panic attack, I will lose it.

For a while, nothing happens. He's still asleep. They bring in different specialists to check on him, but the medical terms they're using don't make any sense to me. I'm so exhausted I can barely think, but I keep trying to ask as many questions as I can. They tell me they've called his mom and she's on her way, but she's not here yet.

I step away to use the bathroom and call my mom to explain what's going on. As I'm walking back, I see Coach and some of the players in the waiting room. Coach is talking to one of the doctors, so I don't interrupt.

I quickly duck into the bathroom, and when I come out, I see a flurry of nurses and doctors rushing around.

There is an alarm going off; it's blasting, "Code blue! Code blue!"

When I rush to try to get to Jake, I see all of them crammed in the room with him. *He* is the code blue patient.

No, no, no, no, no, please don't let this be it for him. Please let him survive this. I pray to someone I don't even know. I pray to God, maybe the universe, but if there's something out there, please don't take him. I stay there in shock from what's happening, and all I hear is "Charge to one hundred! Clear!" Pads are being brought up to his chest. *Hold tight, baby. I still need you.*

"Again!" says the doctor, "Clear!" All hands are off. He's shocked again, and this is when the first sobbed scream comes out of me. It takes me a minute to realize I'm saying my thoughts out loud, loud enough for them to turn their heads to me, and for someone to shout to get me out of there.

A nurse rushes over to me. "Please don't leave me. Please come back to me!" I scream at the top of my lungs. My tears keep falling, and the desperation in my voice is breaking through everything I thought I was holding back.

"Miss, Miss, you have to calm down," the tiny nurse says, and I swear it takes three of the football players and the nurse to drag me out of there. If it were up to me, I would be sitting right next to him, holding his hand and whispering in his ear that I'm still here. That I will love him forever, and I need him to fight and stay with me.

One of the boys pulls me into his arms, and I am so distraught I can't even tell who it is. All I know is the door opens up, and Jake is rolled out with a team of doctors following along with him. One nurse stays behind to talk to us, but she says she can only talk to next of kin. I am still sobbing and shaking, waiting to hear what just happened, and nobody will speak because his family is not here. I'm losing my mind.

Coach talks to them and shows them that he has the release waiver from the parents saying that medical information can be shared with him. They walk away from the rest of us to talk. Coach nods and rubs his face. He looks concerned, but he's not crying, so I take that as a win.

He walks toward us and tells us that they found internal bleeding, and they're taking Jake to surgery, now. They were able to get his heart beating again, but right now, it's touch and go. We should know more in the next few hours about how bad things are. He said the best thing to do right now is wait and pray.

I collapse onto the ground. *Please don't leave me.* It's the only thing on my mind. My sobs flooding my mind and the space. Everything else fades to the background. Nothing makes sense. Nothing will ever make sense until he's out of there and his beautiful eyes look at me again.

25

———

THEN

HEAL, TOM ODELL

Allie

I CLIMB on the bed with Jake, taking advantage of the fact that the nurses aren't hovering right now. I skipped school today to visit him now that he's finally out of the ICU and his visiting hours are longer. His mom is at work, so I don't have to share him with anyone right now. It sounds selfish, but I just want to be alone with him, even if he can't talk to me. Even if he can't look at me.

On Friday, they were able to control the bleeding. He had a lacerated spleen, and they repaired it without having to remove anything. He tore his ACL, and they did a reconstruction on Saturday. They used a part of the muscle and tissue from the other leg to restore it so both his legs are in different types of bandages and braces. Unfortunately, he's still not waking up, but they have high hopes. They say the trauma to his body was enough for his brain to need a longer rest, and they are hopeful he will wake up soon. Of course, they can't promise there's no damage to the brain. I'm choosing to stay positive, though, and praying for the best.

I sit right next to him on the bed and slide down slightly to lay my head against his chest. I start telling him about the weekend. How the team was so distraught this happened, they lost the game. About how nobody is upset they lost but upset about what happened to him. How the hospital has had to turn people away because the waiting room is always full of people here to support him. I talk to him, and I tell him everything, secretly wishing he'll say *anything* back to me.

When I'm not talking to him, it's so quiet. Not the type of comfortable silence you can have with someone you love, but the kind that shatters your heart with every passing second. I try not to cry, but it's impossible to stop the tears from falling down my cheeks. I just want him back, and I want him back, now. Patience has never been my virtue, but right now, it's practically impossible to just wait. I stay lying there with my head on his chest and my heart on the floor as tears stream down my face, quietly drifting off to sleep in this eerie room.

MY PHONE RINGING wakes me up from the deep sleep I was in. This is the only place I have been able to sleep since Friday, but it's never for very long because of the nurses coming in, or my mom begging me to come home. The ringing was thanks to a series of text messages from several people, including my mom and Cara. My mom just wants to know if I'll be home for dinner, which I respond yes to because the nurses will kick me out before then, and she sends a heart emoji. My dad is not in town this week, so I am planning on seeing my mom more.

I take a deep breath, rub my face, and get my ass up from the hospital bed. Stretching my arms, I hear footsteps behind me and turn to see Cara and Cole standing there. Cara has a soft smile on her face that is complemented by her beautiful yellow dress. She always feels like a ray of sunshine. Even though people sometimes say the same about me, I think she is the true representation of that statement. Just looking at her right now makes me feel happier.

"Hey, babe," I say, smiling at her. They both look at me the same way everyone has the past week; with pity. I hate it, but I guess there's no way around it.

"Am I chopped liver?" asks Cole as he walks in and sits on the chair opposite me. He has a smirk on his face that goes away when his eyes wander to Jake. There's no change in his status, so he's just lying there, half here, half somewhere else. His eyes drift quickly back to me, surely trying to hide his hopelessness. Seeing his best friend like that cannot be easy.

"How do you know I wasn't calling *you* babe?" I say lifting my eyebrows hoping to relax the situation a little. I am tired of people walking on eggshells around me, and if I can't be myself with these two, even when I am sad, who can I be myself around? They also don't deserve to just be miserable. We all miss him, but we're hurting ourselves by continuing to drown in the hollowness.

"Because we all know the only person other than me who you're allowed to call babe is lying on that bed," she says, kissing my cheek and sitting next to me. She wraps her arms around me, comforting me instantly.

Cole scoffs a small laugh and adds, "And Jake is a scary motherfucker even lying down, so I'm glad it wasn't me you called babe."

All three of us laugh, and it feels almost normal. I didn't know how much I needed to just talk to friends without talking about Friday or Jake's injuries. Cara and Cole know the same that I do, and I bet if I were to ask, they would tell me they're here for me and not Jake right now. The four of us stay there for the next hour as I try to catch up on whatever happened at school today. We also take turns telling Jake something we don't like about him, hoping he will wake up and yell at us for making fun of him while he's in a hospital bed, but nothing changes.

Visiting hours are over, and we don't have any choice but to leave. We pick up our stuff and start heading out. I turn back around and quickly give Jake a kiss. "I love you. I will be back tomorrow, *mi amor*," I say softly raking my hands over his soft hair. "Please come back to me."

26

NOW

THIS LOVE (TAYLOR'S VERSION), TAYLOR SWIFT

Jake

THE PAST FEW days have been torture trying to stay focused at work. I try to be my best self regardless of how worried I am about Allie alone at the house. I know she's capable of taking care of herself, but knowing how close she was to being seriously hurt makes me go full neanderthal.

"Mr. Clarke?" I hear someone say. Looking up, startled and confused, the whole class laughs.

"Where's your head at, Coach?" Tyler, one of the juniors on the team, asks with a know-it-all smirk on his face.

Was I ever this cocky in high school? Rubbing my face and annoyed at the question I reply, "Want extra work sixty-two?" The class riots in laughter.

There is nothing wrong with admitting when you are in the wrong, so I own up to my mistake, "I apologize if I have seemed off or unfocused these past few classes. Someone close to me was in a bad crash last week, and I'm just worried is all. Now, get back to work."

"Ooh, Mr. Clarke has a girlfriend," Brynlee sasses from the back. I give her a death stare, but the bell rings, and I have never been happier work is over in my life.

I OPEN the door to my house in utter exhaustion after working all day and after a long-ass practice because the offensive line couldn't get their shit together. I've been looking forward to the day being over so I could rest right next to the beauty waiting for me inside.

I walk in and find Allie sitting on the couch with her computer on her lap and a cup in her hand. I would bet money it's espresso bean coffee, two splashes of half and half, and two teaspoons of sugar. The girl could have a coffee IV and *still* go to sleep. What I seem to almost miss is the smell. It smells fucking delicious in here. She looks up from her computer and gives me her megawatt smile. I look around and see the table is set up and in the kitchen, there are some covered pans. It smells like Dominican food mixed with a vanilla scent. *Probably the coffee,* I think. Setting my bag down, I walk to Allie and close the computer on her lap. She keeps smiling at me as she says, "Hey, Jake," shyly.

"What is this?" She says nothing as she smiles and gets up from the couch. She places her coffee on the table and stands to the tips of her toes in a futile attempt to reach higher so she can meet me face to face. I drop lower to meet her where she is and tenderly kiss her sweet little nose. She closes her eyes, fluttering her lashes, and then, as if she loses all the control she has, she throws herself at me in a tight hug. Her arms are around my neck, and her body is flush with mine. Somehow, she's still not close enough, so I pull her even farther into me.

Her lips whisper right in my ear another sweet hello. I want to leave again just to come back and be welcomed like this. "Did you go all homemaker on me and cook dinner, Allie?" I ask her gently, and she giggles.

"Maybe not a homemaker but I did cook some dinner." She tries to let go of my neck, but I pull her tighter against me, not letting her go. Never letting her go. She laughs again and says, "It's nothing fancy, just a little thank you for everything you have done for me. I feel a lot better today, and I wanted to surprise you."

"Oh, I'm surprised alright. You managed to do it with the house intact, too." We both laugh a little more. She kisses my neck and then my cheek on a spot between my beard and my eye. I always thought of it as her spot. I didn't think she'd remember she used to kiss me there when she was trying to cover up what she really wanted to do. Embarrassed that Gma would see her, she would kiss me on the cheek, instead of my lips. Apparently, she remembers it all too well, too.

She lets her head fall against my chest, lowering her feet back to the ground and hugging me around my back. Her warm vanilla scent invades my senses and my head. My thoughts go round and round on how much I love her and how much I love her *here*, with me. "Thanks, Honey, it means the world to me."

She tightens the hug when I call her 'Honey' and that's all it takes for me to stop dancing around the fact I want her, *right now*. I dip my face and kiss her. I kiss her how I often kiss her, worrying she might slip through my fingers again, gently at first and then without reservations. I kiss her like I know this might be our last for right now or even forever. I kiss her like I'm losing my breath, and she is pure oxygen. ⇥

She moans into my lips, and I lower my hands down her body, gripping her ass and lifting her to me. She wraps her legs around me without any hesitation or comments about her body or her weight like a fucking goddess. "Good girl," I tap her ass with a growl. That makes her shiver, and she goes back to my lips. Wild and sweet.

"Jake," a breathy whisper. A silent plea. My hands grab her ass tighter, and she arches against my chest.

I walk to my room without letting her go as she kisses my neck, my ear, and my lips. I bite her lower lip which earns me a whimper and a smile against my lips. I lay her down on my bed —*our bed*—and kiss her lips again. Holding my weight with my hands, I cage her face. I kiss her neck, tasting and licking. She tastes the same, tangy and sweet. A mix of passion fruit, guava, and vanilla. I could drink her up all my fucking life. I continue down her body, lifting her oversized tee, which I notice is my shirt. I hold it in my fist and look at her with an unspoken question.

Biting her lip, she says, "I found it in your closet, and it is so damn comfortable. I always loved wearing your shirts, and I was so happy to find that even after gaining weight they still fit me. I can take it off if you want." She holds my stare, waiting for an answer or my comment.

I give her a devilish smile and say, "Let *me*."

I pull my shirt off her, and she's not wearing a bra. I growl at the view, and she smiles like she knows exactly what she's doing to me. I touch her breast and pinch both her nipples, earning me a little whimper as her legs shimmy under me. "Please," she says, breathy and raspy.

"Please what, Honey?" My voice matches hers, raspy and low, full of lust and want. My dick is hard, but I want to hear her tell me exactly what she wants. I want to hear her say she wants *me*.

"More, I want more." If I were a better man, I would give

her just that, but I'm not, and I don't. I give her *just enough*. I lap at her clit and suck it lightly between my teeth. She writhes and wiggles. I lick and suck enough to get her moaning my name.

When she brings her hand to my hair, I stop. I look at her and ask again, "More of what, Honey?" I slide two fingers into her pussy and feel how tight she is and how fucking wet she is for me. Her body is already telling me what she wants, but I need *her* to tell me, as well. I don't want her to go shy on me, so I say the words that make her shiver under my gaze, "Words, Allie, I need words."

That sentence snaps whatever she is holding back, and she says, "You, Jake, I want more of you. No, not want, *need*. I need you." I think she will stop at that, but she continues, "I need you over me, under me, all around me, and inside me. I need you, now. Please don't make me beg anymore and show me that *you* want me, too."

That's when I snap. I go to the end of the bed and pull her by her ankles to the edge. I keep pulling until her ass is practically hanging off, and I place her feet on my shoulders. "Open up for me, babe," I say, and she does on my command. "Such a good girl," I add before going back down on her pussy, showing her exactly how much I want her. How much I need *her,* too.

I kiss and lick her clit. My beard is covered in her arousal, and I don't give a fuck. I add one more finger to the two already inside her, and she lifts her body off the bed. I lift my other hand and push her back down, holding her in place, my eyes locked on her.

"Too much, Jake, This. Is. Too. Much," she says between gasps and moans.

I stop and raise one eyebrow at her, she shakes her head no, and with a smirk I go back down on her. I flatten my tongue against her clit, and when I feel her tense a little bit more, I bite and tug gently. She drops her feet from my shoulders, and her knees take their place: trapping my head against her delicious pussy. If this is how I die, I will die a happy man. I pump my fingers in and out and then curl them, touching the spot that drives her wild. That touch is what it takes to drive her over the edge. She scrapes my scalp and pulls my hair as she screams my name. In this moment I decide it's my new favorite sound. I keep going until her legs go loose around me, and I get up to grab a condom that I got a couple of days ago from my nightstand, hoping this would happen again.

She follows my every movement, and when she sees what I'm doing, she stops me, grabbing my wrist. I look down at her, raising my brow in question, and she speaks a little breathlessly, "Jake, I'm on birth control. I have not been with anyone since you. Have you gotten tested lately?"

This girl is going to kill me tonight, I'm sure of it. "I get tested every year and always come back free of STDs." I know I should tell her I haven't been with anyone in a while either, but I don't want to open that door. It would lead to too many questions about how long *a while* is and who the last person I was intimate without protection was.

She smiles at me and says, "Then drop it. I want to feel *you*. All of you."

I get back on the bed and kiss her. My hands roaming every inch of her skin. Every part of her. I hike her leg up by her knee as my dick goes to her entrance. She hisses when I am halfway there, but I kiss her deeper, and she relaxes around me.

She pulls me flush against her, and I am terrified to smother her to death, but she says, "I want to feel all of you. Let me feel your weight on me."

I go down as much as I can, but I refuse to let go completely. I keep diving deeper and deeper, praising this beautiful girl as I go. "God, Honey, you take me so well." She moans my name. I drive a little more. "Fuck, you're so tight. So good. You feel so good." She moves under me in gentle circles, making me groan, and I drop my forehead against hers. "Stop for a second, baby. If you keep making those sweet little noises and moving like that, this won't last long."

She laughs at my confession, and I really just want to flip her over and smack her sassy ass, but it won't help my cause either. I am so hard it hurts, but she does stop moving for a while, giving me time to settle all the way in and gather some form of control. I lower my head right onto her nipple and suck, earning me another moan as I drive into her, setting a fast pace. She squirms, moves, and moans under me. Her nails drag on my back as I lick and suck and fuck her how I want to. Like she's mine.

I hike her leg higher, remembering how flexible she is, and place it on my shoulder, freeing my hand to reach her clit. I tease and pinch her clit as I push inside of her, and she shatters again. Her legs tense around me. Her head comes off the bed. Her nails slide across my back. Her pussy clenches around my bare dick as she screams my name. And that sends me over the edge, whispering her name against her skin.

I collapse right next to her as we both pant. Sweaty and spent but sated. I turn my face to look at her, and she looks back at me with glossy eyes. I look at her full lips and skin shiny with sweat. At that moment, I realize how impossible it is not to tell her how I feel about her. In a soft, intimate breathless whisper, I say, "I love you."

She opens her eyes wide and opens her mouth to speak, but I beat her to it, "Please don't say anything right now. It's okay. I just couldn't go one more minute without letting you know." I pull her against me and kiss her softly. I keep kissing her until we're all moans and hands all over again. I won't stop until she's undone under me, coming and saying my name again and again.

27

———

THEN

TAKE ME, ALEX & SIERRA

Allie

"ADIOS, MA, TE AMO." Goodbye mom, I love you. I shout as I try to run out the back door unseen. I have been able to avoid my parents all week, and today should not be the exception. Except when I turn to go out the door, my mom is sitting right by it, newspaper in hand and coffee next to her. I stop as if I had a bucket of ice-cold water thrown at me but try to play it cool.

"Oh, *hola, Ma!*" I say, trying to hide my rush and my nerves. I am sure the school has called her to tell her I have not been in all week. However, I don't have the energy to argue with her right now. I have always been a straight-A student, so this won't affect my grades tremendously, but I know they would have a coronary if I started skipping school.

She looks up at me and points to the chair across from her. I wait a moment or two before saying, "If I sit, I will be late for school."

"*¿Te crees que soy estupida?*[1]" she says, and I have no other choice but to sit down right there and then. I sigh, but she interrupts me, "Allie, what is going on? Why have you not been at school for a whole week?"

"Ma, Jake is still in the hospital. I am not going to keep going on with my life like he is not laying in a hospital bed unconscious."

"Allie," she sighs, "You said it yourself, he's not awake. You can't throw your future away, sitting next to someone when you don't even know if he will ever wake up again."

"He will, and I will be there to see it. I would hate for him to be left there alone like he's not human, Ma," I all but yell at her, and she flinches at my outburst. I am treading in deep waters with this reaction, but I won't let her treat this like an inconvenience, like it is not his life on the line here.

"I'm completing my assignments, and I'll be back at school as soon as he wakes up. In the meantime, I want to be there for him," I say, as calmly as I can manage.

"I know you love him, *mi niña*, but you also need to remember to love yourself, and that means taking care of yourself. Are you eating? Are you sleeping?" her soft gasp takes me over the edge, and tears start falling down my cheeks.

"Ma, how can I when I feel like my whole body is on fire, just trying not to collapse right beside him?" I say between sobs before continuing, "I feel like my heart is being ripped out of my chest with every minute that passes by without him opening his eyes. It is like he is so close but also so far away, and I can barely take it," I gasp. "So, no, I am not eating or sleeping. I'm not worried about my future because my whole future is lying in a hospital bed, lifeless."

She gets up and walks toward me. Sitting next to me, she

---

1. Do you think I'm stupid?

pulls me close to her and drags my head to her lap like she always used to when I was younger. She will always be my safe place, so I let it all out. I cry and sob, asking someone to please heal him all the way. Maybe God or maybe a high lord, I don't care as long as he is completely healed. "Sh, sh, sh. *Esta bien mi niña. Todo va a estar bien.*[2]"

We stay like this for a good while until my breathing is more settled and the tears stop falling. I am a mess of snot and hiccups when she lets me sit back up and hands me some tissues. "Allie, I didn't know you loved him this much, sweetie. This is exactly how I would react if your father was in the position Jake is in. But darling, you need to take care of yourself. I will call the school today to get your absences excused, but you need to promise me you will eat something, and you will get home before 9:00 p.m. tonight."

I nod at her, and after the warmest hug I've had in a long time, we get up and walk to the kitchen where an array of breakfast awaits for me, for us.

I FINALLY MAKE it to the hospital, and I'm practically running to see Jake. I like to be there when his dad or brother are there because they lighten the mood as opposed to his mom, who cries probably just as much as I want to, bringing everyone down. I don't blame her though. I can't even imagine what it's like for her to see her first baby lying there like that. Last night, I was there when the nurses were moving him around, and they were explaining the biggest complication they have with

---

2. It's okay, my girl. Everything will be fine.

patients like him are infections due to sores from lying down for so long. They move his body to let his back rest from laying on it all the time. So, imagine my surprise when I walk into his room, and the hospital bed is empty.

I look around, but I don't see anything, so I drop to my knees practically screaming *no, no, no*. My face in my hands on the cold hospital floor. The contents of my bag are spilling everywhere as I sob hysterically, screaming for him to come back to me. *Take me with you, babe.* I feel cold hands on my shoulder and a soft voice whispering something I can't make out. The world is closing in, and I feel like I am going to be sick. I get up and run to the bathroom, emptying everything in my stomach into the toilet bowl. I'm sitting on the ground, not even caring about how many germs may live here, because what is living if Jake is gone?

The same voice that was talking earlier calls for me again, but this time it's saying my name. I look up toward the door and find Brooke, one of the nurses who has been working with Jake, looking at me with pity in her eyes. I run to her crying some more, and she hugs me tight but tells me to stop crying. How could I? I hug her tight until I hear a raspy deep voice that I have been doing nothing but begging to hear say, "You're scaring the poor nurse, Honey."

Letting go of Brooke I run toward him and stop right in front of him, hands on my chest, begging my heart to not give out on me right now. He's in a wheelchair, with his leg in the cast propped up, giving me the biggest smile I have seen from him. I swear my breath is leaving my body, taking all the air from my lungs. My Jake is completely awake, looking at me with the same love in his eyes as last week.

"Stop freaking out and come give me a hug, baby. I hear you've been waiting for me to come back to you," he says, opening his arms to me, and that's all it takes for my control to escape me, and I leap right into his arms. Fuck hospital protocols.

28

NOW

DRESS, TAYLOR SWIFT

Allie

IT'S FINALLY the weekend again. Although, it feels like it's been a week-long weekend for me since I took some time off and then worked from home for the rest of the week after the accident. It was exactly what I needed to heal my body and my mental health. Being alone in his house, though, not so much. I already cleaned, cooked, read, slept, and tidied as much as humanly possible. I went outside and played with the chickens and helped with the garden as much as I knew how without killing any of the plants. I have the blackest thumb, so I don't want to send my bad mojo to his beautiful garden.

Jake worked long days, and with me not leaving this place at all, and the fact I have no friends or anything to do here is making me be bored beyond existence. Cara and I talked every single day on the phone, and the obvious *I-told-you-so* smirk in her voice is uncontrollable.

Jake said last night, in between lasagna bites and sexy sessions, that he had plans for us today, and I've been beyond excited since. He is already up and about around the house, and I am still lying in bed, contemplating what I will wear. *In his bed.* Since the night of the accident, he has not let me go back to the spare room, and I basically moved into Jake's bedroom. We keep ignoring the fact that there is a ticking time bomb with me eventually getting assigned to another city or state. So far, we're just enjoying every day we can, and for once in my lifetime, I'm giving myself permission to do so.

I hear footsteps, so I look up from the book I have open on my chest but have not been able to read, just thinking about all the little things. I see Jake, walking in with a tray that has a cup of coffee, a plate with what looks like mashed potatoes, eggs, and sausage, *shirtless.* All his tattoos are on display, and his arms look damn edible as they hold onto the tray full of homemade deliciousness. My eyes rake down him from head to toe, and he gives me a cocky, knowing grin as he says, "*Hola,* beautiful, like what you see?"

"Good morning, handsome. And yes, you holding coffee and breakfast is a true vision." He lays the tray of food on my lap, and *holy shit, is this Dominican Breakfast?* "Jake, is this *mangú?*"

He kisses me on my forehead and nods. "I missed eating this when you left, and after a few years, I Googled how to make it."

He smiles and walks away toward the bathroom. I hear the shower running, and thoughts of the other night invade my senses, but I need to focus and eat this before it gets cold. This man can fucking cook, and it has always been my biggest weakness. This breakfast is what people would pay good money for, and he just made it for *me.* On top of that, he made my absolute favorite. Mashed plantains, *mangú,* Dominican sausage, and fried eggs. I bet he didn't even eat. It is a crime that someone who can cook breakfast this good hates eating early in the morning.

By the time I finish breakfast, Jake is out of the shower,

walking around naked without a single care in the world. He oozes confidence as he strolls around, gathering his clothes for the day, and my eyes can't stop tracking him. I sip on my coffee and look at him from under my eyelashes trying to hide how much I am ogling him. *This man could've been mine for a decade now*, is all I can think about.

He starts pulling up his boxers when he says, "Stop looking at me like that, Honey. If you don't want me to do something about it."

I let out a soft laugh and shake my head. "I'm going to shower, so I can be ready. Where are we going again?"

"To run some errands, and I have a tattoo appointment I don't want to cancel, so I wanted to see if you would go with me?"

"Oh, a tattoo? Mm, yes! What are you getting?" I ask, as I get up from the bed and walk toward the bathroom.

"You'll see," he says and winks at me.

I step into the bathroom and close the door behind me. Hopping into the shower, I turn the water as cold as it will go.

AFTER AN HOUR OR SO, we are finally in the truck heading out of the house. Zac Brown Band plays on the radio. Jake is wearing a black Columbia shirt that hugs his forearms perfectly and dark denim jeans that give him a more professional but still casual look. His beard is majestic, and it looks so shiny today, you would think he added some treatment to it. His hand is resting on my thigh, and mine is placed right on top of his. Since he didn't tell me what else we were doing, I opted for a pink maxi dress that flows around my curves, accented with a jean jacket in case it gets chilly later. My curls are cooperating today, holding a loose pattern that is my favorite. Since the accident, I haven't wanted to wear my contacts, so I have my oversized glasses on.

We stop at a few places. The UPS Store to return something, and a nursery to pick up a couple of new plants he ordered. Then Tractor Supply for feed for his girls and the pharmacy to pick up some medication for Jake's dad. We are delivering the prescription to his dad at their car garage since he needs to check in over there anyway. I'm still awestruck at the fact that he teaches full-time, coaches, and also owns his own business. This car garage, which I had not seen before, is one of the things Jake always dreamed of having. A place in which he could tinker with cars but also fix his own stuff if needed. An outlet, and he made it come true.

I'm equally nervous and excited to see Jake's dad again, but he assures me there's nothing to be worried about. He liked me then, and he will like me now. We pull up to the garage, and I see a living image of older Jake walking toward us. He looks just like he did ten years ago but somehow lighter. Jake mentioned his parents got a divorce shortly after his injury, and while it took them a while to be amicable, it clearly was for the best.

"Hi, Mr. Clarke," I say, giving him my hand to shake.

He takes it, using it to pull me toward him, straight into his arms for a hug. "What a treat it is to see you, Allison."

"Please call me Allie," I say when he lets go of me.

"If you call me Joe," he bites back.

"Mr. Joe is the best I can do," I say smiling.

He adds, "Sounds good to me, Allie. Come on in lovebirds, I am sure Jake has questions, and you can be nosy and walk around. See if you can keep yourself out of trouble."

Jake and his dad have a long conversation, mostly about

work, so I stay busy reading a book on my Kindle. I don't go anywhere without it in case of situations like this.

After a while, they say their goodbyes, and Jake and I walk back through the garage toward the truck. On our way out, we see a guy working on something that appears to be a race car. The paint is shiny blue, and it's a two-door with a cage inside of it. Jake and his brother Derek used to race go-karts growing up because his dad worked on them. I am sure he still gets jobs from the racers. Word of mouth goes far in Baker Oaks, and after being part of the racing community for so long, people trust them.

"What's up, Thiago?" Jake says, and the guy under the hood turns his face toward him. He puts the tool he was using on the ground and walks toward us wiping his hand on a towel. He shakes Jake's hand into some sort of man salute that ends in a sideways hug, and then, he looks at me.

This guy has to be at least six-foot-five and built like a fucking machine. He's covered in tattoos, and his dark coffee eyes are intimidating. He looks like a man you don't want to fuck with, but then, he smiles, and he looks every bit of trouble that I'm sure he is. "And who do we have here?" he says, offering me his hand.

"Hi, I'm Allie. I'm friends with Jake," I say as he shakes my hand and raises an eyebrow.

"Friend, huh? I have never met any *girl*friends of this knucklehead. My name is Santiago, but everyone calls me Thiago." He brings my hand to his mouth and plants a kiss on it.

I can pick out an accent in the way he talks, but I don't know from what language, so I ask, "Portuguese or Spanish?"

He smiles and says "Spanish."

"*Mucho gusto, Santiago.*" *Nice to meet you, Santiago,* I say.

"*El placer es todo mio.*" *The pleasure is mine.* He pivots to face Jake and tells him, "I like this one. Keep her, bro."

"I'm trying man, I'm trying," Jake says looking at me. He turns back to Thiago and raises his eyebrows while adding, "Hey, we're actually on our way to see your girl."

"Roe is not my girl, man," Thiago says.

"Funny that you knew exactly who I was talking about, especially since she is not *your* girl and all," Jake snaps back. Savage Jake is my favorite. I love that he keeps zero things hidden unless he has to. He also has no problem letting you know how things are, even when you don't want to hear them.

"She did some tattoos for me, and we train together. That doesn't make her my girl, but keep laughing, I know how it is. Say hi to her for me," Thiago says to Jake, winking at me. Jake gives him the side eye, and we all laugh. We say our goodbyes and make our way to the truck.

On our way to the tattoo place, Jake seems tense, and I don't know why. It can't be because of the interaction we had with his friend, but something is definitely bothering him. I reach to turn the music up, but Jake's hand reaches mine first and puts it down. He then turns the volume knob to the left, silencing the radio completely. I turn my face to look at him, expecting to find him looking at me, but instead, he is looking ahead like nothing is happening. Completely ignoring my gaze on him, which is unusual. I can tell that something is wrong.

"What's going on?" I ask. He takes a deep breath, opens his mouth like he is going to say something, and then closes back up. Jaw tense, he could probably snap something in half with the way his teeth are clenching. He pulls over to a parking lot in a small strip on 6th Street. Puts the truck in park and after a deep breath, he speaks.

"What are we doing, Allie?" he asks with concern in his eyes.

"You said you were going to get a tattoo so that is what I was assuming we were doing," I say.

"What are *we* doing? Not here but in general. What is *this*? I know I said I would take whatever you could give me, but I need to know before I get my hopes up. You damn sure have made it seem like you were right where you belong next to me, but then you called yourself my friend. Is this how you treat all your friends, Allie? Kissing them until they lose their minds?"

Whoa, this took a turn. "Jake." His name is the only thing that comes out of my mouth.

"Don't *Jake* me, Allie. Answer the question, because I need to know before I set myself up to lose every single bit of sanity I have left. I'll take you as my fuck buddy if that's what you want, but I need you to lay it out right now so I can plan accordingly," he deadpans. His gaze is dark and serious, and it's the first time I see the true hurt behind his eyes and his words.

"I don't have fuck buddies, Jake. Never have, never will. I can't separate feelings from sex, which is why I have never been able to sleep with anyone since you." Now, I'm pissed. "And to answer your question, I don't know what the fuck we are doing. I've been telling you since the moment you dragged me to your house from the airport. I usually don't stay more than six months in any place. We've been dancing around the fact that Baker Oaks is not my home. Am I enjoying every single day I'm with you? Absolutely. Do I want to think about what could happen in a few months? Nope, I sure don't. Do I want to introduce myself as your friend? Also, sure don't, but what the fuck do I say? Huh? Oh hi, I'm Allie, Jake's old girlfriend who left forever ago. Enlighten me, Jake."

We are both practically hyperventilating, and I see his resolve breaking, this is not what I wanted. In fact, this is exactly what I wanted to avoid because I knew better. Jake doesn't do shit halfway, he is an all-in-or-nothing kinda guy.

We sit in the middle of this parking lot, surrounded by cars and people who are oblivious to the fire building inside of this truck. My ears feel hot, and I have a feeling both of us could combust with just one spark. The sun is getting lower behind us, letting golden light shine through the window, right onto Jake's eyes, making his skin look more like melted caramel than anything else, and because of the light, I see the first tear rolling down his face. He wipes it off, taking a deep breath before talking again.

"I know that. I'm sorry I snapped at you, but hearing you introduce yourself as *my friend* hurt me worse than I thought it would." He rubs his face and continues, "I know we haven't talked about what will happen, and selfishly, I don't want to because I really want to keep you here with me, forever. However, I know you have big wings, and I'm not going to be the one to clip them. I also have been avoiding the conversation, and I shouldn't have called you my fuck buddy. But *fuck, Allie,* I want to be more than just a friend. My heart doesn't race for friends the way it does for you. My fingers are constantly twitching, wanting to touch you and only you. You are front and center in my mind all the damn time. No friend of mine does that."

I swear I can hear the *thump* of our heartbeats filing the silence of the truck.

"Please don't make me call you that," he finishes with a low voice that sounds so close to a plea it breaks my heart, which is why I don't think before the next words come out of my mouth, because how could I?

"So, is this you asking me to be your girlfriend, Jacob?" I raise my eyebrows.

"I'm done asking," he says, "You are mine, and everyone else should know that, too."

"Okay," I say, and before I can say anything else, he seals my mouth with a kiss, and man oh man, what a kiss. Tender lips with ravenous teeth that bite straight into my lower lip. His tongue swipes against them after the initial sting with a soothing touch. This kiss is not tentative, it contains every single little bit of his possessiveness. Claiming me wholly, and I love it. I open my mouth for him, allowing him better access, and it fuels the beast even more. His hand goes behind my head, pulling me closer to him, and I moan right into his lips. He swallows my cries and then starts to slow the kiss, finishing with a few pecks on my lips. Foreheads together, noses touching, and breathing heavy, we sit in silence. This moment, we are wrapped in reminding us that beyond the scorching kiss, we can also sense the way the other feels by just being here with each other.

"Please don't demote me to the friend zone again. Has a friend ever kissed you like that? Has a friend ever pulled those delicious sounds out of you with just a kiss?" He closes his eyes and takes a deep breath. "You are my friend, but you're so much more than that, Honey. You always will be."

I can't deny him this, so I just nod and pray we will get some sort of clarity on what the fuck we are going to do in the next couple of months. "Okay, boyfriend, let's get out of here before we get a ticket for indecency." He smiles and jumps out of the truck, rushing to my side of the door to open it for me.

29

———

THEN

EPIPHANY, TAYLOR SWIFT

Jake

"CAN you explain more about the injuries?" I ask Dr. Brandon for the third time today. "I need to know exactly what I can and cannot do and when the next time I can train will be," I add. Something tells me I'm not going to like what they have to say considering both doctors and the nurses look as if they were going to tell me someone died.

"Jake. Your injuries are not to be taken lightly. You will need to keep your leg in a brace for four weeks and then do physical therapy for eight to twelve weeks more. We would like to keep you here for another week to run more tests and keep an eye on your healing. Right now, other than in a wheelchair and on the bed, you should not be moving much. Your ACL was destroyed, and we had to replace it with a piece of your muscle. Your recovery will be lengthy, but you should be able to make good progress and be back walking in three months. Running maybe in six," he says. "As for football, I am sorry to have to tell you, but other than recreationally, I don't think you will be able to play ever again."

I throw the tray of food next to me onto the ground when he confirms my worst fear. No more football which also means no scholarship, and my world just fell deeper into the shit storm. "Jake," the doctor says, touching my *good* leg. I should be grateful, I should because it could've ended worse, but this shit right here just fucked with everything.

"Don't *Jake* me, doc. Just go. Please. Unless you have some sort of miraculous cure to get me back on track for my scholarship, leave." They walk out, and that's the moment I start to feel how deep of a hole that this injury will leave me in. Who am I now without football? What am I going to do now?

IT'S evening when I open my eyes again. I have been in and out of sleep all day since talking to the doctors this morning. My parents have both messaged me, but I can't pick up the phone to talk to either of them. I want to go back to sleep, but the smell of vanilla hits me dead in the face. Looking around for the origin, I find Allie sitting on a chair in the corner with her nose in a book. She must have come in while I was sleeping and didn't wake me up. She is wearing one of those long dresses that cover her whole body and gives her an ethereal look. My angel. Mine. I drink her in before I make any noise. Looking at her peacefully reading, with her legs under her, bottom lip between her teeth, and eyebrows pinched in a frown, I wonder how I got this lucky and how the hell am I going to keep her now that I have nothing to offer her. Nothing to promise her.

"*Hola*, beautiful." I startle her, but she quickly sets her book aside and looks at me with nothing but pure joy in her eyes.

"God, how happy I am that I get to hear you call me that again. Hey, handsome." Untwisting her feet from under her, she walks toward me with a showstopper smile, and my heart breaks a little more knowing I don't get to keep her forever. *She deserves so much more than I will ever be able to give her.*

She sits on the bed next to me, leaning forward and giving me a soft kiss on my lips. So damn sweet and perfect. Thinking about ending things with her is killing me, but I need to let her go when I have nothing to offer her other than my potential. Her family will never accept me if I can't provide their daughter the life she deserves.

"What's on your mind, handsome? I can practically hear the gears turning up there." Her fingertips are feather light on my forehead, resting magically on my temple, showing me more love than I have ever felt from anyone else before.

"I got some news from the doctors."

"Oh yeah? Care to share?" she says, grabbing onto one of my hands and placing it between hers. Her warmth reaches my heart, giving me the courage to tell her what I need to. I tell her everything, from the diagnosis to the outcome, and how I can never play again. What I don't tell her is how I know that now I am not enough for her. I'm holding on to the love she has to give me with every ounce of willpower I have and praying to God I find a way out of this mess without losing her in the process.

30

———

NOW

BACK TO YOU, SELENA GOMEZ

Allie

"SO, Allie, how do you know this knucklehead?" Roe asks, prepping for Jake's tattoo.

We walked into the tattoo shop after the whole *'we are more than friends'* conversation in the truck. The place is small, but it has that cozy feel that a lot of businesses in Baker Oaks have. When you walk through the clear glass door, instead of a doorbell to announce your arrival you hear a wind chime made of different-sized sea shells. To the left of the entrance, there is a natural wood-colored entryway table with crocheted items and a book of flash designs for you to pick from. It has real tattoos that I'm guessing she has done and some illustrations of other ones. Everything from tiny tattoos to full sleeves and colorful designs. There is also a picture of her completely dressed in a riding uniform next to a motorcycle and another one of her smiling next to a dog that might be a golden retriever that's basically her size. Toward the back, there are different tables and floating shelves with plants as well as some photographs of tattoos on the walls. The whole place screams bohemian, but when you see her, this five-foot-two, blue-eyed, blonde-haired, beauty covered in tattoos, wearing overalls and vans, you wonder where the bohemian comes from.

"We went to high school together, kind of," I reply. She offered me a glass of wine as soon as we walked in, and it's the same peachy Moscato I had at Jake's. Maybe this is a new brand that everyone loves, but I won't complain, especially not when it is this good. "I went to Baker High my senior year, and we knew each other, then." *Loved each other* is what I want to say. "I came back for work and fate would have it that we would meet again, now."

Jake is looking at me from the tattoo chair with what I can only describe as love in his eyes. I am pretty sure this man loves me, the same way I have loved him for the past ten years. I don't know who I was fooling when I thought I could just move on from this, from him. But maybe I never fooled anyone, and my heart has just been hiding in my chest secretly waiting for my brain to catch up. Jake's shirt is off, showing all his tattoos.

A broken heart across his chest with birds taking the halves away is displayed front and center. An owl, some racing ones, and a heartbeat that slowly dies down to a flat line. I want to ask him about them. Other than the racing ones that he got the minute he turned eighteen to give tribute to his dad and brother, I don't know the meaning of them. Before, it felt intrusive to even ask, especially considering they're not out for the world to see. He let *me* in though, and that right there means the world to *me*.

"Mmm, so high school sweethearts rekindling their love? How second-chance-romance of you," Roe blabs, and we both laugh.

Jake looks confused casting his eyes between the two of us,

sarcastically adding, "You two already have a secret language, great."

We continue laughing, and eventually, Roe adds, "It's a book thing, and judging by her reaction, she reads the same type of books I do. I like this one, keep her."

Jake replies to her but without taking his eyes off me, "I'm trying, Roe, I'm trying."

Same reply he gave the guy earlier, so I say that, "You know, the guy from earlier, what was his name? Oh yes, Santiago, he said the same thing." Roe immediately tenses as she hears the name, and I guess I got it right and my suspicions are true. There is definitely something going on there.

Jake smirks as he says "Yeah, Roe, Thiago said the same thing, you two must be connected on a deeper level." Jake is not done with his sentence when Roe slaps his arm harshly, placing the disinfecting pad she is using to clean the site where she will apply the tattoo, making Jake stop his train of thought and stare at the little pixie tattoo artist. It's all fun and games until that moment, and then, she is all serious business.

He has a large owl on his right upper arm that has black and blue outlines. He said he is adding more color to it to give it more depth and to add hidden items because one day, he will have a whole sleeve. Roe places the new color scheme over it then nods and smiles. She gets up and pulls a cart near her stool. There is a large mirror across from where they're sitting, giving me a direct view of what she is doing on his arm, even though I am sitting on the opposite end of the room.

"Do you mind music, Allie?" Roe asks and when I shake my head and pull my Kindle out of my bag to show her what I plan on doing, she smiles and grabs her phone, turning on some sort of rock music. She moves the stool near him and puts the tattoo gun to his skin. The sharp buzzing sound hums under the music playing while Jake closes his eyes and lays back on the chair, leaving me mesmerized by the whole aura of this moment for too long.

About an hour later, the owl is done. It looks perfect. The colors carry shade, contrast, and highlights, making it look almost three dimensional. She used some techniques on the eyes that make it seem like the owl's gaze follows you wherever you are. His skin is red around the edges of the owl and even bleeding in some places, but the smile he has plastered on his face is worth a million bucks.

Jake pays for the tattoo and hugs Roe. She punches him on the not-tattooed arm and mentions stopping by later at a place called Saddlers. I walk toward her to say goodbye, too, and she gives me the biggest hug I have ever received from a non-Latin stranger. "Come by later, first drink is on me," she says as she waves goodbye.

By the time we are out of the tattoo shop, it's getting darker. The sky shows shades of orange, pink, and purple in the most breathtaking sunset I've seen in a while. The air around us is crisp and not that humid, making me shiver slightly as we walk to the truck. Jake grabs my hand and pulls me to him, wraps me in his arms, and guides me past his truck.

"Where are we going now?" I ask quietly, comfortable in the warmth of his arms.

He kisses the top of my head and says, "To dinner, unless you want to go to the house first and get dressed in warmer clothing, the temperature seems to have dropped."

"You don't have to worry about me, Jake. If you're hungry, we can go to dinner first," I say nonchalantly, even though we both know I could use some jeans or a jacket. I look up to see his face and find him smiling down at me with nothing but love in his eyes.

"Let *me* worry about you, Honey. Let me take care of you, let me show you how you occupy the front of my mind always.

It is all I've wanted to do for the past ten years. I finally have you, let me do my job." He says calmly like he is not shaking my world. He is going to be the cause of my death with his attention to detail and words. He rubs my arms and tilts our bodies turning around toward the truck. "Let's go home so you can change. We'll go to dinner after."

Home, there is that word again, tugging at my heartstrings and pulling me closer and closer to him. I barely survived leaving him once, and I don't know if I could do it again. I don't think I should either.

31

THEN

CHASING CARS, SNOW PATROL

Jake

"You're not helping me with this," I snap. Allie is currently standing in front of me, holding a bag full of toiletries in one hand while looking like a damn snack. Her dark leggings are molded to her legs as if they were painted on her. Her hair is wild, in a loose bun at the top of her head that she calls a *pineapple*. It is my favorite way she wears her curls. Wild and free, barely tamed by a hair tie, just like her. She has on one of my shirts that she stole from my closet, and it could swallow her whole, but she has it tied in a knot right above her navel. Her curves are on display for the world to see, and I just want to scream *mine*. Instead, I am sitting in a wheelchair, shaking my head because my gorgeous, generous, kind, and devoted girlfriend told the nurses she was going to help me shower.

"Jake, you smell. It's time for a shower, and you can't stand up for long. Let me help you."

"I said no. I am not letting you reduce yourself to this. I can do it or a nurse can. Just go, and I'll figure it out," I say, crossing my arms across my chest. They took the IV out earlier today, and it feels like freedom.

Allie stomps her feet around me and pushes the wheelchair toward the bathroom. "I don't give a fuck about what you said, Jake. I am doing this whether you like it or not." This infuriating girl will end me with her attitude.

She rolls me to the shower and locks the chair. Placing the bag of toiletries down, she takes off her white tennis shoes that are covered in doodles, and steps into the shower. She turns the water on as hot as it will go and then steps back out walking toward the door and locking it. Walking back to me with determination in her eyes, she stops right in front of me and puts her hands out so I can hold them. That I do, and she tries her best to help me stand up, but it is a futile attempt. I smirk, shaking my head. This girl. I push myself up from the wheelchair and drag my body to the chair inside of the shower.

"Take the gown off," she says with her bossy voice, and my dick twitches in my pants. What I would give to take the bossiness out of her right here and right now. There is no time for that, so I take the hospital gown off and throw it to the side. She steps in the shower, fully clothed, without a care in the world, and drops to her knees right in front of me. *Jesus Christ.* I growl between my teeth when she pulls my boxers down my legs and tosses them out of the shower too. Seeing her kneeling in front of me has me bothered and hot and my dick standing at attention. She looks at it and laughs.

"What's so funny?" I ask, raising an eyebrow

"The fact that I literally told you I was going to bathe you, but your little friend over here just wants to play," she says, pointing at my dick like she didn't just call it little.

"There is nothing little about it."

"You're right, but I need to keep it light and airy, or else I am going to end up sitting on it instead of helping you get clean."

Another hiss and twitch with those words. I want her to sit on it, too. Maybe I will help her find a seat right on my dick and show her how much I can still do. Even with this fucked up situation. Before I can turn any of those fantasies into reality, she grabs a washcloth and some soap.

She starts washing my feet and my legs. Lathering every single inch of skin with soap while being careful not to let my left leg get wet. The steam from the shower feels amazing, but the sight of Allie at my feet, cleaning me is giving me mixed feelings. I'm in between wanting to love her more for this and being completely mortified that she is doing this. To any other guy, this might be castrating, but I'm trying to see it for what it is, an act of love.

"One, four, three," I whisper with tears falling silently down my cheeks.

"What was that?" she says without stopping scrubbing every part of me, rising from her knees to wash my back and chest.

"I said One, four, three."

"What does that mean? You've said that before, but I don't really know what you mean by that," she says, setting the sponge down. She grabs the shampoo bottle, squirts some on her hand, and stands behind me pulling my head backward gently. She kisses my forehead, smiling at me, and tells me to close my eyes. Following her directions and letting her lather the minty shampoo onto my hair, her fingers massaging in soft circles.

I finally speak again, "It means I love you. '*I*' has one letter. '*Love*' has four, and '*you*' has three. My mom used to say it to us all the time when we were little." I leave out the part in which she told me when I found the one, the woman I could never see myself without, that I would use those three numbers to tell her I loved her.

"Son, sometimes you love people more than life itself, and 'I love yous' just become everyday occurrences. Anyone can say those three words, but not everyone will know the meaning of those three numbers. Save them for the special person who will hopefully cherish your heart the way I cherish yours."

She told me that once, and I never thought at eighteen, in a hospital shower, I was going to say them and explain what they truly mean. "One, four, three," I repeat.

I assume she grabs the shower head because there's warm water running over my hair and forehead as she rubs her fingers aiding the water in rinsing the suds off. She's as thorough as she was putting the soap on me. Every inch of my skin gets touched by the hard droplets of warm water from the shower head and by the fingertips of an angel disguised as a Latina firecracker who stole my heart.

"One, tour, three, two," she says, and my heart almost gives out at the sound of those numbers.

"Wh-wh-what?" I stutter.

Turning off the water and grabbing a towel that she wraps around my head, drying my hair, cheeks, and neck she says, "If one, four, three, means I love you, then one, four, three, two means I love you, too, and I sure do." She gives me a quick peck on my lips. She finishes drying off my body, tenderly and meticulously, until I am as clean as I will ever be again. She officially left a permanent mark on my heart, and it breaks even more at the thought of having to let her go because this gem of a girl, no, not a girl, woman, deserves the world. Sadly, I cannot give it to her anymore.

32

———

NOW

SHIVERS, ED SHEERAN

Jake

GOING BACK to the house to let Allie change clothes pays off when I see her walk out of the room, looking like she came out of my fucking dreams. The girl is absolutely stunning without putting in much effort. The bouncy curls that frame her face with light caramel highlights make her honey eyes pop. I wonder if she knows the reason I call her Honey is not only because she is as sweet as they come but also because her eyes always reminded me of exactly that, honey. She could be wearing my shirt and a messy bun, and she still makes my heart stop. I kind of prefer her like that, natural and free. However, she's walking toward me smiling widely, knowing exactly what she is doing to me. I swear she did this shit on purpose. She catches me ogling her, and it makes her sway her hips even more.

"If you didn't want to go out, baby, you could have just said so. Because the way you look right now is making me want to do many things to you, and none of them can be done in public," I practically hiss. She's wearing dark jeans that are what I think people call high-waisted. They stop right in the middle of her belly, hugging her curves beautifully. She has on a deep red sweater tucked in the front of her jeans, it's loose in the back which probably leaves her ass up to the imagination of whoever might look. It doesn't really help because, with those thighs and her curves, everyone knows her ass is delicious, too. She has some low black boots with heels, making her legs look longer and her steps deadlier.

Instead of replying to my statement, Allie stops dead in her tracks and gives a little spin showing me the whole outfit from all angles. Her long hair falls to her back, and damn it, I was right. The sweater is loose in the back making everyone question what's underneath it. "You like?" she says with a smirk, and that's all it takes for me to lose my cool.

I get up from the couch and stride toward her, practically growling. Her eyes turn from mischievous to full of lust in a blink, and when I reach her and pull her to me, she gasps. That little sound is going to be my undoing. I grab her neck with both hands and lower my lips to her without touching them. The air is thick between us, and her breathing is fast. Her skin is like velvet under my fingers, and her sweet vanilla scent engulfs me in a battle because all I want to do is show her exactly what she is doing to me. I'm close to saying *fuck it* and staying here, but I want to take this woman out. *My woman.* I want everyone in this town to know I am taken. I want everyone to see who I belong to. Who I've always belonged to.

"If you're going to kiss me, go ahead and do it, Jake," she says, almost panting, and now, it is my turn to smile.

"Two can play this game, baby. It's very difficult to see you looking like a damn goddess and not take your clothes off right here and right now, but I have plans for us tonight."

She licks her lips making me lose my train of thought, but I clear my throat and continue, "I am going to kiss you, Honey. But I am letting my heart settle down before I do, because the kiss I want to give you will lead to more kisses. More kisses in more places. We don't have time for that." Raking my eyes all over her, showing her my exact meaning.

She shivers under my gaze, and her lips part in a small plea. I give in and touch her smooth lips with mine. Her burgundy lipstick looks like it would be sticky, but when my lips touch hers, it's like she has no lipstick at all. *Just like magic,* I think, and maybe she is a witch because the spell that I've been under since the day I met her could only be explained by that.

"Let's go, baby. We have places to be." Pulling her by her hand, I walk her out of the house before I decide to lock her up and throw away the key, with me inside of her.

DINNER WAS great at our local Italian spot, La Cucina de Pepa. I know Allie has a weak spot for carbs so Italian sounded like a good idea, and I was right. The girl ate twice her weight in pasta and bread, and I couldn't erase the smile from my face. We had an easy conversation, as usual, and we shared a bottle of wine that paired perfectly with the pasta. I still can't stop smiling every time I look at her. We're walking downtown, hand in hand, smiling like I haven't smiled in years.

We make it to our last stop of the night, Saddlers, the local bar. Partying is not my scene, but Nick is celebrating his birthday tonight, and I couldn't miss it. Stepping into the bar, the walkway is dark and somewhat sticky, it takes a little extra effort to walk but not so much that would make you cringe to be here. The place is packed, per usual on a Saturday night, it's always popular with the line dance lessons they offer. The air is thick with sweat and smoke, maybe from vapes or from cigarettes, who knows.

Allie is walking in front of me, pulling my hand and guiding *me* through the place like this isn't the first time she's been here. Commanding the place with her presence. All I do is follow her closely, covering her back and marking my territory by eyeing everyone who glances our way. I don't know how she looks this confident in places like this but then nervous when nobody's watching. She shows her confidence to everyone else but saves her more vulnerable self for me. I love this version of her, but I adore her other one, too. She turns to look at me, asking something, but I can't hear her voice over the loud country song playing. I pull her closer to me, and she yelps, giggling and raising her arms around my neck.

"What was that?" I whisper in her ear, and I feel the goosebumps crawling under my hands from the sound of my words. Always so responsive to me.

"I said, lead the way now because I don't know where your friends are."

I spin her around quickly in my arms and step in front of her to guide the way. Her arms are wrapped around my chest, leaving not even an inch of space between us. I see Nick's table in the back. I continue pushing through the crowd, nodding to the people I know who are waving or shouting my name. Some are people I grew up with, others are students' parents. I will never get used to hearing *Mr. Clarke* out at a bar. Nick has a couple of tables surrounded by people and drinks. Some of them we went to high school with, and some are work friends. As I approach the table, Nick raises his glass toward me, and everyone else turns their faces around to see us.

After we say our hellos, Nick hugs Allie like he hasn't seen her in ten years—which he hasn't—but she doesn't get the same treatment from Natalie, his wife. She's cordial but less affectionate, and I wonder if it's because she and Tasha got close over the years. Speaking of Tasha, she is sitting at the corner table, farthest from where we're standing. Allie waves at her excitedly, but Tasha's returning wave is barely polite. Before this can turn into a disaster, I pull Allie away from the gathering toward the bar so we can order some drinks.

ALLIE

SEEING all of them after so long is kind of strange. Almost like my brain can't process that they aged. In my mind, they're all still seniors, joking around in the hallways or partying like there's no tomorrow. I was surprised to be pulled into Nick's arms like long-time friends, especially since I got the cold shoulder from Natalie and Tasha, who I thought would be more excited to see me. We used to be close, but maybe me leaving everyone behind caused more problems than I had imagined.

Jake pulls me with him to get drinks, and I see the tattoo girl from earlier behind the bar. She spots us and comes over, placing two napkins in front of us and flashing a wide smile.

"Long time no see, lovebirds. What can I get you?" Roe asks.

"The usual for me," Jake replies.

"Mm, surprise me," I add.

She lifts her eyebrows at me and rubs her hands with a mischievous smile.

A few minutes later she comes back with our drinks and

gives me a flight of little drinks. I have six small glasses, each with different colors and consistencies. Some are bubbly, some creamy. I'm sure my eyes go beyond wide when I see this, earning me a laugh from Jake and a smile from Roe.

"My brain is too chaotic to pick just one drink. I choose drinks from customer's vibes, and my first-timers get a flight so I can get an idea of what they like. After this, I'll never get your drink wrong."

"She's right," Jake says, sipping on some dark-color concoction that I'm sure has whiskey in it.

"You are insane." I sass and roll my eyes playfully.

"Maybe but it works. Go ahead," she adds. She places her rag next to her, and props her elbows on top of the counter and her chin on top of her fists. Intently staring at me while I take my first sip.

All the drinks are different, and three of them are so bitter I have to chug them to finish them. One is thick and sweet with an espresso undertone which I could have as an afternoon drink but absolutely not while out with friends. All four drinks must have been heavy on the alcohol, though, because I'm already tipsy. The last two are my favorites. One is mild in taste but crisp on my tongue. I want to say 'apple something'. It also has some bubbles, and I wonder what it is because I have never tasted a drink that felt like I was biting on a fresh apple.

Roe smiles at my expression saying, "I knew you were a fruit girly. You will love the last one, too." And she's right. The last drink is flat, but it tastes like passion fruit or guava. I can't pinpoint which one exactly, but it brings back memories of going to my parents' country during summer break and having treats and fresh juice that tastes very similar. After I am finished with all of them, Roe takes the tray and returns with a full glass of the last drink. I offer some to Jake, and he takes a small sip. His eyes open wide, and he laughs.

"What did I miss?" I ask, confused. Jake just leans in, brushes his index finger under my chin, and lifts my face so my lips are directly in front of his. He licks my lower lip, and then brings his hand behind my head pulling me closer to him. Closing his mouth on mine, he kisses me deeply. He usually saves these kisses for the bedroom, but he's unhinged right now. He sucks on my tongue and goes back to licking my lips. I stop the kiss because I'm two seconds away from climbing him like a tree. He smiles, pulls his wallet out, and pays Roe.

"Finish your drink, Honey," he says. I pick up my glass, bring it to my lips, and start drinking. He leans in closer and whispers to my ear, "Hurry up and finish so we can go home, because that right there tastes just like your pussy, and I didn't get my fill just from tasting it on your lips." I practically choke on my drink, but he continues, "Watching you enjoy that drinks makes me want to stick my fingers in you until you come around them and then have you suck them clean. So, like I said, hurry up because we have things to do."

With that, I feel my thighs clench involuntarily. I get up quickly, completely flushed, not sure why those filthy words turned me on the way they did, I ask Jake, "Is that a threat?"

"A promise, beautiful." He winks.

I try to walk toward the door, but before we can leave the bar, I am being pulled onto the dance floor by my hands. Roe stepped out from behind the bar area and is currently pulling me and another girl to the dance floor. The instructors at the bar are teaching the dance for Ed Sheeran's *Shivers*, but I already know it. I love dancing, and sometimes, I watch videos online and try to learn them. It's really the only reason I'm on social media.

Since I already know the dance, I can add different moves or give it more flare. Instead of cross-step, I dip and shake my hips in the same direction. Instead of the one spin, I can do a double pirouette and land on cue, and of course when the song says 'shivers,' I shake or drop my head forward and throw it back. After the whole dance floor practices a few times, the instructors let us know the song will play again, and I'm practically jumping with excitement.

I look around and find Jake, eyes blazing and locked on mine. I point at him and jump right on beat, shaking my hips in a circular motion. In no time, I am completely lost in the music. Swaying my hips, shaking my body, hands on my hair, and spinning fast. The whole room disappears. I'm not focused on anything except for the way I feel while dancing and the way I feel with Jake's gaze fixed on me. He hasn't looked away at all. The song is almost over. Smiling at him, I take my moves up another notch, dipping lower, shaking harder, smiling wider, and shimmying as if I were in a dance competition.

The song ends, and I hear applause. I clap too without realizing I am dead center in the middle of the dance floor, and people are clapping around me and a few other girls. Roe and her friend run to me, giving me hugs and high-fives, but my eyes go back to Jake. How could I not when he is looking at me like I'm dessert? He has big bad wolf vibes, and he could eat me if he wanted to.

"Girl, that was impressive. I didn't know you could dance like that," Roe says.

"I love dancing, Roe. The more we hang out, you'll see it's practically second nature to me," I add, eyes still on Jake.

"Well, come back any time, and we can dance some more." We give each other hugs.

And then, Jake is right behind me, holding my hips and pulling me flush against his erection. He sways gently, and I do the same, I lift my hands and grab his neck. His mouth dips right to my ear when he says, "You have thirty seconds to walk out of here with me, or I'm about to take your sexy ass in the bathroom and show you exactly how much I want you." I laugh at his raspy tone but nod and walk us out of the bar. He speeds all the way home, and then, he fulfills his promise.

33

———

THEN

FINGERS CROSSED, ELIJAH WOODS

Allie

JAKE HAS PHYSICAL THERAPY TODAY, and I want to go with him. He has been going for weeks now, and I can finally see the progress. He tries harder when I'm there, which is part of the reason I try not to miss going, but some days, his appointments are in the morning, and I just can't swing it. School is still school, and even though I stopped skipping, my mind is still not completely focused, even when I'm there. My last-period teacher is the most understanding and usually lets me leave so I can make it in time to Jake's sessions as long as I complete my assignments.

Jake has a variety of sessions at Brooks, the rehabilitation facility. He likes some of the therapists, and others, he hates. The flexibility training with Mark is his least favorite, and he has an hour-long session today. Last time he left almost in tears with Mark accusing him of not trying hard enough. He is a tough-love kind of therapist, but I don't think it's working with Jake's state of mind right now.

I walk in the front door, and Lila, the receptionist, greets me by my first name and tells me where they're working today. I smile and wave at her and the other staff I find on my way to Jake. I am about to open the door to room 3B when I hear Mark's voice coming through the door.

"Jake, you need to breathe. Your leg won't move unless you give it oxygen."

"Don't tell me to breathe when you don't know how much this shit hurts. It feels like my leg will snap in half." Jake practically growls at him. I can tell he is in a mood just by the way his voice carries, and who can blame him? He has gone through hell these past few weeks, and he's still not completely healed.

"I do know what it's like, but it's beside the fact that you are in charge of your recovery, and right now, you're only giving me thirty percent. I need at least eighty today, Jake."

"Oh, you know? Do you know what it's like to have everything gone in the blink of an eye due to an injury? My willingness to work goes beyond what I can physically endure. You manhandling patients doesn't give you insight on what it's like."

"We can have the conversation on how much I know or don't know after you do ten more reps—end of discussion. I am not your psychologist. Different type of therapy here."

"Fucking jerk," Jake mumbles and then grunts, which leads me to believe this bickering back and forth is over, so I finally step inside the room. Mark doesn't seem surprised to see me, but Jake does. I don't understand why, he knows I try to make every afternoon appointment. I didn't mention I was coming today, but it still shouldn't be a surprise.

He finishes his session, Mark helps him back into the wheelchair and pushes him out into the yard. I walk by him but we're both quiet. This is not the comfortable silence that we're both used to, this is more of a ticking-time-bomb silence. Any amount of pressure will set it off. And the worst part? I have no clue what happened.

After Mark leaves, I wait a few minutes to ask what's happening. But before I can say anything, Jake says my name in a sad whisper. Now my heart's already breaking by just hearing the emotion in his voice.

"What is it, Jake?" I ask, holding his hand and practically kneeling in front of him.

He can't even look me in the eyes before he starts talking, "We need to talk, Allie."

Allie, not Honey, not baby, *Allie.*

"Did you accept Stanford yet?" he asks without hesitation.

Stanford? What the fuck? Is this what's wrong? "No, I have not. I am considering declining and just taking UF's acceptance."

"Why?" he deadpans, this time looking at me straight in my eyes. Finding deeper parts of me that only he can reach with just a look. He's frowning right at me, and his eyes are carrying so many emotions. The empath in me immediately feels my heart constricting. Sadness, hopelessness, shame. I have never seen him look like this before, and my gut's telling me I won't like where this conversation goes.

"Because I want to be close to you, especially now. I am going to school to be a teacher, I can teach anywhere, even if it's here in Baker," I answer his question, really hoping not to break apart, before letting him tell me where his mind is at.

"What about Teach for America? What about traveling to see the world? How is staying here letting you do that?"

"I am not dying here, babe. I can still do that. *We* can still do that. You just have an injury, Jake. Your life isn't over, but with me staying here and going to UF, I can help, if needed."

"I'm not going to college!" Jake snaps at me in a voice I've never heard from him before. A mix of anger and frustration.

"What? Why?" I ask, completely dumbfounded at his statement. "You might not be able to play, but you can still go to school."

"How, huh? Or did you forget I had a scholarship?" Breathing heavily, rubbing his eyes, and pausing for a second before he continues, "They just sent me the email last night, saying I can still go, but I would have to pay for it. I can't afford it."

"Oh, I didn't think about that." I try to hold his hands, but he is quick to snatch them from me.

"Yeah, not everyone is the two percent, Allie," he bites back.

"That's not fair, Jake. You know that's not how I think," I add, holding back my tears.

"Exactly! You live in your bubble where everything is fine and where daddy can come rescue you. You don't even have to think about how the rest of the world pays for shit. All of us? We need real jobs to be able to live. To pay for basic needs. I can't leave it all to my parents, and now, with all these hospital bills, I'll have to work."

"Jake," I snap at him, "I know you're hurting, and I am so sorry you got that email, but please don't be mean. This isn't who you are."

"Well, maybe I am. Maybe this is the new me," he continues, "I've officially lost everything, Allie. *Everything*."

"You haven't lost me, Jake. You still have me."

He laughs, and I can't take the whiplash I'm getting from his reactions. I get closer to him and try to hold his hands again, this time he lets me.

"You need a whole man, Allie, not a crippled one who can't even go to college. I will never be able to give you the life you deserve. The life you need."

"*You* are all I need. You don't need to go to college. There are trade schools. There are so many options." I'm not able to control my tears this time. They're slowly trickling down my cheeks, but I'm not able to stop them. I wonder what the people around us think is happening. Do they think he is sick, or do they know he is breaking me apart word by word? Do they know he is taking every piece that's keeping me together? Can they hear it? Because pain like this should be seen, heard, and felt. The words he's delivering casually have the power to start a fire.

"You may think that now, but when your family is partying abroad and we can't go because I make nothing, it won't be enough. When you want to spend hundreds of dollars on a purse, and you have to budget, it won't be enough."

"Jake, you will be enough!"

"I WON'T!" he screams, not even looking around to see who might be watching. Not caring one bit about how he is breaking my soul. "How can you say I will always be enough when you haven't even loved anyone before? No one had even fucked you before me, Allie, and you want to tell me that I will be enough, above everything else. I think it sounds delusional, and one of us needs to be rational here." He lands another blow.

"But I love you, Jake. Please—" sob, "please—" sob, "don't—" sob.

Interrupting me, he continues, "We're young, and it was great while it lasted, but I think we're through. You're seventeen, Allie. Go home, email Stanford, and tell them yes. Fly there and forget about me. Forget about this town, and live your dreams."

"Jake, stop it, please," I say between more sobs. "I love you, and I know you love me, too." The tears are everywhere; I'm done trying to control them at this point. "We can figure this out, babe." I'm wiping my face as much as I can without hurting my skin.

"Maybe, but you deserve more, and I'm not going to be the placeholder while you figure it out. This life is enough for me, but it'll never be enough for you or your family. It's done. We're done." He stares at me while I hold in the rest of my sobs with both my hands, blinking rapidly, not even knowing what else to say. I am ready to beg him, again, not to do this, when he says, "Go home, there is nothing else for you here."

I can't hold it in anymore, so I run away from him. I run away from this place. I run until I make it to my SUV, and drive as fast as I can go. I drive for what seems like hours, listening to songs that help keep the tears from falling because what else is there to do? Letting my tears run freely, gripping the steering wheel as tight as I can, I see the sunlight turn into dusk. The sky looks exactly as I feel, turning my desperation into darkness along with the light.

Eventually, the gas light turns on, signaling to me that life goes on, no matter how broken I feel. I make it home and go straight to my room. In the darkness, I find comfort and let myself cry until there are no more tears left.

34

——

NOW

CHAMPAGNE PROBLEMS, TAYLOR SWIFT

Allie

MONDAYS ARE USUALLY my favorite day of the week. It is like a fresh start. My little reminder that not everything is doomed and you get a do-over. I know many full-time working people love Fridays because of the weekends, but have you ever worked with kids? By Friday, you are exhausted, and I find it to be the same in this professional development job. Today is a special kind of Monday because I am working at Baker Elementary this week to train their staff in a new multi-modal reading program. I never went to Baker Elementary since I didn't grow up here, but so many of the people I met in high school did.

Jake had to be at work early, so he already left, and I didn't even get a chance to tell him I was working right in town. Last week, I took some time off and worked from home, so maybe he assumed it would be the same this week. He's usually on top of asking me about work, but Saturday was so busy with errands, tattoos, and Nick's birthday. Yesterday, Jake spent most of the day with Nick, making up for leaving his birthday celebration early, so I barely got to see him. I can't wait to see him tonight and tell him all about my day.

I leave the room and find the coffee pot on, a bagel by the toaster, and a note from Jake telling me to have a good day and to toast the bagel. I adore the way he cares for me, even when he's not here. These little details are the things that stayed with me even when I wanted to forget it all. Taking my cup of coffee back to the room, I finish getting dressed. A loose, above-the-knee dress with a dainty flower pattern and bubble sleeves is the winner for today. My curls are down, and for the first time since I've been back in Florida, they're somewhat tamed. I add a clip to take some of them off my face. Going back out into the kitchen, I pour myself more coffee into a to-go cup, finish the bagel I left on the counter, and head to work.

"HI, I'm Ms. Z. I'm here for some meetings with Mr. Ryan today," I tell Lisa, according to the nameplate on her desk. I'm smiling and looking around, trying not to look as nervous as I feel right now. No matter how much I do my job, I still get nervous when I start with a new school or new teachers, and today, I have both. Mr. Ryan walks into the yellow-painted front office and takes me back to meet my first group.

He explains that they often do Professional Learning Communities (PLCs) in the lead teacher's classroom and asks if I'm comfortable with running them on my own. Nothing new for me, so I'm happy to follow along. PLCs are my favorite way to share tidbits with teachers because they have the meetings already planned. When I taught, I hated losing planning time in weekly meetings. So, I love it when I get to work with teachers during those times instead of adding to their schedules with extra meeting days.

This new program I'm presenting today is one of my favorites that my company offers. It gives the teachers data on the students' progress every week. Things like fluency and vocabulary acquisition, which are so hard to assess in a full classroom, are assessed weekly with this program. Having a team working together makes a huge impact in students' progress. I couldn't have imagined having this much support when I was in the classroom.

My day goes fast, and before I know it, it's 2:00 p.m., and I only have one more grade level. I'm meeting with the second grade last, and I'm pumped. Second grade was my favorite grade level to teach, so I can't wait to share with these teachers all the tools at their disposal with this program. I love knowing they will be able to take the kids to the next level, ready for deeper multisyllabic words and comprehension.

Looking at the map, I search for Mrs. Clarke's room. Room 212 on the right. It's been easy to navigate because the floor plans of this school are almost the same as the high school. I haven't set foot in those halls since I was seventeen, but I could never forget them.

I find her classroom empty, yet, I still walk in and start setting up my small station. I love bringing multiple samples with me to the first meetings to get a feel for what the teachers may or may not like. I bring pens and stickers with me, too, because who doesn't love free swag? I continue setting up and grab my phone to shoot Jake a text.

ME:

> Hey, I hope your day is going well. Do you have practice tonight?

He doesn't often reply right away. I have a feeling he's all-in with his students, the same way that he-s all-in with me and all-in with everything he does. I have never met a person more present than him.

FUTURE HUSBAND:

The offensive line is off today, so my practice will be shorter. I'll see you soon. 143

I freeze looking at the numbers on that text. He has not only told me he loves me, but then, he goes and writes 143 in there? Like it won't make me have palpitations. Like I'll be able to breathe easy afterward. There's no doubt in my mind that I love him. I always have, and I always will, but do I reply with the numbers, too? Knowing what they mean to him?

At some point, I have to let go of my fears and finally give in to my heart. Stop punishing myself for the past and embrace the future. We're both adults, now, and if we want to make this work, we should. It all starts with a step, even if it's not small, and it takes every single inch I have to give at this moment, but I take it. I take it, and I grab the opportunity to love this man wholly, the way I've wanted to for a decade.

ME:

1432 ♥

While placing my phone down, I hear steps and look up to see Tasha right in front of me. Her gorgeous blonde hair looks pristine right now in loose curls. She has on a black dress that fits her incredibly and white tennis shoes, accented with a jean jacket. *I am obsessed with this outfit.* I plan on telling her just that, but when I get up and smile at her, her blue eyes turn icy as she walks toward me and takes a seat at the desk. I turn around to face her, confusion in my eyes but before I can say anything she opens up her journal and a pen and says, "I'm listening, get started."

"Hi, Tasha! I didn't know you were a teacher! How cool."

"You never knew what anyone else wanted to do with their lives other than Cara. So, are you really surprised you didn't know I wanted to teach?" Her tone is harsh, and I don't understand why. She's talking to me like you would talk to the mean socialite who took the job you wanted without deserving it.

She stares me down, leaving me no choice but to apologize. "I'm sorry, high school was such a blur, sometimes I forget details. Take your name, for example, I completely forgot your last name is Clarke," I say.

"Oh, it wasn't when we knew each other." She continues sneering before adding, "I took my husband's last name, and it was a bigger hassle to change it when we divorced. The kids were already used to calling me Mrs. Clarke, so I kept it."

"Neat! I mean, not about the divorce but about you being able to keep it. I'm sorry about the divorce, though." What a blabber mess, Allie. There's something about this whole exchange that feels odd. We were never close but definitely friendlier than this.

"Yeah right, I'm sure it opened the door wide open for you to crush his soul. *Again*," she bites.

And until now, I had not put two and two together.

I gasp, and she smiles. "Oh, you poor thing, you didn't know? I guess he *can* keep secrets from you, after all. Here, I thought I was the only collateral damage from your fucked up love story."

"Wh-wh-what are you talking about?" I am aghast by her words and the delivery. My train of thought is completely lost, and if Tasha notices, she doesn't care because she continues.

"Jake. He was a wreck after you left. We all saw him lose himself. He did end up in college, but he fucked his way through it. Women, alcohol, parties, you name it. He even stopped going to football games. One day, he finally snapped out of it, and we all started seeing the Jake we knew come back to us," she continues with her voice getting more irritated. "You see, we all knew and loved him before you came and destroyed him. You were a wrecking ball in his life and smashed everything in your path, but he eventually got over you, or so we all thought."

We stare at each other for another minute, but she continues, not letting me get a word in, "I will skip the way we fell in love with each other because I do believe he loved me, in his own broken way. But there was no competing with you in his heart. He tried, oh how he tried, but it was almost like he was looking for you in empty places. Like he was lonely even with people around him because you took his heart, dropped it, stomped on it, and never gave it back. Eventually, I got tired of living in your shadow. I got tired of competing with a ghost."

She takes a breath, and when I think she is done, she adds, "You did a number on him, Allie, and I never thought it could be mended. Seeing him with you again on Saturday proved me wrong. He was just too broken for anyone *but* you. So, yeah, your love story—" she says with air quotes "—fucked more than just the two of you. I hope you know that. And if you didn't, I'm damn glad to be the one to tell you."

That's what it takes for the tears to start falling, and for me to lose every single word I know other than, "Excuse me." Somehow, between broken sobs, I make it to the bathroom with my heart breaking all over again.

35

———

THEN

HEART LIKE YOURS, WILLAMETTE STONE

Jake

THE MINUTE ALLIE LEFT, my tears started falling. I was beyond cruel, but how else would I get her to understand that I am not good enough anymore? Before this injury, I didn't have much to offer, but at least I had potential. How do I let her waste her heart on a man I don't even *like* anymore? A man I don't recognize anymore. Mark found me in the garden, still crying, an hour later and called my mom. The fact I'm eighteen, and these doctors still call my parents is beyond me.

As I lay in bed thinking about today and how I managed to fuck my whole life in these past weeks. I went from having everything to being completely detached from it all. I just want to go to sleep and wake up when this is all over. Before I attempt to do that, I make the mistake of looking at my phone. I see a line of texts and missed calls. This damn town can't mind their own business. Everyone is so nosy. It annoys the hell out of me. I don't have time for this now, nor do I want to deal with it, so I click the button on the side of my phone, turn that shit off, and go to sleep.

A WEEK PASSES before I attempt to deal with real life. I go to physical therapy and back to the house. I don't answer the door for anyone, and I'm pretty sure my parents argue about me every single day. I hear their muffled arguments behind closed doors, but honestly, I don't care anymore.

I thought my life had meaning beyond football and my friends, but that was true only before Allie. Thinking about never seeing her again might be breaking me more than anything else, but I managed to mess that up too. There is no way I can undo the words I said to her. I can't just patch it up with an apology and call it a day.

My phone buzzes on my nightstand, so I pick it up and see a text thread with Nick, Cole, and Billy.

NICK:

Dude, stop moping and just call her.

ALEX:

If I have to hear any of the girls saying they will kill you again, I might cut your balls off myself. Allie is heartbroken, bro, and she doesn't deserve it. You should see her, she's like a shell.

NICK:

Honestly, you don't deserve this shit, either. Whatever happened, fix it.

ALEX:

I still don't know what you did to fuck up the best thing that ever happened to you. We could all see how lost you were in her, so I know that it wasn't anything dumb like cheating.

COLE:

No, it was worse. He told her she didn't know what she wanted and he was done with her.

NICK:

WTF

ALEX:

Why?!

COLE:

Who knows, that's all Cara told me.

NICK:

We can see everyone read the messages, asshole. Just reply or answer the damn phone.

I don't know why I finally decided to reply today. Why not all of the other hundreds of messages I have? I had no problems ignoring everything else. Maybe it's seeing that even the boys think that Allie isn't okay. I know Cara's pissed. She let me know herself as soon as Allie called her, and every day after.

ME:

I'll text Allie. Get off my back.

ALEX:

DO NOT TEXT HER, MAN. You wanna be dead? Go to her. Show your face and apologize like the man you are. This ain't you, we all know it, it's time for her to know it, too.

ME:

and if she brushes me off?

NICK:

> Then you show her every minute of every day how you feel about her until she forgives your ass. I would do the same for Natalie. When you know, you know, man.

When you know you know. And damn it, if I don't already know. I knew the moment I met her she was special, and the more I got to know her, the more I wanted to know the real her. I'm so out of her league, but she still gave me a chance. She gave *us* a chance, and now, I'm not missing any chances and letting her go.

She said she wanted to figure out where we go from here, and maybe I should let her. Maybe, this once, I get to be selfish and take what she's offering. I'll have to find a way for her to live her dreams. You can't cover up a firefly and pretend they can shine just as brightly. I refuse to be the shadow that covers her light.

I pull my body from the bed, using my arms to get on the chair. I wheel myself to the bathroom to take a shower, wash all the funk away, and head to my girl's house to try and get her back.

36

———

NOW

THE LAST TIME (TAYLOR'S VERSION), TAYLOR SWIFT FT. GARY LIGHTBODY

Allie

BY THE GRACE of everything that is above, I was able to finish my meetings. After my crying session, I returned to her classroom and pushed through the worst training session of my career. Tasha's smirk at the end was not lost on me, she took pleasure in making me hurt. She took pleasure in seeing me cry at work. I never thought of her as cruel, but according to her, I never thought of her at all.

Jake was married, is all I can think about on the way to his house. Funny how I called this place home in my head, multiple times, but now it's suddenly *his* house. Do I even know this man? Why would he hide something like this from me? *Breathe, Allie, breathe.*

I'm determined not to let my emotions drive my reactions more than they already have. Yes, I was surprised—and still am —but I am sure there's a reason why he didn't tell me. Of course, I didn't expect him to be celibate, but the fact he didn't mention he was married before bothers me. I'm not going to act like a seventeen-year-old right now, and I *will* talk to him about this.

After arriving at the house, I take a shower, wash my hair, and put on comfortable clothes. There is something about washing my hair after a day of feeling like the world hates me that makes it feel less heavy. Right now, I need to remove all the weight I can off my shoulders before I talk to Jake.

I've been sitting on the couch, trying to read but not being able to make any progress for a couple hours, when the door opens, and Jake walks through. Jake, with his perfect smile that can light up a room. He holds a couple of grocery bags in his hands, places them on top of a table, and walks straight to me. He always does this, and lets everything go as soon as he sees me. He makes me feel like nothing else matters but me. Like I am all he can see, and nothing else is as important as having me in his arms as soon as he can, as often as he can. Then why, oh why, did he keep this from me?

The second his hands touch mine, and he truly looks in my eyes, he sees right through the fake smile I'm wearing. His eyebrows scrunch in a frown. His gaze darkens, and he asks, "What's wrong?"

He's waiting for my reply and searching my eyes as he sits next to me without dropping my hand. He shows me patience with his silence. He shows me he would wait for ages, if needed, for me to tell him what's on my mind.

"I went to work on-site today. We didn't get a chance to talk yesterday, so it slipped my mind to tell you."

"Okay? Are you hurting? Was it too soon to go back to work?" he says worriedly.

"No, not really. They assigned me to Baker Elementary. I spent all day working with the teachers there." I pause when I notice the color leaving his face before adding, "With *all* of them."

He breathes heavily and closes his eyes. I see his throat bobbing as he swallows. His body immediately tenses, he opens his eyes, and says, "You talked to Tasha, didn't you?"

"I did. Jake, why didn't you tell me? I was so blindsided, and it wasn't even the worst of it."

"What did she do? I was trying to avoid leaving you alone with her at all costs. It's part of the reason I pulled you away from the crew on Saturday."

"You still didn't answer my question, Jake. Why? Why didn't you tell me?" I ask, my voice breaking as the first tear falls.

"God, baby, please don't cry," he says. I swear I hear panic in his voice. His hand comes up, wiping my tears away, and then remaining right on my cheek. This just makes me even more upset, so I shake my face away from him.

"Don't make this about me, Jake."

"Allie," he sighs.

"Don't *Allie* me, either. I asked a simple question." My tone is anything but friendly. I'm done dancing around this. I want answers, and he is purposely trying to avoid giving them to me. *I hate it*. It's almost like the lie is worse now. Omission and now evasion.

"When was a good time to tell you I got married, Allie?" He pauses briefly, and I assume he's done, but he continues, "You walked back into my life, and it was both like no time had passed and like a century had gone by. When should I have brought it up? Sometime in between me losing you and you coming back to me? How about the moment I saw you at the airport? Or how about when I practically showed you how fucking gone for you I am? I never stopped loving you. Trust me, I tried, but I failed at that, too."

His voice turned thunderous and shaky at the same time. Like he's holding on to every ounce of restraint he can. He's showing me his pain, but you can tell he didn't want to go there.

Like the gentleman he is, he's putting me first again and letting me in.

"Jake," I try to whisper, but it comes out more stern than I hoped for. It sounds like I'm upset when in reality, I'm hurting. I'm hurting for me but also for him. For this beautiful man, who has loved me for years, even when he didn't want to. Even when he shouldn't have. I thought my actions only affected him for a few years, but maybe they did more than that. Clearly, it's been so much longer, apparently the whole time we were apart. I owe him at the very least to listen to him, now. I stay quiet while letting him gather himself and continue. He doesn't though. The man who keeps talking is not *my* Jake, but a very angry version of him.

"At first, I tried to get you back. I was hurt when you first left. And I didn't even attempt to ask you to stay. Then, I was pissed. I drank. I partied. I fucking did it all to try to get you out of my mind, all while still recovering from the injury. I didn't come home some days. I didn't eat. I was a wreck because how are you supposed to move on from the love of your life?" He sighs. "I finished college and started teaching here. I found purpose again, but I was numb if I wasn't coaching or in the classroom."

"One day, the boys and I got drunk at Saddler's. When I woke up the next day, there was a blonde in my bed when all I wanted was to see golden brown skin and soft curves. I didn't remember shit, but every message on my phone said how glad they were that I was finally enjoying myself. That blonde, as you might guess, was Tasha. That one night turned into another one, and another night turned into more."

"I don't want the details on how you fell in love with someone else, Jake," I snap.

"What the fuck was I supposed to do, Allie? Wait? For what? For you to finally show up again? Because I fucking waited, Allie. I waited for years before I let my guard down again. I waited for years before I realized you told me you were better off without me, and you meant it. I'm not going to sit here and apologize for attempting to move on!" he shouts.

"I DON'T WANT YOU TO APOLOGIZE!" I practically scream at him, getting up from the couch, stomping into his bedroom, and slamming the door. I start moving all my stuff I can find into a pile. Tears falling down my face. I'm shaking, unable to control my breath. If I don't get myself in check, I'll be useless soon. I take a moment, close my eyes, and practice my breathing. In, *one, two, three, four. Out, one, two, three, four, hold.*

Jake walks into the room, and I snap my eyes open. Closing the door behind him, he says, "I'm not done with this conversation, Allie. Do you want to know why I never told you? Buckle up, because you're about to find out. I'm tired of not sharing every part of me with you, and I'm tired of waiting for you to be brave enough to share every part of you with me. So, I'll go first. I'll be brave enough. I will put my heart on the line again. I will lay it all out, and then, you can scream at me if you want. Even though you have no reason to."

With that, he sits on the edge of his bed and pats the spot next to him. I sit beside him but as far away as I can be without falling off the bed. He wants me to sit here and listen to his love story with someone else. Fine, but I don't have to be near him while he does. I wipe my eyes and look at him, "Go ahead," I say.

"In the beginning, I didn't date Tasha, I fucked her. I fucked her the same way I fucked many women after you. I used her the same I did them, to try to fill the void you left. It wasn't fair to them, and I wasn't the man I had been. I lost sight of who I was when my lifeline was taken away from me. I justified the way I used her by saying I was trying to get over you. One day, she called me out on my bullshit. I felt like an asshole, so I told her I was done with the mindless sex and I wanted to take her out on a date. So, we went. She was kind of fun. She was funny, kind, and sassy. Which I'm sure you know. She was entertaining, too. After a few dates, we fell into a comfortable friendship of sorts."

He pauses and looks at me. Then gets up and leaves the room. Leaving me in ominous silence. *Who does that?!* He comes back holding a glass of wine in one hand and a beer in the other one. He hands me the wine and sets his beer on a coaster on the nightstand. The room has warm lighting that usually makes it feel cozy, but right now, it feels threatening. Unwelcoming. He removes his shoes, sits across from me on the bed, and grabs his beer.

After a swig of his beer, he continues, "I never really thought of her as my girlfriend. Every time I thought I could let my guard down and call her that, your name would come to mind, and I couldn't do it. After months of stringing her along, she finally snapped and asked me to label things. She cried, and I would've done almost anything to make her stop because, at that point, I did care about her. I guess in the midst of it all, I started healing my wounds. I told her I was serious about her, and we moved in together. She didn't want to live in this house, so I moved in with her and rented this house out. At some point, it became bearable to share my everyday life with her, so I married her. No wedding, just me and her."

I'm looking at him sharing all of this, and I can tell he is hurting. This hurts him, but it hurts me, too. It's like seeing him share his life with someone who is not me. The pieces of my heart I thought were glued back together, crumble all at once. Like a sand castle being washed away by a wave.

"We had a routine. Wake up, work, come home, eat dinner, fuck, go to sleep. Every. Single. Day. We would hang out with

Nick and Natalie and some of the other guys, but that was it. All this shit happened between August and June, so by the time Cara came back for the summer, we had dated, gotten married and divorced. It was all so quick. We shared no interests. We had no long conversations. No new topics to discuss. Eventually, it became a chore. Living with her felt like a job, so I drank to try to feel something. I drank every night just so I could tolerate her because even though she was a good woman, she wasn't you. I don't think I ever even loved her, and I am sure she knew it, too."

"One day after work, she found me drinking, and tried to kiss me hello, but I turned my face. I could barely even look at her at this point, let alone kiss her. She ran crying to the other room, and when I went to try to stop her, the words that came out of my mouth were, *Allie, wait.*"

I gasp loudly. Covering my mouth to try to contain my sobs and my surprise, I look at him. He's tearing up, too. Barely noticeable, but I can see he's torn. He's not looking at me anymore but at the bottle in his hand.

"I didn't have it in me to go after her. I didn't deserve her forgiveness, not after that. It was then I realized I had become everything I said I would never be, and she deserved better. She thought maybe I was cheating on her, but what she didn't know was that I'd never chosen her. I had always been in love with you, since the first moment I saw you, and there was never room for anything else. There was never room for anyone else. Because she thought something was going on, she grabbed my phone and looked for your name. She couldn't find a contact, but she found you in the texts I never deleted. She saw your number was saved on my phone as *Future Wife* and lost it. She packed my stuff and kicked me out. We got divorced a few weeks later."

I keep crying silently. Listening to this man bare his soul to me. Listening to how much I *actually* fucked his life up, beyond what I ever considered and probably beyond repair. He seems to be done, and because I don't know how to stop pouring salt over the wound, I say "I still don't know how we could be doing whatever this is when you kept something like this from me!"

"You're one to talk about keeping things hidden!" he yells, and I flinch. "I'm sorry Allie, but fuck! How can you in good conscience say that to me, huh? At least you asked, and I answered. When will I get my answers? When will you finally tell me what drove you away from me? What did I do that was so unforgivable you had to disappear from my life and leave me with nothing but dust?"

We stare at each other, but I just shake my head and look down. He moves toward me and lifts my chin with his finger.

"Look at me, Honey. Please be honest with me. Just tell me what I did," he says with the most broken tone I have ever heard. "I've spent ten years of my life punishing myself for hurting you. I know I fucked up, but if you knew me as well as I thought you did, wouldn't you would have seen through the bullshit? I said sorry. I was stupid, but you still left. What did I do, Allie?

"You didn't do anything, Jake."

"Then why the fuck did you leave me?! If I wasn't enough, if this town wasn't enough, why did you come back? Why did you let me open my heart and my life up to you again? If you were just planning on packing your bags and never looking back again, you're more cruel than I thought you were." He gets up and walks away from me.

Seeing him walk away is heartbreaking. Mind-altering. I'm panicking, so I yell, "I DID IT FOR YOU!"

He stops but doesn't turn his body and between sobs, I add, "I left because I loved you. Everything I did after the day I last saw you, I did it for you!"

37

THEN

AFTERGLOW, TAYLOR SWIFT

Allie

HAVE you ever walked through life feeling like you lost all purpose? Like suddenly, everything you thought mattered doesn't anymore? My mom tells me every day how worried she is about me. I barely eat, I don't sleep, and with the amount I cry each day you'd think I would've run out of tears by now, but they keep coming. Cara is ready to kill Jake, but she's worried it might hurt me more.

My room smells like death. Containers of leftovers are piled everywhere. I won't even let Rosalia come in and clean. If I could just close my eyes and sleep until my heart stops hurting, I would. If I wasn't terrified of the way my dad would react, I would ask for something to take this pain away.

There is a firm knock on my door, but before I can yell to leave me alone, the last person I am expecting walks in: my dad. I sit up and stare at him in a daze, wondering what in the actual fuck he's doing here. He usually doesn't step one foot in any of our rooms. It's almost like we're beneath him, and other than my mom, we're undeserving of his time. This is his world, and we're all just living in it. He makes sure we feel it, too. He does something even more surprising and sits on my bed, looking at me with tender eyes.

"*Hola, mi niña.*"

"*Bendición, papi*[1]," I reply—such a Dominican thing to say, but it means so much to my parents. They take pride in knowing their kids keep the traditions, even if it's just a word.

"I wanted to come in and check on you. Your mom is really worried about you. She said you haven't even left your room. That's not like you, *mi niña.*"

This is the second time he calls me his girl, and he usually doesn't talk to me like that unless he's trying to sugarcoat something.

"I'm just going through a lot right now, *Papi.* I'll be okay though. *Te lo prometo.*"

"Why don't you tell me what's going on?" he says.

"Because it is about Jake, *Papi.* I know you hate him, and I don't want to add more to that feeling."

"I want to know what's bothering you. Just tell me. Chances are what I'm thinking is worse than what he did, so tell me."

So I do. I tell him everything. I tell him about how much I love Jake. I tell my dad about how Jake makes me feel and how he treats me. I tell dad about Jake's injury and how he lost his scholarship. I tell him about how it broke my heart knowing Jake wouldn't be able to attend college. I tell him about how Jake broke my heart.

Dad lets me finish without uttering a word, also unlike him. Once I'm done showing him all my cards, he rubs his face and

---

1. It's a Dominican tradition. It translates to blessings dad but we say it to say hello to close family members.

looks down. I see he has something to tell me, and I've never seen him hesitate to share, so this must be important.

"What is it?" I ask.

"Allie, what do you want with this boy?" he asks.

"Honestly, *Papi?* I thought he was the one. I thought we were going to be together forever, but apparently, he didn't feel the same way." In between sobs, I continue, "I only want what's best for him, though. I wish he could continue with whatever's left in his life without feeling like he lost it all."

"What if I tell you there's a way he can still go to college? I can't promise you he will be able to move on with everything else, but at least he can have that. I know his family can't afford it, and he won't let them go into debt."

"How do you know that?"

"Just know that I do," he replies.

"What do you mean there is a way?"

"What if I pay for his college tuition, full ride? He won't have to worry about any college expenses, not even housing or food."

"You would do that?" I ask astounded.

"*Si, mi niña.*" Yes, my girl.

"*Papi,* that would mean the world to me! I can't wait to tell him!" I sit up and practically jolt in excitement, but his expression falters. Confused, I ask him, "What is it? This is great news!"

"The thing is, Allie, I don't want you to tell him. My one rule with this is you don't talk to him again. He hurt you, sweetie, and I don't ever want to see you like this again, or your mom worrying as much as she has these past days."

"Dad, I *will* tell him. How could I not?" The way he's looking at me makes me feel like the *help* he's supposedly providing, that previously felt like a soft place to land, is quicksand, and I'm slowly slipping away.

"Then, he won't get anything. If you want him to get this, it'll be anonymous, and you won't see him again. If you break that promise, he'll lose the money," he adds like he did not just pour more water over the quicksand.

"Is this you making me choose, Dad? Are you making me choose between him having a future or being with me?"

"I guess I am," he says without any ounce of remorse. "The decision is ultimately yours. Let me know by the end of the week."

With that, he stands up and walks out of my room. Leaving me more shattered than when he found me.

I HAVE BEEN THINKING about dad's proposal for the past few days. I have not left my room much, and I have zero reasons to leave the house, meaning all of my time has gone to thinking. My heart wants to tell him to fuck off, but my brain is thinking about what this could mean for Jake and his family. For Jake and his future. Because of his whole *'don't tell anyone about this'* bullshit, I can't even talk to Cara about it. I can't even talk to Jake at all.

My mom came in a while ago and asked me to get dressed and come downstairs. She said it all in Spanish, in her *'I mean business'* voice, and I am not playing with that. She is such a gentle soul, so when she's serious and uses that tone, nobody wants to find out what will happen if you don't obey. So, here I am, getting out of the pajamas I've lived in since who knows when.

My hair is wet, pulled up in a messy bun. I put on some jean shorts and a T-shirt that's too big for me but extra comfortable.

She said to be out of pajamas, she didn't specify what to wear, so comfortable clothes it is. I head downstairs, straight to the kitchen to get some of Rosalia's snacks before meeting my mom. I am assuming she's either in the studio or in her library.

My mom is a huge snob for books, and I'm sure that's where I got my love for them too. My dad builds her a library everywhere we move without exception. He hires people to just pack her books and ship them to wherever we're going next. If my mom says she needs an extra room for books, he makes it happen. He may be a dick to us, but he sure makes my mom feel like the queen she is.

I find her exactly where I thought she would be—crossing the French doors into a sunlit Florida room, or sunroom as most people call it, with floor-to-ceiling bookshelves. They're full of incredible books, some I never want to read, and some I'm dying to read. She has a whole system on how I can check out books. She writes her rating in the top corner, the main tropes for the book, and the age she thinks is appropriate for me to read. She has a whole shelf full of 'Eighteen or Twenty-One Plus' books that I am salivating over reading, but she won't budge. "*I want you to experience real relationships, Allie, before you read about all of these,*" she always says. I know most of them are spicy books, but it's not that much different than health class or what happens at parties, or at least I don't think so.

She sits on a recliner, facing the doors with her back to the large windows. She has a blanket over her legs, and she's sipping on her coffee with a book open on her lap. Across from her, there is a large lounging chair—*wait, there's someone there.* When I take a better look, I find Jake sitting in the chair. Leg propped up and his wheelchair next to him. He is looking down at what seems to be a book.

They're both so lost in whatever they are reading they don't notice me standing there completely blown away by what I'm seeing. I clear my throat, signaling to them that there's someone here, and Jake startles. My mom, on the other hand, doesn't even look up from her book. She sips her coffee one more time, closes her book, places it on the table next to her, and gets up from the recliner. She walks toward me, coffee in hand, and a gloomy look on her face.

She kisses me on the cheek and whispers, "I hope you make the right choice." She walks away with my thoughts and closes the double doors.

Looking at Jake, I see the torment in his eyes. Why is he the one looking like *that* when I'm the one carrying the weight of the world on my shoulders? Then, I remember the main reason I've been crying and heartbroken did not start with my dad's proposal but with Jake breaking my heart. Now, I'm mad all over again.

"What are you doing here, Jake?"

"Can we talk?" he asks with his puppy eyes. How can I say no to that?

However, I don't reply and just stare at him, waiting. He points to the recliner my mom was sitting in, and I take a seat. "I'm listening," I say.

"Allie, I don't even know where to start. There are no excuses for how I acted and the things I said to you the other day. I've been sick to my stomach thinking about it."

"Uh-huh."

"I wish I could say I can't believe I said those things to you, but I can. I was a complete asshole to you, and you didn't deserve it. But I have been hurting a lot. It's not an excuse for how I treated you, but pain clouded my judgment. You know I love you, more than words can even describe. I'm going through a lot right now, and I thought I was doing the honorable thing by letting you go." Tears are streaming down his face, but he continues, "The only thing I did was break both our hearts in the process. I came here today to apologize and to beg you to take me back."

Silence. Deafening silence. Heartbreaking silence. Earth-shattering silence. I've been praying for these words to come, but now with the decision I have to make, I'm not sure I want to hear them anymore. Now, I'm in a spot I never wanted to be in. Choosing him or choosing my heart. I can't have both. If I tell him right now that I love him and that we will conquer all the challenges of life, what will happen to him? Will he be able to follow what's left of his dreams? If I tell him I'm done, then he gets his future, but he doesn't get *me*. Tears fall down my face now.

"Oh, Allie, please don't cry. Don't cry anymore for me, please. Please let me back in, Honey. I love you, and I will do everything I can to show you, every day, for the rest of my life, and in whatever comes next."

At that moment, I finally find clarity. There's never going to be a winner here. We lose either way. But I can't be selfish. I can't let this good man lose everything he has always worked for. He deserves the world, even if I'm not in it.

"Jake, sorry won't fix it. Just telling me you apologize is not going to change things, it will not erase the things you said."

"I know, Honey, I know. But I will die trying to show you how much I didn't mean it. I will prove to you over and over again how much you mean to me. You are all I need, let me show you I can be exactly what you need, too." He sounds desperate. Broken. Sad.

Looking up, past Jake, through the glass doors, I see my dad. He's standing, leaning on the counter, wearing a dark suit with his eyes focused on me. The minute he sees me staring back at him, he raises an eyebrow, and I know what he's wondering.

What are you going to do, Allie?

I take a breath, close my eyes briefly, and when I look back at him nod. To let him know with that small gesture, that I'll do what he says, as long as he can keep his end of the deal. *Un contrato con el diablo*[2].

"I know you're hurting, Jake. I can see it, I can feel it. I'm not going to lie, what you said to me hurt, and it still does, but it opened my eyes to some things I believe were true. I still have a lot of life to live. I also don't think I want to settle in Baker. I want to travel and explore. I want to meet different people. I am not ready to just stay here and live happily ever after." Now, it's his turn to look stunned.

If I am about to break his heart, I need to do it in a way that won't give him any hope. I don't want to hurt him, but I need to destroy him to save him. To give him a future.

"I don't blame you for what you said, I might need to thank you for it. I was willing to let an opportunity like Stanford pass by because I didn't want to leave you, but honestly, this might be what we both need. A clean slate and a fresh start. I love you, and I always will, but I think this is goodbye." I get up before he can see the tears about to burst from my eyes. I don't know how I was able to hold it in for so long.

Opening the doors, without looking back, I say, "Have a nice life, Jake. It was great having you in mine." Then I run, straight to my dad.

He's waiting, and when he sees me, he extends his arms and wraps me up in a hug. We walk outside toward his car and get in as fast as we can. When I look back, I see Jake right outside the door, looking absolutely destroyed.

---

2.   A deal with the devil

PART 4

MAYBE NEXT TIME, JAMIE MILLER

I thought you were it,
I thought we were meant to be.
Maybe in another life,
You'd be mine.

38

NOW

I ALMOST DO (TAYLOR'S VERSION), TAYLOR SWIFT

Allie

"SO, yeah, Jake, I did it for you. Maybe at some point in the past few years, I could've reached out again, but how was I supposed to just call you? My dad's trying to make amends for the ultimatum he gave me because after that, he lost me, too. It was never easy to even think about how differently it could've gone. I actually imagined you were married and had the children you always wanted. Living in your precious town, with a deserving woman. I was so certain you were happy, I never even asked Cara. After the first five years, I stopped wondering. I didn't want to know how happy you were, but I sure wished you were. I never thought I would find you single and willing to give me another chance. Willing to fall in love with me again." I sob.

He gets up and walks toward me, wrapping me in his arms. Wrapping me up in him. His hand goes to my head as I lay it right on his chest, and let it all out.

"Shh, Honey, I got you. Let it all out. I'm right here," he continues, using a soothing voice and gentle caresses. I let the tears fall, and my heart pours out all the angst, fear, and secrets that it has been holding for so long.

"You silly girl, you thought I was willing to fall in love with you again? I never fell out of love, Allie. I found love in you once, and it never let me go. I belong to you, my Honey, whole-heartedly. There is no love without you in the equation. I fell for you the moment I first saw you, and you, my love, caught me. There is no more falling after you hit solid ground."

He kisses the top of my head then grabs my face with both his hands and pushes me back so he can see me. So I can see *him*. Looking me right in my eyes, he says, "You are my solid ground, Honey. Don't let another earthquake take that from us." With that, he kisses me. He kisses like he always does, gentle at first, and then ravenous. As if the time he has with me is fleeting, and he won't waste a single moment playing it safe.

His lips go beyond my lips, to my neck, to my collarbone, and my ear. He kisses, licks, and nips like I'm dessert, and he has a sweet tooth. He starts pulling my dress up and continues to kiss me, on my chest, right below my bra, going down toward my belly button. We should stop to finish the conversation, but I can't seem to gather the strength to make him. "Jake, I—"

"Honey, you can tell me what you want, or I can show you exactly what you need," he says, stopping halfway to my navel and looking up at me with pure lust in his eyes. "Let me show you how well I know you. Let me show you you're exactly who I want and who I have always needed." His fingers move up to palm my breast. His eyes not leaving mine, he pulls my bra down and takes my nipple in between his index finger and thumb. Rubbing slowly and then pinching hard, he elicits a moan from me. I arch my back and close my eyes, and I swear I feel his smirk. I shimmy under him, and it's all the confirmation he needs before he lowers his head and devours me.

His fingers are teasing and pulling, rubbing, and pinching at my nipples. His tongue is deep in my pussy, licking and teasing my clit.

"Look at you," he rasps. "So fucking wet for me." He lowers his hand from one of my breasts and pushes two fingers into me. He continues licking and rubbing, and I squirm.

"More," I whisper.

"So demanding," he snaps back.

He uses his free hand to angle me up, putting his arm under my ass, tilting me more toward his face. The sounds coming out of me are indecent, and they seem to fuel him even more. When he curves his fingers inside of me and bites right on my sensitive clit, I lose all control I have and crash into pleasure. Heat floods over my body and pools in my belly. My skin is tingling with goosebumps everywhere. I shake under him, and he doesn't relent. He continues until I'm limp against his mouth.

He looks up, undoing his jeans, never taking his eyes off of me for one moment. "Goddamn, Allie," he says before his mouth is clashing against mine. I taste myself on him, tangy and somewhat sweet. He smirks against my mouth, almost like he knows what I'm thinking. I want to roll my eyes at him, but instead, he grabs me and flips us over, with me straddling him. My pussy sliding right onto his dick. "Fuck," he growls while looking at me, intensely, passionately.

He can sense I'm going to say something about my body. I hate this position because he can see all my curves, soft or not. He can see how my breasts sag and how many stretch marks I have. It makes me self-conscious, but with his eyes heating the more he looks at me, it makes me hesitate before I say anything else.

This man has never said anything negative about my body, and he looks at me like there is nothing else he would rather look at, like there's no one else. He makes me feel desired and it gives me a funny feeling all over my body. I put my ankles under his ass, using his muscles for leverage. My hands grip his headboard for balance, but he wraps his arm around my back, unclasps my bra, and slides it down off my arms, forcing my hands to let go of the headboard so he can remove the bra completely. I balance on my knees and gasp when he touches my nipples.

Touching them and fluttering his fingers to my back, he applies pressure, pulling me to him. He can see the hesitation in my eyes. He knows what I am thinking, and what I'm feeling before I can even reply. "Allie, unless the words coming out of your mouth are going to be positive about your fantastic curves, your smooth skin, or your delicious ass, save them. You. Are. Fucking. Perfect," he says, dragging a nipple into his mouth. Letting it go with a popping noise, he adds, "Perfect and *mine*."

Our mouths clash against each other. Licking, sucking, desperate. Silently saying 'sorry and I forgive you.' I start moving with the same rhythm he set. Matching his cadence, the way my heart is matching his. I push his chest down, earning me a scowl, and his eyebrows rise. "My turn, Jake. Let *me* show you how much I want *you*."

"Yes, ma'am," he says, licking his lips.

And I do. I ride him like I'm unhinged. My pussy is as wet as it's ever been. The slickness makes filthy, perfect sounds, causing the most delicious friction. He brings his hands to my ass and squeezes hard, making me shiver and moan. "So fucking responsive to me, baby," he says, and I show him exactly how responsive I can be.

I increase my tempo, moving to a new rhythm I've never felt before. Showing him how much I want him.

"Eyes on me, Honey. Look at me while you ride my dick."

I do just as he says, letting out a small moan and licking my lips. My eyes on him, his hands on my body, and the way he feels inside of me is too much. "Jake, I—" he knows exactly what

I need and places a finger on my clit. Applying the right amount of pressure, making the pressure building in my stomach grow and burn so good at the same time. He can tell I am almost there, and with his other hand, he pinches my nipple. I'm done for. I let out a moan and a gasp when I contract around him.

I close my eyes, lost in pleasure, when I hear him say, "Look at me, Honey, watch what you do to me." I feel him come inside me. Filling me up. Making a mess of both of us, not letting go of my eyes for one second.

Our breath catches, our rhythm slows, he pulls me to him, and I collapse on top of him. Sated and filled, in more ways than one. He kisses my cheek, flips me back over, and tells me, "Stay there." He stands up and walks to the bathroom. Comes back out with a small wet rag and a victorious smile.

"Hi," I whisper.

"Hi back at you. Lay on your back, Honey." I obey, looking at him, wondering what on earth he's doing. He kisses me softly and uses the rag to wipe down every inch of my skin, cleaning up the mess we made together, and my heart flutters. I am not sure why I didn't let him show me before how he could take care of me, but I'm tired of letting this man put himself last. I am ready to put him first. If he lets me.

39

———

NOW

THE ALCOTT, THE NATIONAL FT. TAYLOR SWIFT

Allie

I WANT to get dressed so we can finish the conversation we started, but he won't let me. He tells me he needs to go put the groceries away. After a while, he comes back with a bottle of wine, a tray of snacks, and a few beers. He places the food on the bed while I wrap my body in the sheets. I feel completely self-conscious about my naked body, but wearing my clothes doesn't feel right either. Like always, he seems to read my thoughts and notices when I put an arm across my chest. He lowers his body and hands me one of his T-shirts. I put it on, and it immediately feels like he is hugging me. His scent enthralls me, and it's the best feeling in the world. "Thank you."

"I should be thanking you. I love seeing you wear my clothes. I don't think I will ever get tired of it."

"I love wearing your shirts. Since I was a little girl, I always looked at magazines and movies of girls wearing their husbands' or boyfriends' shirts, but I always thought it was only for smaller girls, not for me. Until you. Makes me feel like I fit somewhere."

"You just needed to find the right person for you, Honey. You fit right here, with me. You don't need to make yourself smaller to find comfort in things that you want. You are just the right amount of everything," he says, making my heart melt even more.

All the anger I felt when this evening started is gone. My eyes hurt from crying, but I feel content. I feel safe. All I want to do is clear the air and figure out where we go from here. I grab a piece of—*Wait, are these potatoes? When did he make these?*—a very crunchy potato skin with cheese and bacon, no sour cream. I take a bite, close my eyes, and practically moan at how delicious these are. A little cold but still perfect.

Jake chuckles, "Was I right on getting those, huh?"

"First of all, where did they come from? Second of all, is this a whole plate of just potatoes? Third of all, no sour cream! You are speaking my love language here."

At that, he laughs a little harder, and his shoulders relax. "I got them at Publix, when I saw all the types of potatoes they had as sides, I had to get them."

"You don't even like potatoes, Jake."

"But you do."

This man. Who wrote him? Because in real life, they don't come like this. They don't say the perfect thing at exactly the right time. I finish a couple more potatoes and keep drinking the peachy wine I have come to love. There's a small silence, and I know that means one of us is gathering the courage to speak, to ask the hard questions. With questions come answers, and I'm not sure if I'm ready for them. Not to give them and not to hear them.

"Allie, I don't want to keep dancing around this. Can we just talk about, well, everything?"

I nod, placing my glass down on the side table. I sit criss-cross, pull my hair up, and tie it with the Invisibobble that never leaves my wrist. I swallow, take a deep breath, and ask, "What do you want to know?"

"No, no, no," he says, shaking his head and his hands. "We're clearing up the whole marriage thing first, and then, we can talk about the decision you made for me without my input." I sigh, and he continues, "What do *you* want to know?"

"Do you love her?" I ask without holding anything back.

"No. Plain and simple. I don't think I ever did. I did care about her, though, and I have felt like the shittiest human for years after what I put her through," he answers honestly.

"How long ago were you guys married, and why, when I was probing, asking if I was going to run into someone, you didn't even mention it?" Wow, I really came on strong, holding nothing back.

He chugs his beer and tosses it into the trash bin, landing it right in the middle. He does a little celebration shrug and says, "I was twenty-two when I first got together with her, right after your birthday. We got married the following year, and we were divorced by twenty-four." He swallows before he continues, "Everyone in this town knows about our history, Allie. About hers and mine. And yours and mine. Very few people will bring it up. Natalie might have, but I know Nick talked to her, so I wasn't worried. The two of them are inseparable. I know I hurt Tasha, and Natalie was the friend she confided in, so it affected the way she feels about you and me."

Taking a deep breath, he finishes, "And, Allie, how was I supposed to tell you? *'Hey, by the way, I was married to one of your old friends, and we might run into her in town'.* I just got you back. Haven't you realized by now that I am willing to do whatever it takes for just another day with you? Hell, for another minute with you? I would give it all up."

"I love you," I say before I can stop it from coming out of my mouth, but what is the point in keeping it in now?

He holds my face with both hands and kisses my lips tenderly. "You have no fucking idea how long I've wondered if you still love me."

"I never stopped. I loved you then, and I love you now, Jake."

"Yeah, but how was I supposed to know? You disappeared on me, Allie."

"I HAD TO," I shout, frustrated again. "Your future was thrust in my hands, Jake. Everything else was already taken from you, and I had the chance to give you something back, so I took it."

Putting space between us, he shakes his head and closes his eyes. His jaw clenches, and his shoulders rise again. I am losing him again.

"What was I supposed to do?!"

"You should have asked *me!* You should have let me make the decision with you. I don't care that your dad said you couldn't tell me, you were supposed to trust me. We could've figured something out."

"You had just dumped me, Jake. I don't know if you have any idea how broken I was. For weeks, I barely ate, I was hardly surviving. Then, my dad made that proposal, and I just wanted to make sure you didn't lose everything," I say, exasperated.

"But I did lose everything, Allie. I lost it all. Yes, I have a career now, but I've been numb for years. You were hardly surviving for weeks? I have been in survival mode for ten years. This isn't living, this is barely getting by. You took my life with you when you left. I didn't know I was barely living until you came back, and suddenly, colors are brighter, grass is greener, the sun is warmer, and days are longer. You do that to me."

He lets out a big breath, and rubbing his eyes, he says, "I was just being. I wasn't living. I missed you so damn much, it was fundamental. Not only did my heart miss you, but my soul did, too. I got a glimpse of what it was like living as a whole when I found you, and then you left, and I was only a shell of myself. I see it even clearer now."

He truly loves me. This sweet, kind, caring man truly loves me. Still. Even after everything. Even after the time that's passed. He loves me. I'm not sure why I am so surprised, he shows me every day how much I mean to him. With his touch, kisses, and longing stares. With the coffee he makes just for me in the mornings. The random texts with songs that remind him of me. The way he cradles me at night. His never-ending patience. He shows me every day.

"I do have a question," he says. He looks unsure like whatever he is about to say might throw us into the fire again. I don't think I can deal with the whiplash of emotions, but I'd rather get this over with.

"You left that day and never came back. You didn't finish school, you never replied to my texts and calls. Your social media disappeared eventually. Your family moved. It was like you never existed, but then, you texted me from the same number, so I know your phone number was always the same. You never blocked me because the text messages went through and so did the phone calls, at least until the last time I tried. It seemed like you just forgot about me."

"I didn't forget about you, Jake. That would be impossible. You also made it really hard to even attempt to move on with all your calls."

"But you never answered the phone," he says in a defeated voice.

"I know," I reply. I stand up quickly and ask him to give me a second. I go back to the spare room and find one of my suitcases. At the bottom, there is an envelope I bring with me everywhere I go. Since I travel for work, I don't own much. I have some stuff at Cara's and some stuff with my parents, but everything I own is usually with me. Including this envelope. I grab it from the suitcase and bring it back to Jake's room, handing it to him.

"What is this?" he asks.

I reply with the only answer I have and probably the one he was least expecting, "The whole truth."

40

———

THEN

STICK SEASON, NOAH KAHAN

Allie

IT'S BEEN months since I left Baker Oaks. My parents were able to get the school to use the credits I had to finish my transcript, but I didn't walk at graduation. My dad sent me to Europe to spend the rest of the school year and the summer with my *tia* and her family. We traveled, we ate, we cried, we laughed. I was able to spend time with her little ones and clear my head.

I left Baker Oaks and erased everything about my life there except Cara. I messaged her to let her know where I was going. And even though I deleted social media and turned off my phone, she knew I would be back in time to start college with her. We also email now and then, which is nice. She only mentioned Jake a handful of times, but eventually, she got the gist and stopped.

I am ready to go back to the States tomorrow, but something in me is not entirely sure I'll be okay when I get back. I don't want to go anywhere near Baker Oaks, but I do have to face regular life eventually.

I grab my phone, which I haven't used in months. I have around fifty missed calls and a couple of voice messages, all from Jake. I don't want to deal with this. I don't want to remember the life I thought we could have. I just want to forget it all and start over. I delete the call log and open the voice message list.

There are four messages from him, not a lot compared to the amount of calls he left. But I'm sure they're all about the same thing. I don't want to hear his voice again. I try to swipe left on the first message to delete it, but instead, I accidentally click the play button, and his voice comes through my speakers.

> "Allie, answer the damn phone. I know you're
> upset, and I know I fucked up, but you have
> to know I didn't mean any of it. You know
> me better than this, Honey. Is there
> anything I can do to show you I meant my
> apology? I know you said 'Sorry doesn't fix
> it', but you need to let me try and fix it."

Beep.

His voice may torment me from now on. He sounds miserable. He sounds broken. *I did that, I broke him.* There is no going back from this feeling of guilt, so I might as well listen to the rest of his messages.

> "It's been a month, Allie. I've tried to give you
> space. Your brothers won't tell me anything.
> They say they don't know what happened. I
> saw your mom, too, by the way. She smiled
> at me casually, like I was a stranger, and

walked past me. Did she forget about me too, Allie?"

BEEP.

There are some sobs in between words, and hearing him cry breaks me in half. My tears start falling, too.

> "I guess I never meant the same to you as what you meant to me because if you loved me, at least half as much as I love you, being away from me would be destroying you. Just like it's destroying me."

BEEP.

It is destroying me, Jake. You have no idea.

> "Do you know what it's like to lose the one thread of hope you have? I went to check your Instagram, and it was gone. Your Facebook is gone. There is not one piece of you left anywhere. Except, you're everywhere here. I'm sitting on the bench on 6th Street right now. If I close my eyes, I can almost feel you sitting next to me, just like all those times we would sit here before. If I focus, I can almost hear your laugh. I can almost see your hair flowing against your face. If I truly wanted to, I bet I could even smell you. Your sweet tropical scent. But when I open

> my eyes, you aren't here. Did I imagine it
> all? Did I imagine what we had, huh? Or
> did you trick me? Are you that good of a liar,
> Allie? Did you make it all up? Were you
> ever even here? Because if you were—"

Beep.

The message cuts off, but he doesn't call again. I know because the last message he left was a week after that one. He sounds sad, yes, but more than anything, he sounds angry. I don't think I've heard his voice like that ever. Knowing I caused him that much pain makes this situation worse. What would happen if I called him right now and told him the truth? Could I call my dad's bluff?

Somehow I wish I could tell him the way I feel. I wish I could talk to someone, anyone, about what it feels like to be burning inside. My life went up in flames. It looks perfectly fine from the outside, but the truth is, nothing will ever be the same. I will never be the same.

I have one more message from him, and I don't know if I should listen to it. Tears are still falling. I let out little gasps in between. If I don't gather myself soon, I might end up having bigger issues. My anxiety has been barely hanging on to sanity, and I can't let myself spiral anymore than I have. One last message, it can't be worse than the rest.

> "I got a scholarship, Allie. I don't know how, but
> UF called and said my tuition and living
> expenses would be covered for a whole
> degree. I decided to change tracks a little,
> though. I'm picking a degree I can use here
> in Baker. Maybe coach one day. But you
> know the worst part of all? I can't even be

happy about this because the one person I
want to tell, the one I want to celebrate
with, to cry with, to talk to, won't answer the
phone. I get it. You don't want to be with me
anymore, but you're my friend. I really
could use my friend right now. Maybe I was
never the one for you, and I can learn to
respect that, but don't take my friend away
from me, too. Please call me back."

Beep.

I wish I could do something about this pain. It's torture.
Plain and simple.

That night I cried myself to sleep. I replayed his voicemails
over and over again until I had memorized every word, every
pause, every sob he left in them. I promised myself I wouldn't
reach out or find out more about him, but if he's going to be
leaving me messages, maybe I should listen to them. And keep a
part of him with me forever. I delete all the other messages I
have, so my voicemail doesn't get full.

It's now time to head to the airport. My family drives me,
and after the usual hugs and tears, we say goodbye and see you
later. Walking through the airport, I feel like a zombie. I'm sure I
look like one, too. There's a crater-sized hole in my chest that
won't go away and now refuses to be ignored.

I find my gate, and right next to it, there's a small kiosk that
sells the usual. Candy, books, key chains, and swag with *'Thank
you for visiting Switzerland'* everywhere. There is also a box
with journals with things written on the cover. I walk toward
them to check them out. I was wrong, these aren't journals,
they're stationery kits. I don't know who writes letters anymore,
but they're adorable, and calling my name. I buy a couple of
them and sit down while I wait for my flight to start boarding.

I stare at the clear plastic bag holding the stationery, and I suddenly get the urge to open one and write. I want to write Jake a letter. A letter I will never send but a letter with the answers to his questions. I grab a Tül pen from my purse. Those always live there because they are my favorite, making it easy to start this idea before it becomes another thing I don't want to follow through on. Placing the open kit on my lap, I grab the first piece of paper, lay it flat on top of the clipboard included and write.

41

———

THEN

LITTLE DO YOU KNOW, ALEX & SIERRA

Allie

Dear Jake,

I don't even know what this will end up being like. What the words I write will end up meaning to me. I know exactly what they'll mean to you, nothing, because you will never see them.

I listened to your voice messages, and I don't know what hurts more: hearing your voice or knowing that I was the cause of the pain. I know nothing makes sense to you, now, but in five years, when you have a successful career and are able to provide for your family the way you always wanted, you'll appreciate it. Hell, in five years, I'm not sure you will even remember me. You might be going around town and barely remember that once upon a time, you loved a girl who loved you back. Because whether you want to believe it or not, I love you. I love you so fucking much.

I know that is the reason this hurts so much. My heart opened up to you, completely. Wholly. It beats solely for you, but you are not here, and it hurts. I know it's my fault. I know I made my bed, and now, I have to lie in it. It just fucking hurts so damn much.

I miss every single thing about you. I miss talking to you. I miss sharing lazy moments with you. I miss your mouth on mine and your hands on my body. I miss you, and I have a feeling, I will spend the rest of my life missing you.

I hope you never forget that. I hope you never forget that you are my favorite person in the world, even when I won't be able to see you ever again.

143,

Allie

42

THEN

SEE YOU LATER (TEN YEARS), JENNA RAINE

Allie

Summer, Eighteen Years Old

FUTURE HUSBAND:

I saw in Cara's stories that you're back in the States. Answer the damn phone, Allie.

FUTURE HUSBAND:

It is not beyond me to come and hunt you down. We need to talk.

FUTURE HUSBAND:

I will never get tired of calling you. I will do it every day if it means that at some point you will answer the fucking phone.

FUTURE HUSBAND:

I'm patient. I will wait.

FUTURE HUSBAND:

I will wait for you. I'll be right here.

43

THEN
TEE SHIRT, BIRDY

Allie

Fall, Eighteen years old

Dear Jake,

You called again. Ten missed calls this past week. You left three messages. You told me about your life and about how much you miss me. You told me about running into Cara and how awkward it was. You told me to take care of her because she broke up with Cole. You told me you loved me. Past tense. You didn't say you still do, and that hurt.

I deserve it, I guess, I deserve everything you're throwing my way, and I should just take it. I should ignore your calls or block your number, but I can't seem to be able to do it.

Classes start next week. I will get my degree in Early Childhood Education. I don't think I will ever want to teach older kids, so I am going to opt for the safe choice. Cara will do the same with a minor in Special Education. She said and I quote "It takes a weirdo to work with the highest special needs, and I happen to be that weirdo."

Speaking of Cara, I don't think she is hurting like you think she is. Or at least, she doesn't seem like it. She seems okay, like she made peace with her decision.

Will we ever get to that point? Will we ever be at peace with each other? Will I ever forgive myself?

Time will only tell, I guess. In the meantime, I am keeping your messages so I can replay them every morning. I have one of your T-shirts, and I sleep in it almost every night. Waking up with you surrounding me and listening to your voice, even if it's sad, gives me hope that maybe one day I will find a love like ours again. If I don't, at least I was lucky enough to experience it once. How magical it was.

143,

Allie

44

———

THEN

ALL I WANT, KODALINE

Jake

Summer, Nineteen Years Old

"Hola, *this is Allie. You know what comes next. Leave me a message or send me a text. I probably won't call back, but I'll know you love me. Bye!*"

"*When you are done recording your message, hang up or press pound for more options. Beep!*"

"Happy Birthday, Allie. Nineteen. How has it been over a year since the last time I saw you? I know I said in my last call I wasn't going to call again. Well, I guess it makes me a liar. The Gators won tonight. I should be happy for my friends playing, I should. But I'm not. I miss playing, and I hate being on the sidelines.

You know what I hate the most, though? How
much I still fucking love you. I don't want to
love you anymore. I don't want to keep
living with the thought you might show up
and tell me it was all a nightmare. It doesn't
matter how fucking mad at you I am, if I
could see you just one more time, I would
die happy, I'm sure.

Why did you fucking leave me, Allie? If you
loved me, why did you leave me? If you
truly loved me, why did you take my heart
away with you? I might as well have died on
that field because being without you is not
fucking living.

Somehow I have to be a supportive friend. I
have to go be the life of the party. Be the
good friend I've always been, but I don't
know who that is anymore. I guess he left
with you."

BEEP

45

THEN

BIG GIRLS DON'T CRY, FERGIE

Allie

Summer, Twenty Years Old

Dear Jake,

I fucking hate missing you. I hate missing you more than I hate the series of text messages you send. I get them all by the way. The nice ones in which you promise to wait for me. The hard ones in which you tell me how much I fucked up your life.

Do you want an update, Jake? Or do you only call when you're drunk and lonely? Do you even miss me or do you miss the ghost of me? You don't even know me anymore.

I am tired of fighting this, Jake. The more we

hold on... The more calls you make and messages you send, the more it continues to hurt.

You need to let me go. You need to move on. You will be a catch for whoever gets you. You are every girl's dream boyfriend. You will be someone's dream husband one day, but that won't ever happen unless you let it. You need to let me go. You need to forget about me.

I won't be able to forget you, Jake, but I sure am trying to find some happiness, too. I am tired of crying and hurting. I even started therapy because I couldn't continue going through life like this, a shell of who I was. Utterly broken and shattered into tiny pieces that exist everywhere but within me.

I have to put my big girl pants on and stop crying over something neither of us can change. I will forever love you, though. I hope you know that since I won't ever get to tell you again.

143,

Allie

46

———

THEN

21, GRACIE ABRAMS

Jake

Summer, Twenty-One Years Old

"Hola, *this is Allie. You know what comes next. Leave a message or send me a text. I probably won't call back, but I'll know you love me. Bye!*"

"*When you are done recording your message, hang up or press pound for more options. Beep!*"

"Twenty-one, huh? I guess you're finally old enough to be considered a real adult. I wish I could say I wasn't thinking of you last night, but I was. I was thinking about you out drinking without me. I was thinking about what you were wearing. I was thinking about what you were drinking. If you were happy while out celebrating with your friends, and then I didn't even have to imagine it. Cara's Instagram showed me exactly how happy you are.

In every single picture, you look blissfully happy. You look at ease and full of life, just like you used to look right here in my arms. I hate it as much as I hate being away from you. I hate that someone else might be putting that smile on your face. I hate that I am still so far away from you, that I don't know what your life is anymore.

Are you still funny, kind, and smart? Do you still like dancing in the dark? Do you still read? Do you still love that espresso bean coffee that drove me crazy with energy? Are you ignoring me because it hurts, or are you ignoring me because I never meant anything to you?

I really want to wish that every drink you have tonight reminds you of me. I would be lying if I said I wish you were as miserable as I am, but the truth is I just wish you the best. Would I want to be the one making you smile? Do I wish I was the one buying you your first legal drinks and dancing with you, even if I didn't want to? Yes, I do, but it doesn't change the fact I'm glad you're happy, even if it is not with me.

I finally see it, now. Love—true love—shouldn't hold you back, ever, even if it means holding your heart back. It's not about forgetting you, that won't ever happen, it's about knowing I just want you to be happy. I can spend my time wishing for unfulfillable promises, or I can use my wishes to hope you get the best life that you can. If there's anyone who deserves to be happy, it's you, my love.

You probably think I'm pathetic. Calling you and leaving messages. I would think I'm pathetic, too, and as much as it kills me to say this, I think this will be the last time I call you. I can't keep doing this to myself. At some point, I have to face the fact you moved on. That you are better off without me and that you and I don't belong anymore. At some point, I have to push forward.

I think this is that point.

I never wanted anything else for you, other than

you being the happiest version of yourself you can be. It seems like you got that, now. I do feel fucking lucky to have gotten you in my life once. Some people spend a lifetime looking for something an ounce of what we had, and I got to experience it fully, whole-heartedly, and all-in for a while.

I love you, Allie, and I always will.

Goodbye, Honey."

BEEP

47

———

THEN

FORGET ME (COVER), CELINA SHARMA

Allie

Summer, Twenty-Three Years Old

Dear Jake,

It's been two years since the last time you called. I haven't heard your voice since, and I just realized it. It took me a while to figure out the small changes I felt and the fact that your calls stopped. I still missed you everyday, but I wasn't mad anymore. This feeling of acceptance happened in the same way we fell in love. Little details at a time, and then all at once.

At first, I realized you didn't call for a year when it was my twenty-second birthday, and I didn't get a message from you. It bothered me, but not as much as I thought it would, so I let it go. I didn't write again either, and I didn't question it. After all, maybe you were ready to move on, which is exactly what I asked for.

This summer, Cara came back from visiting her parents and her summer job and said that some of your friends were talking shit about me because of what I did to you, like I had a choice. Then ,she said you stopped them and said it wasn't worth it, and I was torn. Destroyed, again. That's when I realized it has been two years without hearing from you. I thought I was okay with it all, but hearing you thought talking about me wasn't worth it hurt. A lot.

I would be okay with you moving on, with you not picking up the phone anymore. It would be easy to understand why you hate me or why you would never want to see me again.

What I don't understand is, how could you say what we had wasn't worth anything? Did I mean nothing to you that you have to even stop all talk about me? Cara said you didn't ask, not even once, about me? Is this true? Was I not a crucial part of your life like you were to me?

Move on all you want but forgetting me? Erasing me? That fucking hurts because I sure as hell can't erase you.

I guess it's time for me to try and do the same, but wish me luck because I can't seem to even move on. Not when everything comes back to you.

I guess it's time for me to try and do the same, but wish me luck because I can't seem to even move on. Not when everything comes back to you.

48

NOW

TIME TO BE YOUR 21, ALEXZ JOHNSON

Allie

"YOU DIDN'T WRITE 143 on the last letter," Jake says, wiping the tears off his face. He read them all, *twice*. He read every single letter, every unhinged comment and thought I had about us for years. Every tear. Every heartbreak.

He went through all the emotions as well. Little by little and then all at once. Right now, I can't tell if he is heartbroken or if he is upset. Either way, seeing him crying on his bed, with my letters strewn all over, might be the most hurtful image in my brain.

"You know I never stopped loving you, but I was completely torn that day." My hands are clammy from clenching my fists while he was reading. I laid all my cards on the table. The truth never spoken finally shared. Now, the ball is in his court.

"I think I remember that day. Cara was hanging out with us for the first time in a while. Everyone was drinking and grilling her about so much, then your name came up. I had to shut the conversation down not only because I wasn't going to let anyone talk shit about you, but also because it was like a slap to the face. I hadn't brought up your name in a long time, so I could pretend you didn't exist. I could pretend." Sighing with relief and complete calmness in his eyes. "I knew in that moment what I know now, Allie."

"And what's that, Jake?"

"I thought it was as clear as day, but I guess I need to put it into words. I love you, Honey. I always have, and I always will. There was never anyone else who could replace you or make me forget you. The question is, are you ready to let me love you?"

I let out a sob and can see the surprise on his face. He comes closer to me, putting one hand on my face and moving a ringlet behind my ear. His forehead lands on mine. I close my eyes, more tears fall. Tears he wipes away with his thumb tenderly. I don't deserve his never-ending patience. I don't deserve him.

"Shh, it's okay. I'm not going anywhere," he coos.

I move until I am straddling his lap. His hand instantly going to my ass while he pulls my neck forward with the other. He peppers kisses on my lips. Delicate kisses like he's afraid he might break me. His eyes are closed, his eyelashes brush his cheeks. His nose touches mine, and he's holding on to me for dear life. Not rushing this moment. We shut out everything else that may be happening, leaving only the two of us in existence. He sighs, and I can almost hear my own heart shattering like glass.

He's afraid. He's afraid of letting me in all the way. He is afraid I might break his heart again, and who can blame him?

He wraps his arms around me, bringing me closer to him. He holds me tight in his embrace. A warm hug I never want to escape again. He lays us both down, climbing on top of me, and kissing me softly. When I try to deepen the kiss, he won't let me in, instead he lifts slightly, whispering against my lips, "Let's go to sleep, Honey. We can continue this conversation tomorrow. Right now, we need to let it rest." He kisses my forehead and lays down beside me. Pulling me flush against his chest, fitting perfectly behind me, murmuring, "I love you."

THE NEXT MORNING COMES ROUGHLY. I am in a daze, and he's rushing to get out the door. We overslept big time. He's flustered, I see it in the reddish tone on his cheeks and how his movements are abrupt and all over the place.

"Hey," I whisper. My voice is rough and dry, so I clear my throat. "I'm sorry you're running late."

"Why are you sorry, baby?" he asks, taking a second to stop and look at me. I have on one of his shirts and nothing else. My bare legs are showing, and my hair is a rat's nest, I'm sure. I know he's late, but he's still taking his time, drinking me in from head to toe. He smirks ,and I roll my eyes.

"Eyes up here, Jakey." We both laugh. The tension fleeing the air, helping us relax a little. "I should've set an alarm or been mindful of my word vomit last night."

"I wanted to hear all of it. I needed to know, Honey. I do have to go, or I'm going to be later than I already am. I can't cancel practice today. We have a big game Friday, so the boys need me. But I do want us to continue the conversation from last night."

I nod, letting him know I understand, and that it's okay. "I'll be here when you come home."

"Please be." He jogs toward me, bag in hand, and drops a kiss on my lips. A quick soft peck before he turns around and walks toward the door. The house suddenly seems smaller with him almost out of it. I wave at him, and he winks. "See you later, Allie."

I haven't checked my email, but I planned to work from here today. My meetings at this assignment are getting less demanding, so I'm waiting for them to let me know my next one. Usually, when I start having more days where I work from home, it's a true indicator my time is up, and I'm being sent somewhere else soon. But for the first time in my career, I don't want to be on the move.

49

———

NOW

ANYONE, JUSTIN BIEBER

Jake

I love teaching. I love my job, but more than anything, I love the kids. I especially enjoy teaching the same guys I coach. Somehow, it brings us closer together, making it a fulfilling profession. Some days, I might be tired, but I still enjoy being in my classroom. Today was not one of those days.

I'm tired from not sleeping. *Who could have slept after that whole shitstorm of information?* On top of that, practice today was a disaster. Every player who cares is all in their head about the game Friday, and they all care. We haven't made it to States since I was playing, and we all know how that ended: with nobody playing and everyone losing. The team was on edge and playing like they've never been coached a day in their life.

Now, I'm on my way home to have a conversation that should've happened years ago. So much time lost when we could have just made the decision *together*. It's easier to say it now, of course; now that we're mature and have had time in between to reflect on all the dumb shit we did in our teens.

Walking into the house, my heart is beating fast, and my hands are sweaty. I feel like a teenager walking to pick up my date for the first time. Except, I'm a grown-ass man, walking into my own house, where the love of my life waits for me, ready to discuss what might change the rest of our lives.

Sitting on the couch with her legs tucked under her, a book in her hand and a blanket over her, Allie looks up when she hears me walk in. "Hey, handsome," she says with a grin, closing her book and placing it on the end table next to her wine glass.

"*Hola*, beautiful." I walk toward her, placing my bag on the ground, I sit on the couch by her side. I want to kiss her, but I don't know if that's where we're at right now.

She must sense my hesitation because she untangles her legs from under her and comes tome, kissing me gently on the lips before whispering, "How was your day today?"

I fucking love this comfortable side of her. The Allie who's not worried about being herself. The one who waits for me to come home after we both go to work. The one who makes this house a home.

Kicking my shoes off my feet, I put them on the rustic coffee table in front of me and tell her about my day. She listens attentively. Her hand on mine, rubbing small circles on the top. She seems at peace. I hope it's because of me.

"How about your day?" I ask without even knowing what she did today. Did she go back to the elementary school? Has she been home crying the whole time? Did she leave the house at all?

"It was fine, pretty normal. I was given some news, though," she says with panic in her eyes.

"Oh, really? What kind of news?"

"It depends," she says.

"On what?" Raising my eyebrow at her.

"On where we are going from here."

In this moment I realize she's making quicker circles on my hand and shaking her leg. Both are signs she's nervous about whatever she's about to tell me. My heart skips a beat, waiting for her to break my heart again. I can sense it.

"They're asking me to go to Atlanta to train at another school for a few weeks. My flight leaves on Friday around 10:00 p.m. I think it means I'm going to miss your game."

"That's okay, there will be other games." I'm not sure where she's going with this. Is she leaving Friday and then never coming back? Or is she leaving for a few weeks and then coming back to me? "What are your plans for after that? Are you coming back to Baker?"

She looks at me with sadness in her eyes. Dropping my heart again like it weighs nothing. She alone can destroy me without words. This is the moment I might lose her again.

"What are we doing here, Jake?" she asks after taking a deep breath.

There are no right answers here, but I'm ready to beg her to give us another chance and not leave. I'm laying all my cards on the table. I am not making the same mistake twice.

"I don't know, but I want to fucking find out, Honey. I don't want to lie to you and tell you I can drop you off at the airport and wish you well without feeling like my life slipped through my fingers, again. I want to be with you. Even if it means packing my bags and following you wherever you go next. I am not willing to find out how to move on after I know exactly how you feel in my arms again."

"Jake, you are not quitting your job to come with me," she blurts out, crossing her arms over her chest.

"Well, I don't want you to leave my life, so my life will have to adapt to yours. I can do this with no issues, I just need to finish the school year. Then, I'm all yours. In the meantime, we need to try something out because I am not letting you go again. I refuse."

"Jake."

"Allie." I grab her arms and pull her toward me. "I made this mistake once, Honey, I'm not making it again. I'm willing to do whatever it takes to have you in my life."

"Jake, I don't want you to give your life up for me." Tears start falling down her face. Fuck, I hate seeing her cry, but I swear she has an open faucet on her face the minute she has big emotions. She's like a cup that's always full. Full of love and passion, so the minute another drop falls in it, she cries.

"Honey, don't you understand? There is no life without you. *That* was not living. I was barely existing. Hold on to me, hold on to us. For once, choose me. I know it's scary, and maybe this town won't be enough for you, but I love you more, so I am willing to give it up."

"I always chose you. I made that decision because I was choosing your future."

"I know that's what you thought, baby, but my future was always you. So now, I am begging you to let me have a future with you. If I'm enough for you, if my love will be enough for you, then let me make the choice. Let me follow you and your dreams. Let me choose you."

"What about your dreams?" she asks in between sobs.

"My dream has always been you," I say, unapologetically. She looks at me with stars in her eyes. Her swollen but beautiful honey eyes.

"I love you," she whispers.

"I love you too, baby. Now what?"

"Long distance until we can figure some things out? I don't

want you leaving your school or Baker abruptly. We can Face-Time, we can talk on the phone, right?" she asks, putting all my cards on the table.

"Yes, we will figure this out," I say, holding her hand and kissing her knuckles gently before adding, "Together." Reassuring her with more than words that we will be okay.

50

——

NOW

SAY DON'T GO (TAYLOR'S VERSION), TAYLOR
SWIFT

Allie

JAKE COULDN'T BRING me to the airport because the playoff game is tonight. The Sharks are playing The Commanders, the same team they played the night Jake got injured. I'm still in between cloud nine and terrified about trying this long-distance thing with Jake, but I love him, and I am only fooling myself into thinking that I could move on from him twice.

I took an Uber to the airport, the trunk loaded with my bags. Phone in hand, I look out the window, when I get a text message from Cara.

CARA:

Why are you getting on that plane?

ME:

Because I have to.

CARA:

Says who?

ME:

The fuck? My JOB!

CARA:

You're telling me right now that you are picking your job over the love of your life? You were fucking miserable for years. Don't do it again, Allison.

ME:

Don't 'Allison' me. This has been my dream job my entire career.

CARA:

But what is your dream? Not your dream job but your dream life?

ME:

Idk

CARA:

I think you do, you just don't want to admit it.

ME:

Oh but since you know me so well, friend, enlighten me.

CARA:

For once in your fucking life, Allie, put yourself first. I'm not telling you I know what you want in life. You need to find it yourself in you. You know the answer, you know it in your heart.

ME:

I don't have a choice. I have to go to work.

Cara:

Babe, you're a teacher. You can teach literally anywhere. You also have more money than any adult would need at our age, just sitting in your bank account. Why don't you stop being the responsible one, and for once in your life be the selfish one. Put yourself first.

ME:

I'm not touching that money.

CARA:

FML

ME:

WHAT?!?!?!?!?

CARA:

We all make mistakes. You need to let that shit go. Your dad is trying to make amends.
Let him.

CARA:

And fine, let him doesn't mean let him control your life because the independent bitch that you are now won't go backwards

CARA:

Let him make amends, though, or at least try.

CARA:

<3

ME:

K

She's not wrong, though. Why am I going to this job? I do love my job, but do I love it more than I love Jake? No. Why am I putting him last again? I thought helping him have professional stability was what he wanted. But I was wrong. He just wants me to pick *him*. To put him first. And that's exactly what I am going to do.

I text Cara one more time.

ME:

Actually, fuck the job. Fuck responsibilities. I will figure that shit out.

CARA:

••••

ME:

I'm going to show this man, exactly how much I love him.

Cara:

YASSSSSS QUEEN!

Go.
Fucking.
Show.
Him.
I put my phone in my bag and tell the driver, "Sir, change of plans, let's turn around."

51

NOW

TAKE ME HOME, US THE DUO

Jake

"TEN!"

"NINE!"

"EIGHT!"

The crowd is cheering as our running back steps away from the touchdown. We've been tied for the past five minutes, and with the clock against us, this is the last chance we have to make a touchdown and win this game. This has been a hard game. The Commanders are good, and they showed up to this game. But. So. Did. We.

"SEVEN!"

"SIX!"

The running back is almost there. Some of the other guys are running behind him, pushing everyone else away. Guarding him with their lives. He doesn't dare look back. Five more steps and he'll make it. A Commander is right behind him, practically breathing down his neck. The air in the stadium shifts. People are on the edge of their seats.

"FIVE!"

"FOUR!"

"THREE!"

TOUCHDOWN! With three seconds left on the clock, he made it. He fucking did it. A touchdown. We won! We fucking won the game. The crowd goes wild. People are cheering, clapping, screaming, and crying. The Commanders are completely defeated. Their coaches are shaking their heads, throwing their hats down, and yelling at their players. I could never understand why coaches get so angry at kids when they lose. Yes, it is disappointing but they played a damn good game, and at the end of the day, they're kids. They're going to beat themselves up enough.

Running toward the team currently gathered at the end zone, I can't help but smile wide. We did it. They did it. They deserved this, and they got it. They played well, but more than that, they put in the time and effort to work through the things that needed improvement, and this is their reward. All I can think about is how I can't wait to call Allie and tell her about this.

Walking back toward the locker room, I have to blink a couple of times and rub my face because I think I am hallucinating. Walking across the middle of the field is Allie, wearing a fucking Sharks Jersey, looking like a damn vision. Curls flowing in the wind, tights that hug her perfect legs, and the Sharks Jersey acting like a half-fitted dress around her curves. She's smiling big, and when she sees that I notice her, she starts running toward me. *What on earth is she doing here?*

"Allie? Baby, what are you doing here?" I ask, completely dumbfounded and a little out of breath, both from running and because this woman takes my breath away every time I see her.

"I couldn't leave you again. I wanted to show you I would be happy here. Baker is enough. You are enough. You always were, and you will always be. I'm tired of fighting it. I love you, and I don't want to go another day without you."

I kiss her. I kiss her and show her exactly what those words mean to me. Pulling her closer to me. Holding her head, breathing her in. When she lets out a little moan, I pull away, suddenly remembering we're on a football field, and a high school football field at that. I kiss her nose and her forehead and look down, smiling like a fool. An in-love fool.

"Jake, you guys won! I am so proud of you." Her hands holding my face and her eyes looking right into my soul. I nod and smile. I wouldn't want to celebrate with anyone but her right now. Or ever. For the rest of my life, she is the only thing I need. My only constant. Everything else can change.

"Do you feel on top of the world right now, baby?" she asks with giddiness in her voice.

"With you by my side, I do," I reply. We don't say anything for a moment. Both just standing in this moment together. Taking it all in. Her hands are still holding my neck. The brightest smile on her face and her eyes glossy with emotion. Hope, happiness, *love*. It is all there.

"Take me home, Jake Clarke," she says.

"And where is home, Honey?"

"Home is wherever you are," she says, and my world stops spinning. I am about to show this woman how she is *exactly* that. My home.

"I've been waiting a lifetime to hear you say that." I hold her hand and pull her straight into the parking lot. "Let's go home, Honey."

EPILOGUE

Timeless, Taylor Swift

Two years later

ALLIE

"YOU LOOK STUNNING," Cara says, wiping her tears away. We have been waiting for this day for a year, but if we're both being honest, we've been dreaming about it since we were in high school. Today, I get to marry my best friend.

We're hosting a small ceremony in a venue by the river. Beautiful oak trees surround an open area of grass that's lit up with fairy lights. White chairs face forward to an arbor with beige and orange drapes right in front of the water. My dream venue with my dream man.

A lot has changed in the last couple of years. I officially

moved to Baker and quit my job. I went back to the classroom for a little bit, but after everything that happened last school year, I couldn't do it anymore. Now, I work from home for a professional development company. I travel a few times a month, but not for more than a day or two. Jake is still coaching and teaching at Baker High. It has been a dream, and although he asked me to marry him a few months after I moved in with him, we wanted to wait until all the turmoil that took over Baker Oaks settled before we said 'I do.'

"Thank you, babe. I feel like a princess," I tell her. My dress is perfect. Exactly what I wanted. It's an A-line cut that accentuates my body type perfectly with lace and beads making a floral pattern on the top. My hair is pulled to the side in a loose braid, with some curls framing my face, just like Jake loves it.

"You are a fucking queen. Feel like it!"

WALKING DOWN THE AISLE, Taylor Swift's *Lover* is playing in the background. With my brothers holding my hands, I walk toward the man who has always had my heart. He's smiling from ear to ear in his black tuxedo, standing alone since we decided not to have a wedding party, especially since Nick is not here with us today. It felt wrong to have groomsmen without him, so we decided for it to just be me and him standing up there. Tears fill his eyes, locked with mine. He looks at me the same way he always has—like the world ceases to exist, like there is only me.

My brothers walk me to him, giving him the usual spiel of, "Take care of our sister." His rough hands hold mine tenderly, the biggest oxymoron. He looks at me and mouths *hi*. We're lost in each other until we hear the officiant clear his throat, and we both giggle looking at him.

JAKE

"Now, Allie. It's your turn to share your vows with Jake," the officiant says. Going first was a good idea because I was already overwhelmed, and Allie hadn't even started. I know she will kill me with her words, as per usual. She looks nervous, and it's the most adorable sight. Again, I'm glad because it helps me breathe easier to see a little of her nervous self come through this fucking vision of a woman in front of me. Talk about making my heart stop, with that dress and her hair framing her face perfectly. Minutes away from being completely mine, from being my wife.

"Twelve years ago, we were two kids who fell head over heels in love with each other. People thought we were going to be the ones who would stay together forever. Voted most likely to run away together. Unfortunately, mistakes were made, and we were apart for too damn long. I don't want to keep beating around the bush on why or how, but I am so glad we found each other again."

"You were great for me then, and you're pure perfection for me now. In the big gestures and in the little everyday things that make my heart skip a beat every time. The way you wake up early and quietly let me sleep longer. The way you cook me breakfast and make me coffee the way I like it, when you don't even drink any. The way you always smile when you see me, like you missed me even if you just walk away for a second."

"We have built millions of memories. Laughing. Arguing.

Crying. Sleepless nights. Months apart. Years together. New friendships gained. Old friendships lost. Broken pieces of each other healed through love, hard work, and time."

"And we're still here, not only with a beautiful strong relationship but also ready to start the next chapter in our love story. And I wouldn't trade any single moment, especially if I get to keep calling you home."

"People ask me if I regret leaving my job and my lifestyle, settling for the slow-paced, small-town life, but they don't know that my answer will never change; I will never regret *you*. I will never regret us. I don't have to miss home because *you* are my home, and wherever *you* are is where I belong. The best decision I have ever made, hands down, is choosing you. And I still can't believe I get to love you every day, but even more, you choose to love me too."

"You are my best friend ,and sometimes that means giving me reality checks and telling me hard truths, and although I might not seem to appreciate it in the moment, I will be forever grateful for it. And for your faith in me even when I've lost all faith in myself. For loving me as I have changed from the naive cheerleader to the woman I am now. For being my constant. For being my rock. My listening ears. My favorite hug. The coziest pillow. And my laugh on the hardest days. So, I guess what I am trying to say is thank you. Thank you for choosing me every day. For making me see the best parts of me through your eyes and for holding my hand while I fight the worst ones."

"And here I am, promising that I will. I will always love you on this journey even when the load gets heavy. Even when we turn gray, even when I get so mad I don't want to, I promise I will. I promise I will stand by you in parenting, business endeavors, and life decisions; even with deciding what's for dinner. I promise I will be the very best friend you could ever ask for. I promise I will guard your heart with all I have and then some.

But above all, I promise to choose you, unapologetically, through rough or smooth terrain, in sunshine, and rain, from sunrise to sunset, when we're happy and when we're mad, and everything in between; I will choose you. You know I'm obsessed with love stories, but ours is my favorite forever and ever until wherever we end up."

"One, four, three, Jake."

The crowd is silent. She not only took my words away, but she took them from everyone else. This fucking woman is incredible, and she is completely mine.

"Jake, you may now kiss your bride." The words I've been waiting a lifetime to hear. I pull her to me in one swoop, hold her by the neck, dip her low, and kiss my wife.

ACKNOWLEDGMENTS

Oh my gosh, thank you so much for reading my book. I have so many words I wish I could say, but more than anything, I just want to say thank you. Out of the millions of books out there, you took time to read mine, and that means more than you know. Jake and Allie are close to my heart, and you giving them a chance is filling my heart with love.

I want to take this opportunity to say thank you to everyone who made this book possible. Sure, I wrote it, but so much more goes into creating a story and publishing. Way more than just having a story in your heart, even though that's the right place to start.

Thank you, Joey, for your never-ending belief in me. For being my solid rock and for not once asking me to close my computer when I was elbows deep in drafting or editing. Thank you for being my number one supporter, and when I start to doubt myself, you remind me how incredible I am.

To N. and M., because when you both heard I was writing a book, your little jumps and claps made me keep pushing to show you that you should always go after your dreams.

To Adriana, for being more than a best friend and alpha reader. Thank you for proofreading tons of my words and changing all my "its" for "it's" when they were necessary. Thank you for hyping me up after I shared my unhinged ideas and for helping me be completely delusional.

To Jen and Crystal, for willingly reading this book as it was being written and not letting me give up with your sweet comments.

To my beta readers: Jayné, your grammar corrections, sweet comments, and suggestions made this book better. Thank you for giving me feedback gently but also helping me make this book what it is today. Mikayla Hornedo, your whole author self, gave this baby book a try and gave me valuable feedback. I will never be able to repay you. Mandy, you beta read for so many big authors, the fact that you took time from your busy schedule meant the world to me, too. Kelsey, your input was incredible, and I loved your overall help in making this book even better. Thank you so much.

To Wonder and Wander Editing, for dealing with the hardest part of writing and doing it graciously. Thank you for your never-ending work, making sure this book the best possible version of itself. Thank you for making me feel like I knew what I was doing even when you had to flip the order of my sentences so many times (my bilingual brain chaos). Sophie, you are an angel, and more people need you in their lives.

To Ever After Cover Design, for taking my thoughts and putting them on a gorgeous cover. More than I could've asked for. The tears of joy I shed when the final design came were infinite. Aliyah, you were incredible to work with, thank you so very much!

To all the ARC readers who read and review my baby book, thank you from the bottom of this indie author's heart. Thank you to all, especially to Colleen, Sarah and Beth.

To my author friends, Veronica, Nicole, Emily, Bella, Mikayla, and Rachel. Thank you for answering my million questions and for showing me that this job can be so rewarding but also challenging. Thank you for never making me feel like I was bothering you with all my comments and for walking me off the ledge multiple times without even knowing it. Thank you for showing me we all thrive better when we work together, and there is room for everyone in the publishing world.

To my mom and brothers, for always making me feel like I could do anything I set my mind to. *Gracias de todo corazón.*

To YOU, reader, for giving me a chance and making my wildest dreams come true.

Last but not least, thank you, Joey, again. I hope when you read this, you see all the little and big parts of you in Jake and know that you are such an incredible husband, I had to find a way to share parts of you with the world. Even if it's just in the form of a fictional character. You deserve the world, babe, just like you have given the world to me.

Now off to cry in baby author tears and on to the next book.

143,

Ambar

WHAT'S NEXT

Do you want more Allie and Jake?

Scan or click here for a bonus epilogue! PS: There are babies included <3

Or read Santiago and Roe's story, The Trail Often Crossed here.

You can also read about Alex, the quarterback in Baker

High's team love story, in a sweet and spicy Christmas novella here.

Are you itching for Cara's story? Click here to read The Road Sometimes Taken.

Ambar Cordova is a romance author whose heartfelt stories have touched readers around the world. With a focus on raw, emotional storytelling, she creates relatable worlds with flawed characters that feel real. She grew up in the Dominican Republic and brings diversity as inspiration to her stories. Ambar writes books that readers not only escape into, but also find themselves in.

Her debut series, Baker Oaks, features a cozy small town in Florida showing multicultural stories that bring butterflies to her readers. When Ambar is not writing, she's teaching, spending time with her family, and reading. Ambar enjoys boat rides, traveling, and spending time outside.

ALSO BY AMBAR CORDOVA

The Baker Oaks Series

The Truth Never Spoken—a heartfelt second-chance romance where her sexy ex says she needs to go home with him after they have not seen each other in ten years.

The Trail Often Crossed—a fast-paced sports romance where the hot new-to-town tattoed man finds out the spitfire and afraid-to-love bartender from the night before is his new rival.

The Gift Rarely Given—a hot and spicy Christmas novella where an ex-QB with a bad reputation proposes to fake date a confident plus-size Latina to help him fix his image and get her mom to stop setting up with bad dates.

TLAT—an angsty age gap, secret relationship romance! Preorder NOW!

www.ingramcontent.com/pod-product-compliance
Lightning Source LLC
Chambersburg PA
CBHW022007310726
48972CB00006B/1561